The Prince of Warwood
and
The Rise of the Chosen

J. Noel Clinton

The Prince of Warwood
and
The Rise of the Chosen

J. Noel Clinton

Chapter 1

The Dark King Lives

'I'm a murderer!' The thought hammered into Xavier's head. Sighing, he rolled onto his side and closed his eyes willing for sleep to come, but it remained elusive. He couldn't shake the dark thought already seeded in his brain. He was a murderer! He'd killed not one but two men. Alas, William LeMasters had been an evil, horrible man, and he had wished him dead numerous times, but if truth were told, he hadn't really meant to kill him. He'd only meant to drain him of his powers so that he would no longer be a threat, but he hadn't been adequately prepared for the power of the King's Key. This small, gold staff was possibly the most potent object on Earth, encasing every power known and many unknown in the empowered world. It not only had the ability to empower individuals with additional powers; it also had the ability to abolish powers, sometimes with deadly consequences. The prophet had failed to mention that to him. But then, the prophet had failed to mention a lot of things!

Although LeMasters' death hadn't been intentional, the death of his father's long trusted assistant was another matter. Milton Bailey had been brutally tortured and morbidly maimed by LeMasters. The excruciating pain as he was dismembered alive chopped away his resolve, and he feared that he would betray his king by renouncing him. He begged for Xavier to end his life so he could die with honor knowing he'd stayed true to King Wells. In the end, Xavier had killed Milton, not William LeMasters. He had murdered an innocent man!

Xavier rolled onto his stomach, buried his face in his pillow, and tried to swallow past the painful knot growing in his throat. Guilt and despair ran rampant inside him. The more he fought to hold back the feelings the harder they pounded in his thoughts. He whimpered into his pillow as tears erupted in torrents. But, crying didn't help. It only left him miserable and congested. Inhaling a shuddering breath, he pushed his feelings down, deep down and wiped his face on his pillow.

With a sigh, he thought back to all that had happened over the past year. It had been nearly a year since he had learned the truth about himself, his father, and the strangeness in his life. From that moment on, his life had become a strange and deadly whirlwind. He longed for a normal, simpler life, but he simply wasn't a normal boy. He was special. It wasn't his unusual white hair that made him special. It wasn't that he possessed powers that common people could only dream of. It wasn't that he would someday be king of a kingdom full of empowered people just like him. No, what *really* made him special was that he was the Chosen. Although few knew this, Xavier Wells was the future of all mankind. He was responsible for defeating the Dark King and saving the world from years of oppression and cruelty that his rule would bring. *This* is what made him special, and he would trade everything he had: all his riches, all his powers, all his abilities, if he could just be *normal*. He didn't ask for any of this! He didn't want anything to do with it! It was because of this destiny, this impending conflict that the people closest to Xavier had died: his mother, Dublin Minnows, Maggie Applegate, and Milton.

Accidental or not, at least the man responsible for their deaths was dead. William LeMasters had made Xavier's life miserable. He had kidnapped him and held him captive at a facility called the Institute, which imprisoned, brainwashed, and tortured empowered children until they yielded to his command. Then, he brutally assaulted and murdered his mother and beheaded his girlfriend's father. He had been an evil man who spread terror wherever he went, but none of that mattered now. He was dead, and Xavier was glad. Many believed that with William LeMasters gone, there would be no Dark King to rise up to dominate the world. But Xavier knew the truth. Nothing had been avoided or prevented. Nothing had changed. The Dark King would still rise, and he would rise with an all-consuming fury the likes of which the world had yet to see! He would extract his revenge and devour those who stood against him, inflicting pain and agony on those they cherished most. He would want to even the score. Nothing had been avoided by William LeMasters' death. If anything, it had ensured the inevitability of war.

Of course, no one knew that William wasn't the Dark King. He never was. He had been molding and grooming his son, Fox, for that role. All the harsh words, the abuse, the confrontations he put his son through had been carefully designed and orchestrated so that Fox would become the man he was prophesied to become: The Dark King. It had worked. The look in the older boy's eyes following William's death mirrored the dark coldness that had always been present in his father's eyes. In the end, William LeMasters had beaten Xavier in that cell. His death had made the war between the Dark and the Light irreversible. Fox LeMasters would rise to power and seek revenge and global domination over all mankind.

He had to tell his father. The kingdom had to prepare.

"Son?" his father's voice pulled him from his thoughts with a start, and he bolted upright in bed.

Shadowed from the light pouring in from the hall, the king's face was unreadable, but Xavier knew from the lingering coolness in his body that his father had been listening to his thoughts. Only royal heirs had the ability to penetrate the minds of others, and the king was a very powerful telepath. Although Xavier had the ability to detect a breach in his thoughts, he still lacked the ability to refuse or guard himself against such infiltrations. He felt a wave of irritation, first toward his father and then toward himself for not remaining alert to the warning signs. He groaned inwardly.

"God, Dad! Stop invading my thoughts! It's not right! I don't do it to you!" he hissed grumpily.

The king didn't respond to his son's grievances as he moved into the room and stopped next to the bed. The hallway light played hauntingly across his features, casting half his face in a soft, warm glow. Finally he whispered with quiet authority, "It seems that it's necessary. This information should not have been kept from me."

"I wasn't keeping..."

The slight movement of his father's hand stopped his denials short, and he expelled a long breath of defeat.

"All right, maybe I was keeping it from you, but I *was* going to tell you. I just... I guess I wanted to believe, just for a few days, that everyone was right. The battle with the Dark King was avoided. I didn't want to have to think about Fox and what it all would mean, what it would mean about you."

His father sat heavily on the edge of the bed. After a moment of silence, he spoke softly. "I know all of this, your new life, your role, your destiny, has been overwhelmingly difficult for you. But you must stay the course and focus on your training. If we are to be victorious over the Dark Army, we must continue the training we began at the mountain, and our people must be warned."

"Yes, sir. I know." Xavier paused taking a deep breath.

"There's something you wish to ask?" Jeremiah asked.

Of course his father knew there was more. He shook off the chill still lingering in his bones and looked up at the familiar shadowed figure sitting on the edge of his bed.

"Well, I was wondering, what happened to the Key after I — after LeMasters died?"

"It was found clutched in your hand. We had a hard time prying it from you," the king remarked.

"Where is it now?"

"Loren has it well hidden and protected," he answered, patting the boy's shoulder.

Xavier nodded thoughtfully, expelling another long breath. The Key was safe. "But, what about my...I mean, the sword? Did you find it?"

His father shook his head. "No, the sword was never found. If I were a betting man, I'd say Fox took it."

"Fox took it? But why would he want the sword? He has his own, and it's not like I couldn't get more swords..."

"Xavier, that sword glows whenever you are near it! Think, son! Why would he not want it?"

"Oh," he muttered, feeling stupid.

Both father and son sat for some time, drifting into their own thoughts and fears. Finally, his father patted his leg and stood. "Try to get some rest. You still have a lot of healing to do."

He nodded and watched the king cross the room and pause at the door. "Goodnight, son."

"Night, Dad."

Chapter 2

Rebuilding Warwood

Warwood was still in shambles, and normal kingdom life had been suspended until essential repairs were completed. Since Xavier couldn't physically lift and move things due to his injured hand, his father had assigned him to one of his most trusted friends, General Loren Hardcastle, who was organizing telekinetic citizens. Today, their task was to clear out the rubble and assist masons and construction workers in rebuilding the gatehouse, which had been demolished during the initial onslaught of LeMasters' invasion.

Rebuilding the gatehouse would be a simple task and Xavier was looking forward to doing something constructive, regardless of how tedious or boring it might become. Although his powers could be intense at times, he felt confident that he had a secure command over them and could summon them without difficulty. He didn't like to brag, but there were few kids in the kingdom who could rival his empowerment level and strength.

However, there was one power that still proved challenging for Xavier: that of impediment. He struggled to block telepathic advances, especially when faced with a strong, capable telepath. His confrontation with William LeMasters only punctuated this deficiency. Although he had made gains in impediment and could, at times, hoodwink Uncle Mike, his father was a different matter altogether. The king was the most powerful telepath alive. For this reason, when the new school term began, Uncle Mike would no longer be teaching him telepathy; his father would. He wasn't sure if he was happy about this change in professors or not.

When they arrived at the gatehouse, Loren began dividing up the telekinetics with specific jobs. Xavier was assigned to Loren's group, and he was sure this wasn't by accident. No doubt the general had been told to keep an eye on him. Loren led him and half dozen others to the rubble that once was the magnificent entrance to the kingdom. Their task was to raise massive stones into place while masons quickly secured them with mortar. In no time, the gatehouse was taking shape and before noon they had the structure half built.

"It's boring work," Loren remarked as if reading Xavier's mind. "But, there are so few telekinetics, and we are the only means the kingdom has to lift and move heavy objects."

He nodded in response as his mind began to wander. He looked at the group of telekinetics sorting through the rubble finding stones that could be reused. When a usable stone was found, it would be tossed into a growing pile twenty feet to Xavier's right. The first few times a stone crashed to the ground next to him, he had jumped, but the men's unparalleled accuracy quickly eased his nerves and the clattering and cracking of falling rock became trivial background rhythms of the work. Still, he couldn't help but marvel at the inherent skill and accuracy the men possessed.

"Hey! Am I flying solo on this job?" Loren teased, nudging him with his elbow.

"Oh, ah, yeah... I mean no. Sorry," he mumbled.

He watched as the general settled another stone on top of the structure before turning his attention to a stone weighing close to 500 pounds. He lifted the stone into the air, but before he could place it on the gatehouse, a fiery sensation snaked from the pit of his stomach and shot into his outstretched hand. His body shook visibly with effort as the stone suddenly felt like it weighed, well, 500 pounds. Then a chill rushed through his body as the telekinetic energy drained from him. No longer in his power, the massive rock began to plummet. He desperately tried to recapture the stone with telekinesis, but he couldn't engage the ability, and the stone continued falling to where Harry's dad worked.

"Look out!" he screamed at Mr. Sims.

Simultaneously, a hot draft grazed Xavier's cheek as Loren's telekinetic force whisked by him and caught the boulder less than a foot above Mr. Sims, who hadn't even had time to cower. Slowly, he lifted the boulder into place before looking down at Xavier.

"Let's take a break," he declared quietly, clamping a hand on his shoulder and leading him toward Center Square, where several vendor booths had been set up for food and drinks. Without a word, he grabbed two bottles of water and handed one to Xavier. Then he moved to a large aspen and lounged in its shade. Patting the earth next to him, he beckoned, "Come on, kid. Take a load off."

Xavier settled next to the general and watched as he drank half the bottle in two swallows. He took a sip of his own water, but it did little to clear the lump embedded in his throat.

"Sorry about that. I guess... I was... wasn't paying close enough attention. Maybe I'm still kind of tired and not quite a hundred percent yet," he rasped.

"Is that what happened?" Loren asked, looking at him thoughtfully. "Well, I guess it's possible. You haven't been out of the hospital very long, and we've been working on the gate house for nearly three hours." He studied the boy next to him.

Xavier tensed. The general's intense stare nearly made him forget that he wasn't telepathic.

Finally, he smiled. "What do you say we take a lunch break? Maybe a rest and some food will reenergize you. You stay put, and I'll get us a couple of sandwiches."

"Okay," he muttered, slumping against the tree trunk as Loren stood and ambled toward the long table of sandwiches, fruit, and tidbits in Center Square.

His mind reeled over what happened. Why had his power quit on him like that? Concentrating intensely at a small twig a few inches from him, Xavier attempted to reconnect with his power, but nothing happened. Trying not to panic, he closed his eyes and tried the relaxation techniques Uncle Mike had taught him when he got frustrated with his impediment exercises. After a moment of breathing evenly and "listening" to his biorhythms, he slowly opened his eyes and glared determinedly at the twig. Purposefully, he stretched out his hand and the twig flew twenty feet into the air. Relief flooded through him and he leaned back against the trunk once again.

By day's end, the gatehouse was fully rebuilt and the group cheered in triumph and pride.

"Well, done, young sire," Loren called jovially, draping an arm around his shoulders.

"Thanks. And thanks for catching that stone. I thought for a moment that it was going to crush Mr. Sims," he muttered ruefully.

"Anytime! Besides, I'm used to covering for you Wells boys," the general teased.

"Hey!" he laughed, punching the man in the gut.

Loren doubled over and feinted injury. "Lord! Is that how you repay your gratitude?" he gasped melodramatically. As Xavier started toward him again, he chuckled and effortlessly held the boy at arm's length. "It seems that all the Wells boys have short tempers, too."

Xavier laughed. "Yeah, but I'd say Dad's is the worst."

He chuckled and nodded. "I've known your father and uncle all my life. It's true. Your father always had the hotter head but only barely. Speaking of which, we better head back to the palace and see how the brothers are getting along with the trials."

"The trials? What trials?" he questioned.

"Well, not necessarily trials today. They were working on the charges against LeMasters' men who surrendered: mostly preliminary stuff, organizing the crimes by severity, separating the children's crimes from the men's crimes, that sort of thing. Your dad wants you to be present when the trials begin," Loren concluded, looking sideways at the boy. "I guess he thinks it would be educational in being a king."

"Oh. Yeah. I guess he would," he muttered.

Once they entered the palace gates, his eyes settled on Lana's house. Sadness weighed heavily on his shoulders as he slumped past it, frowning. He missed her terribly and longed to go back in time to King's Mountain when all was well between his father and Lana. He treasured the time spent at the mountain. There was always a sense of urgency among the citizens, but there was also a deep sense of belonging, loyalty, and family. It was as if the mountain ceiling held them all together. But, now that they were back in the kingdom with nothing but sky above them, those familial feelings seemed to drift up and away, lost. Lana was lost to them.

"Do you think Dad will ever make up with Lana?" he asked miserably before he realized he had spoken aloud.

Loren studied him before answering. "I don't know, Xavier. That's up to your father."

He sighed despondently. "Great, that means no. He won't apologize. He always thinks he's right and that he knows best." He looked up at Loren imploringly. "But, he doesn't know best, Loren. Not about this! He needs her! I need her! Couldn't you talk to him? Maybe if you told him what an ass he's being he'd listen to you."

"No, Xavier. No, no, no, no!"

"But, Loren..."

"No, Xavier. It's not a good idea."

"Then what am I supposed to do? Dad's too proud...they'll never get back together if they're not nudged in the right direction," he complained. "If you could just talk to him..."

"No! Xavier, I said no!" he barked, stopping and turning the boy to face him. "Your dad will have to decide for himself what to do about Lana. We have to stay out of it. I know it feels unfair to you, but this isn't about what *we* can do! It's not up to us to save their relationship. It's up to your father and Lana. Stay out of it!"

"Okay, okay," he moaned and stalked away.

"Come on, Xavier. Don't be that way," Loren called, falling into step with him. "I didn't agree with his decision to push her away either! I understand why he did it, but it wasn't the right thing to do!"

"But now that William LeMasters is dead, why isn't he trying to get her back?"

Loren sighed and ruffled the boy's hair. "Believe me, kid; when your old man decides he wants Lana back, he'll move heaven and Earth until he has her. Just give him some time."

"If I can survive life with him until then," he muttered.

"Sorry about that. Your dad was never that great under emotional stress. He tends to get a bit cranky," he explained, draping an arm over his shoulders. "Why don't you spend the night with Court tonight? I'm sure I could swing it so you have tomorrow off."

"Do you think he'll let me?"

The general nodded with a grin. "Sure he would. Just because he's miserable jackass doesn't mean he wants you to be one too."

"Can I quote you to Dad on that?" he snickered.

"You can try, but I'll deny it. I sure don't need the king on my butt more than he already is." Loren's deep laugh echoed down the long hall as they entered the palace, but it quickly evaporated as harsh, angry words bellowed out of the royal residence, echoing through the palace's chambers and passages.

"Damn it, Mike! We can't just pass sentencing without an executive session!" Jeremiah's voice boomed.

Loren and Xavier exchanged a look of apprehension before bounding up the stairs and through the door.

"Don't give me that, Jeremiah! If you hadn't passed the amendment to limit the king's authority, we could hold trials and sentencing in the same setting! But, no, you and your petty insecurities..."

"What in the hell does that mean?" Jeremiah spat.

"You know what I mean! You're so afraid you'll turn out like *him* that you make knee-jerk decisions!" Mike shouted.

"You don't have the foggiest idea what you're talking about!" he retorted viciously.

"You've got to be kidding me! I don't know what I'm talking about? Lord, Jeremy, I lived in this palace too! I know how he treated you. I know the harder he tried to control you, the harder you fought to defy him. Even now, with Father long gone, you're still trying to outrun his shadow!"

"Enough, Mike!"

"No! It's the truth. But hear this brother, the harder you fight against becoming our father, the more you *act* like him!" Michael spat.

"I said, enough!" he shouted, lunging at him, but Ephraim and Loren jumped into action and kept the brothers apart.

"Well, done, *Your Highness*. You just proved my point, but of course, you've proven it repeatedly over the years. Starting with that stunt you pulled in Cleveland."

The king instantly stilled and gaped at his brother.

Michael sneered. "What? Did you honestly think I wouldn't find out?"

"I don't know what you're talking about," he muttered unconvincingly as he shrugged out of Ephraim's hands and walked over to the bar to pour a drink.

Mike shook Loren off of him and stepped toward his brother. "Bullshit! I know that after you verbally spanked me about leaving my kingdom and shirking my responsibilities, you returned to Cleveland and coerced Natalie into leaving the city. She left! She left and there wasn't a trace of where she went!" Michael yelled, barely taking a breath between his words. It was obvious even to Xavier that Michael had been stewing over this for years. "I asked her to marry me, Jer! I could have brought her back *with* me!"

"You were only nineteen! You had no business getting married!" Jeremiah snapped.

"THAT WASN'T FOR YOU TO DECIDE!"

"Yes, it was Mike!" Jeremiah slammed his drink onto the bar, its contents sloshing in the glass and spilling over the rim. "It was my responsibility to look out for you after Quinton died. Only God knows why, but you were hell-bent on self-destruction, and I thought it was best that you returned to the kingdom where I could keep an eye on you. You weren't mature enough or in the right frame of mind to get married! Besides, you're my brother...and I needed you! My *family* was gone! I was grasping at any splinter of family I had left, damn it."

Michael stared at his brother, incapable of responding to the truth and emotion he felt behind the king's words. The fiery anger in his eyes extinguished, and he looked away.

"Jer," Loren whispered. "Maybe you should..."

"Loren," Jeremiah hissed in a tone that was clearly a warning.

Michael's head whipped up. His piercing glare darted between the two men before settling and boring into Loren. Suddenly, he exploded with fury and tackled Jeremiah. The abrupt movement stunned Loren and Ephraim, catching them off guard. Although Michael had a maimed leg and the king outweighed him, he managed to ambush him with two good thumps to the face before Loren and Ephraim hauled him off. Jeremiah slowly got to his feet, wiping his bloody mouth with the back of his hand.

"God, Jeremiah! I take it all back. You don't *act* like Father! Hell, you ARE him!" Michael spat with raw anguish. "You should have...you should have told me about the baby! Where are they? Where did you send them? Have you been sending them money?"

"I only know where she used to be, Mike. She moved on before the baby was born and refused to accept any money," he whispered.

Michael looked at his brother in disgust. "I'm leaving."

Ephraim nodded and muttered, "That's probably a good idea. I'll stop by your place tomorrow morning so we can discuss the trip, Mike."

"No, Ephraim. I'm leaving the kingdom. I'm not going on the scouting mission to Coasta. I need to find Natalie and my kid," he growled and looked at his brother, who still avoided his eyes. Then without another word, he stomped to the door.

"Uncle Mike?"

He looked down at Xavier with surprise. He hadn't realized the boy was there. He tried to smile as he ruffled his nephew's hair. Then, without a word or a backward glance, he left the residence.

"Jeremiah, I'm sorry…I didn't change my thinking fast enough. Maybe you should have told him…"

"Loren!" Ephraim interrupted, giving a slight nod toward Xavier.

Loren nodded with understanding before changing the subject. "Sire? The boy worked hard today, but with his hand still healing I think it would be for the best if he rested tomorrow. He shouldn't overdo it. Why not let him spend the night with Court? I think both boys have earned a day off."

"Thanks, mate," Ephraim muttered dryly. "I noticed you didn't volunteer to let the hooligans spend the night at your house."

Loren grinned. "There's no way I'd trust your boy with my daughter. I have to protect my little girl."

Ephraim coughed as he winked at Xavier. "Protect Erica? It's the lads who need protecting from her! That girl is too much like her father."

"Thank you, buddy. That's the best compliment you've given me in a long time."

"It wasn't a compliment," he muttered before

addressing the king. "But, I agree. The boys deserve a day off. Xavier is always welcome at my home."

The king smiled down at his son. "I heard that the gatehouse has been completely reconstructed. Well done, son."

"Thanks. I had a little help," he answered snidely, nodding at Loren.

"A *little* help? I'd say it was more than a little help, you little brat!" he spat playfully, chasing him around the receiving room.

Chapter 3

Family and Friends

Xavier exited the royal residence, dragging an overstuffed backpack and carrying his pillow. Ephraim stood just outside the door with Henrick.

"Ah, Xavier. Good! Rebecca is holding dinner for us." he announced, draping an arm over his shoulders and steering him down the royal staircase. "I must warn you, your highness. In a household with four growing boys, food doesn't have time to get cold. So if you plan to have any dinner tonight, you better grab it when you can."

The moment they walked through the door, Xavier was struck by how loud the residence was. Mrs. Hardcastle was yelling for Caleb to get his shoes out of the dining room. Drew and Court were arguing about the latest rugby match.

"Oh, come off it, Drew. It wasn't a foul, and you know it! You're just sore that your team lost and you lost a bet with Jonas!"

"Bloody hell I am! It was a foul as plain as the pimple on your ass!"

"ANDREW EPHRAIM HARDCASTLE!" Mrs. Hardcastle yelled. "I will have your father wash your mouth out with soap if you don't clean up that language!"

"OW! Mum, Courtney hit me." Caleb whined.

"And I'll do it again if you keep waving that foul sock in my face, you git!"

"Boys! For the love of God, would you act like you had some sense! Your father is due home any minute with Prince Wells, and he doesn't need to witness how barbaric you lot truly are!"

Ephraim looked down at him and winked. "It's not too late to back out, sire."

Xavier grinned and shook his head. "No way."

"Okay. Don't say I didn't warn you."

Still smiling, he followed Ephraim into the living quarters and took in the chaos of a normal family preparing for dinner. Loren was right. This was exactly what he needed.

"Hey, X! Just in time!" Court bellowed from the large dining room table. "Here, sit next to me."

As Xavier shuffled his way toward Court, Ephraim detoured into the adjoining kitchen, swept his wife into his arms, dipped her, and planted a noisy kiss on her lips.

"Hello, love," he whispered.

"GET-A-ROOM," Drew coughed loudly.

"Hey now," Ephraim growled playfully, as he threw an oven mitt at his oldest son.

"Dad?" the Hardcastles' second oldest boy, Dennis, called from the table where the boys sat waiting. "Terry invited me to spend the night after the bonfire celebration. I told him I'd have to run it by you first. Is it okay?"

"Sure, son. I don't see why not," Ephraim told him as he settled at the head of the table. "But the celebration is still a week away so I want you to keep your nose out of your books long enough to help with your chores and duties. Understand?" Dennis nodded as Ephraim continued, "We must all pull our weight to get the kingdom back in order."

"Yes, sir," the boys chimed together.

Once Mrs. Hardcastle was seated, Ephraim took his wife's hand and then Drew's as he announced, "Let's give thanks."

The boys all joined hands and bowed their heads in near unison.

"Bless us, O Lord and thy gifts, which we are about to receive from thy bounty, through Christ, Our Lord, Amen."

"Amen," the family chimed, crossing themselves with the sign of the cross.

Ephraim began dishing out helpings of roast beef and passing plates around the table to each person. "How did your day go, sweetheart?" he asked his wife as he passed Xavier a plate of roast beef.

"Good. The hospital wasn't damaged much, but a lot of the supplies have been destroyed or stolen. So, Healer Dorne and I will be making a trip to the mainland tomorrow to replenish our stocks."

Ephraim nodded as he passed another plate to Drew.

"Dad? Can Xavier and I go camping at the lake tonight?" Court asked.

Ephraim paused briefly, his gaze fluttering between Xavier and his son. "Who's going to be there?"

"Beck, Garrett, and all the guys."

"I don't know, son. King Wells gave Xavier permission to spend the night here in the residence, not in the woods."

"Come on! We haven't had much time to be with our friends and to just goof around. We've been working our tails off; we need a break. Please?" he pleaded.

Ephraim passed a plate to Dennis.

"Well, I don't see why you couldn't go, but Xavier needs to ask his father. He needs to know about the change in plans." Ephraim passed the remaining plates to Court and Caleb before looking at Xavier. "If your dad tells me you can go, then I have no problem with the camp out."

"Yes, sir," Xavier responded before turning to Court. "I'll ask him after dinner."

The moment the last plate of roast beef was distributed, the boys immediately scrambled to fill their plates with potatoes, green beans, rolls and butter, and fruit salad. Xavier had little experience when it came to large family dinners and found himself watching in awe at the sights and sounds. Everyone was talking at once, and the silverware clatter was like a chorus of wind chimes. If Court hadn't kept prodding him, he wouldn't have had a crumb to eat but the meat on his plate.

"Xavier, here mate. Have some potatoes before Drew gets a hold of them," Court called, nudging him.

"Mum, tell Caleb to stop doing that!" Dennis complained as Caleb stuck out his tongue coated with a mixture of half-chewed food.

"Caleb Walter Hardcastle! Mind your manners or you'll go to bed without dinner!" Rebecca chided.

"Dad? Can I go camping with Court and Prince Xavier?" Caleb asked, shrugging off his mother's reprimand.

"NO! You're not going, bogie miner!"

"Courtney! Don't call your brother that!" Rebecca snapped.

"But, Mum! If Caleb goes, it won't be a break for me, and that's the whole point of the campout! I'll have to babysit him so he doesn't drown himself," Court argued.

"Dad! I need a break too! Can't I go camping?" Caleb persisted.

"Dad!" Court whined.

"Dad!" Caleb mocked, and Courtney thumped him on the arm.

"Ouch! Mum!"

"Ouch, Muuuuum!" Court mimicked and a shoving match between the younger sons ensued.

"You know, for once, I'd like to have a peaceful meal without a major row at the table!" Rebecca stated.

"That's enough, boys," Ephraim called firmly, and his sons fell silent. "Caleb can go."

"But, Dad!" Court bellowed.

"Courtney! I've given my decision," Ephraim stated, his eyes pinning his son into silence.

Court ate the remainder of his meal without another word, sulking and throwing murderous glances at his younger brother.

After dinner, Xavier followed Court into his room that he shared with Caleb.

"Blimey! I can't believe Dad's letting Caleb go! I swear to God, if that little git..."

Caleb entered the room with an enormous grin. "Hey, guys. What should I take?"

"Your bible and rosary," Court hissed. "You're going to need them to pray that I don't kill you in your sleep."

Caleb rolled his eyes dismissively and looked at Xavier. "Did King Wells say you could go?" he chirped.

"Oh, ah...not yet," he muttered and looked at Court. "I better go ask."

Court nodded as he began scrounging in his closet for his sleeping bag.

When Xavier entered the residence, he found Mrs. Sommers restocking the wet bar in the receiving room.

"Hey, Mrs. Sommers. Where's Dad?"

"Hi, sweetie. What are you doing home so soon?"

"Well, there's been a change in plans. The guys and I are going camping at the lake if it's okay with Dad. Where is he?" he gushed.

"Oh, that sounds like fun. He's in his room, I believe," she replied, continuing with her work.

Xavier bounded up the steps two at a time and hurried

into his father's room, but he was nowhere in sight.

"Dad? Dad?" he called, moving toward the open patio door. He found the king leaning against the patio wall watching the sun set.

He looked up at him in surprise. "Hey, kiddo. What are you doing home?"

"Well, Court and the guys are going to the lake to camp and I was wondering if I could go with them. Please?" he pleaded.

"I don't see a problem with it, but you'll need a good sleeping bag," he answered, leading the way back into the bedroom and crossing to his closet. "Here, take mine. It should keep you dry and warm." He pulled the bag from the closet and handed it him.

Xavier hugged the sleeping bag against him, smelling his father's scent on the fabric. He smiled up at him. "Thanks, Dad. I'll see ya in the morning, okay?"

"There's no hurry. I have an early meeting with Governor Bracus and the rest of the High Council. So if you and your friends are still going strong tomorrow morning that will be fine. Just be home for lunch, okay?"

"Yes, sir. Goodnight, Dad."

"Goodnight, son. Stay out of mischief," he warned.

Five minutes later, Xavier, Court, and Caleb slipped through the secret passage in the palace's wall. The academy's windows were ablaze.

"Hey! What's going on at Wells Academy?" Caleb asked.

"God, Caleb! Do you live in a cave or something? It's where they're keeping all the kids in the Dark Army until their trials."

"Oh," Caleb whispered.

"About time! How slow can you get? We've been waiting for *hours*! What's the matter? Did you girls have to do each other's hair or something?" Beck called from the edge of the woods.

"Shut up, Beck! You nag worse than my mother," Court bellowed with

a laugh.

As they approached the group of boys, Beck's grin slipped as his eyes drifted on Caleb. "Damn, Hardcastle! We're not running a nursery!"

"I know," Court groaned, giving Caleb a shove. "The little git whined to the old man until he made me bring him."

"I didn't whine..."

Court moved in on his brother. "Shut it, Caleb! You invited yourself along, but that doesn't mean we have to listen to your mouth all night."

"You can't make me..."

"You want to bet? See Harry there?" Court asked, nodding to the dark-haired, dark-eyed boy leaning against a tree trunk. "He's a glaciator. All I have to do is give him a sign, and he'll freeze your mouth shut."

Harry nodded, but didn't say a word, which was more intimidating to the younger boy. Caleb visibly gulped and gave a nervous nod.

"Okay...okay. I won't say a word. I promise."

This seemed to satisfy the group, and they began their trek into the woods. When they arrived at the lake, the sun had set, and its fiery glow was beginning to fade into the horizon.

"Okay, mates. We should build a fire first, and then we can go skinny dipping," Beck announced, plopping his sleeping bag and duffle onto the ground.

"Skinny dipp..." Caleb began, forgetting his promise and was met with half a dozen piercing glares. "Sorry, I forgot."

"Well, don't forget it again," Court spat. "And for your information *baby* brother, we skinny dip because it's fun. We skinny dip because we can't just run home for dry clothes."

"Oh," Caleb muttered.

It didn't take long for the group to gather firewood and start the fire, and within minutes, they were stripped and splashing riotously in the lake.

"Hey, Hardcastle. I hear you and Jefferson have a *thing* going. Are you really that sick in the head? I mean, why would you want her for a girlfriend? She's bossy, pushy, and a complete pain in the ass!" Beck asked.

"Hey, I like my women with spirit!" he defended as he splashed Beck.

"What about you, Xavier? Are you and Robbie still sucking face?" Beck questioned snidely.

"Back off, Beck," he warned quietly.

The other boy shifted uncomfortably, but not another word was said about Robbie.

The boys were so preoccupied with swimming, mucking around, and splashing each other that they never noticed their clothes had mysteriously disappeared until they were ready to dry off and enjoy the warmth of the fire.

"Hey! Where are our clothes?" Frankie piped up as they swam toward shore.

A muffled group of giggles brought the boys to a halt before climbing ashore.

"Who's there?" Court demanded.

"Who's there?" a high voice mocked before bursting into snickers with at least three other voices.

"X? Can you *listen in* and see who it is?" Garrett whispered.

Xavier paused and stared into the dark trees before finally smiling. "It's Erica, Robbie, Rene Jones, and

Melissa Dorne."

"Melissa Dorne!" Garrett exclaimed, looking at Beck. "I told you she was sweet on you!"

"Shut it, Bracus," Beck hissed before bellowing into the wood. "Hey, Jefferson. You better give us our clothes back, or you'll be sorry!"

There was a loud giggle. "And just what are you going to do stark naked, Wilson?" All the girls burst into laughter and started squealing out catcalls at the boys.

"What do we do?" Frankie asked, and every boy looked at Xavier.

"Hey, Xavier. Why don't you just summon our clothes back," Court suggested, and the other boys nodded eagerly.

"Uh, yeah. Okay."

After a deep breath, he closed his eyes and extended his hand toward where the girls were hiding. Almost instantly, he felt tingling in his fingertips, and their clothes flew from the trees and landed in a pile next to the fire. The group cheered around Xavier, but he didn't have time to bask in the glory of his success for his fingers were still tingling. He couldn't seem to disconnect his summoning powers. Suddenly, four girls flew screaming from the wood and splashed into the water in one tangled heap. The boys around him burst into uncontrollable laughter.

The girls, on the other hand, were livid.

"Who did it?" Erica blared, her soppy gaze darting from boy to boy before settling on Xavier.

"Xavier? Why did you do that? That was mean!" Robbie asked, her voice hard and hurt.

"Oh, come off it!" Beck bellowed. "You girls had it coming and you know it. Do you really think that swiping our clothes wasn't a bit mean?"

The girls didn't have a comeback for that and simply stared at Xavier.

"I thought so," Beck declared triumphantly. "Now, if you don't mind, we'd like to get dressed."

"Oh, no, we don't mind at all, Beckley," Melissa replied with a coy smile.

"Come on, come on, turn your backs so we can get out and get some pants on!" Frankie bellowed.

"Turn our backs?" Erica teased. "What on Earth do you mean?"

"Fine. Turn your backs or don't, but I am getting out," Xavier spat irritably and waded through the water toward the girls in the shallow end.

The girls squealed, ran out of the water, and disappeared into the trees. The group of boys burst into triumphant laughter.

"Way to go, Xavier!" Garrett cheered, clapping him on the back as he made his way to the shore.

"Wait! How do we know they're really gone and not hiding in the wood?" Caleb asked.

"Caleb, try not to think, would you? It's just too hard on your feeble brain," Court mocked, climbing ashore and pulling on his undershorts and pants. "Xavier has telepathy. He'd know if they were, you git."

"Oh," the younger boy mumbled and climbed from the water and dressed.

However, Xavier wasn't sure if the girls were gone or not. His telepathy had suddenly gone silent. He couldn't connect with the girls or any of the guys. What was happening to his abilities? In one day, he had lost his telekinetic grip on a boulder nearly crushing Harry's dad, unintentionally dunked his girlfriend and her friends, and no longer seemed able to read thoughts. But he didn't say a word to the others as he settled in his sleeping bag near the fire.

Chapter 4

A Kingly Mistake

Late the next morning, the boys packed up and went their separate ways. As Xavier, Court, and Caleb scrambled sleepily through the secret passage and circled around the palace, Erica skipped up from behind them carrying an overnight bag.

"Hello, boys," she chirped with a wide grin. "My, my, it's good to see you actually *wearing* clothes, but I must say you have adorable backsides."

"Yeah right, Jefferson. Just keep pretending like you saw something. We know Xavier scared you off. But, seeing you in a wet t-shirt was definitely worth the price of admission," Court teased, blowing a kiss at her.

Erica's confidence faltered briefly, but within a fraction of a second, it was replaced with smug satisfaction. "And what makes you think Xavier scared us away...completely away."

Court laughed dismissively. "Fine. You say you were there; prove it!"

Her grin widened. "Well, Beck has a scar on his left hip. Whereas, you have a birthmark on your left cheek, and I don't mean the cheek on your face."

His jaw dropped as Erica flashed him a brilliant smile and walked ahead toward the palace entrance.

"Oh, and Xavier? Robbie is really mad at you for throwing her in the lake. You better go and see her. She doesn't see you nearly drowning us as fair play, like I do. She thinks you've betrayed her."

"Betrayed her? I didn't..."

"Don't tell me," Erica retorted impatiently. "Tell her!" Then she entered the palace.

"Holy Hell, X! Why didn't you say something about the girls still being around? When the other guys find out, they'll go barmy. Those girls are never going to let us live it down! We're talking a lifetime of snide remarks and taunts," Court hissed.

But Xavier wasn't listening to Court. His father and Loren had just exited the Governing Hall and were stalking across the horseshoe-shaped drive. It was clear by their expressions that they were both in foul moods and Loren was glaring lividly at Jeremiah's back.

"Sorry, Court. I've gotta go," he mumbled and scrambled after the men.

"Wait Xavier!" Court called after him. "What are we going to do about the girls?"

"I'll talk to you later," he yelled over his shoulder and hurried into the palace after the men.

He heard the men before he saw them. Loren's shouts flooded out from the royal residence. Xavier scurried up the steps, and when he opened the royal door, he found them toe to toe.

"This is none of your business, Loren."

"You were out of line. Jesus, Jer! What were you thinking?"

"JEREMIAH WELLS!" Lucy shouted as she pushed by Xavier and into the room.

Jeremiah paled at the sight of the furious woman storming across the room. She pushed herself between the men and poked the king in the chest.

"You have gone too far this time! I just got off the phone with Lana. She was crying hysterically. I could barely understand her."

Jeremiah sighed, turned, and walked to the small bar near the hearth. He poured himself a drink and muttered without turning, "If she weren't so stubborn, if she'd just listen to reason..."

"Jeremiah Xavier Wells! Do not make this out to be her fault!"

"Lucy." Jeremiah turned to face her, his face set and stony. "I am your king. I would appreciate a less accusatory tone and more respect!"

Lucy glared at him unflinchingly. "Then, act like it! I should have known your pride and ego would win out. I'm disappointed in you, *King Wells*." The woman spun around in a huff and stomped to the door.

"Lucy, stop!" Jeremiah called after her. "Please stop."

Lucy paused before turning back toward Jeremiah. "Remember when we were kids, Jeremy? Remember what you used to say about your father? You used to tell me that he was overbearing, insensitive, out of touch with the common man, and an outright bully? You promised, no you *swore* on your mother's grave you'd never be like him. Well, sire, you broke that promise today," she spat as she pointed accusingly at his chest. "And, if you continue as you are, you'll not only rival your father's cruelty, you'll surpass it." Lucy turned and exited the residence, slamming the door behind her.

At the insistence of Mrs. Sommers', later that afternoon Xavier begrudgingly began cleaning his room. He dropped the last of his dirty clothes in the hamper when his father strolled into the room.

"Wow," Jeremiah exclaimed, announcing his presence. "What on Earth drove you to do this?"

"Mrs. Sommers," he explained, grinning sheepishly at his father. "You know what she's like. She's a bit scary when she gets demanding."

His father nodded with a grin. "Yes, I know. She still scares me."

He laughed.

"I know school doesn't start for another couple weeks, but I think, under the present circumstances, we'll start your impediment lessons today," Jeremiah told him, crossing the room to the plush armchairs next to the windows and settling in one. He motioned to the other.

"What? You mean now? But, Dad...I was going to take a shower. The guys and I went swimming in the lake and..."

"Xavier, I have time in my schedule right now. Please sit, so we can begin," his father replied shortly.

"Yes, sir," he muttered and moodily collapsed into the armchair across from his father. He wasn't looking forward to this. Impediment lessons usually left him with a bit of a headache, and now that his father was overseeing his lessons, he knew the headaches would be undoubtedly worse. Not to mention, since the silence he experienced at the lake, he hadn't tried to use his telepathic abilities. What if he couldn't engage them? What would his dad say? Maybe he wasn't the Chosen after all. Would the Chosen experience faulty powers?

However, all his fears left him as he began to meditate and felt the power responding inside him. Overwhelmed with relief, he nearly laughed out loud.

"Ready?" Jeremiah whispered.

Xavier gave him a brisk nod and the session began with a jolting shock. His father was in his thoughts with no effort at all, and before he could even begin to repel him, he was penetrating the surface layer of his thoughts and accessing his memories. Suddenly, Robbie came into his mind, and their first kiss.

"Dad! Stop!" he shouted.

Jeremiah withdrew and stared at him placidly.

"What was that?" he snapped, standing and glaring down at his father.

"It's what any telepath could do if he refines his skill," he answered calmly.

"Yeah, well, I don't think Fox even has telepathy!" he hissed angrily. "So why are we even bothering?"

"Xavier..."

"No, Dad! This is stupid. I'm taking a shower!" he blared and stomped toward the bathroom.

"Xavier Wells!" his father's voice held such unwavering authority that the boy froze. "Come here and sit down."

He obeyed.

"Son, do you really think we should base your preparation on what powers you *think* Fox has?"

He huffed bitterly before finally muttering, "No, sir. I guess not."

"Good. Now, let's continue. When I infiltrate your thoughts, do not panic. Panic clouds your concentration. Instead, and I can't believe I'm telling you this, think of a believable lie. Think of something that would interest the intruder and lead him astray. This is the first step in impediment, as I'm sure Spencer has taught you," Jeremiah concluded.

He took a deep breath and tried to relax. He closed his eyes and concentrated on a lie he thought his father would believe. He thought of Lana. He knew he was playing dirty, but he figured it didn't matter since he would need to practice any and all means necessary to impede Fox's attempts.

"Okay, I'm ready."

Instantly, he felt the coolness of his father's presence in his thoughts, but the force connecting them shuddered. Suddenly, his head began to spin, and he found himself in his father's thoughts. Slowly, a white veil dissolved and he found himself in his father's office at the Governing Hall. His father and Lana stood tensely facing one another.

"Lord Lana! You know why I did it! Why are you being so stubborn? I know you still love me; I can feel it in your thoughts," his father demanded.

"Good Lord! You only seem capable of repeating the same lines over and over again," she spat. "Yes, Jeremiah! I know why you pushed me away, but what you don't seem to understand is that you were wrong!"

"Wrong? I wasn't wrong! Or didn't you hear what LeMasters did to Milton? He butchered the poor man! He would have done the same to you...or worse!"

"Yes, *King Wells*. I know all of that! You don't get it, do you? You really don't see how badly you handled this at all! Well, fine. Keep thinking your holier than thou thoughts, but I'm not listening anymore," she yelled and stomped toward the door.

"Lana!" his father called, rushing after her and grabbing her arm. Not another word was said as he pulled her to him, trapping her against him with his arms. Her struggling stopped the moment he kissed her. After a moment, her senses returned, and she began squirming in his grasp. Finally, she shoved him away and swung an open hand at his face. He swatted it away lazily and kissed her again. Again, she wiggled loose.

"You do that again and I'll scream bloody murder, *Your Highness*," she growled.

"If you didn't like it, why did you kiss me back? Why did you even come to my office to see me?" he asked smugly.

This time her hand found its mark on his cheek, and she spat, "You boastful, egotistical pig! How dare you! I didn't come to *see* you; I came to give you my resignation! I am resigning from my High Council position and judgeship." She thrust a piece of paper into Jeremiah's hands before turning and storming from the room.

"Xavier!" the king boomed.

The memory of his father dissolved away and Xavier found himself staring into the genuine article's enraged eyes.

"Da... Dad? I'm sorry. I...I don't know how I did that! I...I..."

His father's eyes softened marginally. "No matter. I wasn't prepared for you to be capable of doing that yet," he grumbled. Then after a deep breath, he continued more steadily, "I know better now. I won't underestimate you again."

The brief success of infiltrating his father's thoughts and memories wasn't repeated. His father had been restraining his telepathic strength before, but he didn't make the same mistake twice. Soon, Xavier had a pounding headache and couldn't stop his father from invading memory after memory.

Finally, the king sighed and announced a bit too happily, "Well, I think we've done enough today. A hot shower will help ease your headache, son. But before you do, can you tell me what that last image was about? Did you truly throw those girls into the lake?"

Xavier rubbed his head and answered sheepishly, "Yeah...well, you saw they stole our clothes...what was I to do?"

Jeremiah eyed him astringently. "Okay, okay. Granted, you were in a tough situation but, son, a king must rise above being goaded into actions that can be perceived as strong-arming."

"You mean like what you did when you forced Lana to kiss you?" he challenged, irritated at his father's pompous, know-it-all tone.

The expression of superiority slipped quickly from his father's face as he stared coolly down at him. After several long moments, he stood and ordered brusquely, "It's nearly dinnertime. Get a shower."

As his father reached the door, Xavier blurted, "I'm going to Robbie's first. I have to talk to her."

"No, you are not. Shower. Dinner's in twenty minutes."

"It'll only take five minutes!"

"Son, I said no. You'll have to do it tomorrow after the trials."

"But, Dad!"

"No, Xavier!" he barked, and the pair stared bullishly at one another for several long minutes until Xavier's eyes dropped to the floor.

"Downstairs in twenty minutes," his father commanded before turning and opening the door to leave the room.

Xavier made a face and a rude gesture at his father's back.

"If you do that again, boy, you'll be in a world of hurt," his father warned without turning and left the room.

Chapter 5

Midnight Visit

Xavier tossed and turned in bed that night. The thought of Robbie being mad at him, hating him again, made it impossible for sleep to come. He tried calling her after dinner, but she wouldn't come to the phone. He had to talk to her tonight, or he would never sleep. With his mind made up, he hopped from bed, pulled on jeans and a t-shirt, and crept to the door. It wasn't quite 11:00 pm, and his father was surely still up. He slowly pulled the door open and peered down at the reception room below. His father sat in an armchair next to the fire with a drink in hand and a small stack of files on his lap. But, he didn't seem to be working. He sat staring at the flickering fire, sipping the amber liquid.

Holding his breath, Xavier tiptoed down the walkway to his father's bedroom. He closed the door with a soft click and expelled his breath before hurrying out onto the patio. Once there, he closed his eyes and concentrated on Robbie's bedroom. He had been there only once. Last fall, they wrote a history paper about Hurricane Andrew which struck the east coast of the United States in 1992. After cross-referencing the disaster with newspaper clippings from both common and empowered sources, they determined that the hurricane had been the result of an undocumented empowered teen who had no idea he was causing the extreme weather patterns.

But, it had been months since the project, and it was extremely important to have an accurate mental picture of the environment he was teleporting into, or he could end up stuck in a wall or something. After a moment of breathing evenly and concentrating on the memory of the room, Xavier felt the familiar tug as the power actuated. Within his next breath, he teleported from his father's patio to Robbie's room. Slowly he opened his eyes and waited for the dizziness to subside. He saw Robbie's sleeping figure a foot from where he stood. Grinning triumphantly in the dark, he knelt next to her bed.

"Robbie?" he whispered, shaking her lightly. "Robbie, wake up."

She jerked awake, and he clamped his hand over her mouth to keep her from screaming. "Sh! It's just me."

"Xavier? What on Earth are you doing in my bedroom?" she hissed.

"I had to talk to you...to apologize for what happened at the lake," he whispered. "I'm really sorry if I hurt you. I didn't mean for it to happen. It was an accident. I was only trying to get our clothes back; I never meant to toss you into the lake. Really!"

"Then how did it happen, Xavier?" she asked softly.

Relieved that she didn't sound mad, he sank to the floor beside her bed and sighed. "I don't know how it happened. It was like I couldn't turn my power off. I think something's happening to me, Rob. Weird things keep happening to my abilities. Like, I didn't know that you were still hiding in the woods when I...when we all got out of the water."

"Yeah, I thought that was strange," she whispered, as she climbed from her bed and sat on the floor next to him.

"I just figured maybe you wanted us watching..."

"Why would I want that?" he hissed moodily. "Would you?"

"No. I'm sorry. It was one of Erica's harebrained ideas. I swear, she's getting worse than her dad. I'm sorry, Xavier."

"It's okay. There's nothing that can be done about it now. But, Robbie, I didn't *know* that any of you were still around. My telepathic ability was...gone!" he continued.

"Gone? Is it still?" she asked, alarmed.

Xavier shook his head before he remembered in the darkness she couldn't see him. "No. I got it back just in time for impediment lessons with Dad today. Whoopee! But, that's not all Robbie. Yesterday, I nearly killed Mr. Sims. I lost control of my telekinesis during the reconstruction of the gatehouse and a stone nearly crushed Harry's dad. If Loren hadn't caught it..." his voice wavered at the thought. He felt her hand searching for his before grasping it and giving it a reassuring squeeze.

"Xavier? Have you told your dad about this? It might have something to do with the prophecy..."

"No, I didn't tell him and I'm not going to. He's being a complete jerk all the time. He yells at me for no reason. Well, not just me, he yells at everyone really." Then he snickered dryly. "But Lucy gave him a verbal smack down this morning." He sighed miserably, throwing his head back against the softness of the mattress. "Lana resigned from the High Council today!"

"Oh...well, I think most people had kind of expected that," she noted.

"I didn't!" he hissed.

"Well, Xavier, what did you expect her to do? She couldn't very well stay on the High Council and make judgments on your father's actions when she's feeling so distraught over him. It wouldn't be fair to the throne. Lana is a very honorable woman. She wouldn't taint the Council in that way," she explained.

"Yeah, I guess. It just feels like she and Dad are growing farther and farther apart. I really miss her."

"I know. I'm sorry," she whispered, squeezing his hand again.

"You won't tell Dad about the problems I'm having with my powers; will you?" he pleaded.

She was silent.

"Robbie, please!"

"But your dad might be able to help!"

"No, please. He's got enough going on. Please, don't tell him."

She sighed loudly, "All right, all right. I promise."

"Thanks." He draped an arm around her and pulled her close.

The couple cuddled into each other enjoying the closeness. With the kingdom in disarray, there had been too much work to do and little time to be together. Xavier stared into the darkness deep in thought with Robbie's soothing warmth next to him. Soon her breathing became loud and even. She'd fallen asleep. He grinned and muttered sleepily to the girl beside him, "It's nice to see I have such an intense effect on you. It does wonders for my ego, but I really should go."

She moaned a protest in her sleep, and again he smiled.

"Okay, I'll stay a few minutes longer." But his eyes were growing heavier, and he was having difficulty keeping them open. Finally, he gave in to the slumber with the thought, *"I'll just close my eyes for a few minutes."*

The next morning, as he began to stir from sleep, his entire left arm and shoulder felt heavy and numb.

"What's wrong with my arm?" he wondered and

opened his eyes. Bright sunlight blared through his bedroom window and he blinked. But, it wasn't his window, and it definitely wasn't his bedroom! Befuddled, his eyes drifted from the boy band posters on the purple walls to the unicorn figurines and stuffed animals cluttering bookshelves before finally to the white-washed dresser with purple lilacs painted at the corners of a large vanity mirror. Where was he? He looked back at the blinding light pouring through the window like a spotlight before finally looking at the sleeping girl nestled against his left side. Then, he remembered. Oh God! He was still in Robbie's room!

"Robbie! Robbie, wake up!" he hissed, shaking her.

She yawned and stretched before blinking up at him and frowning.

"Xavier?"

"Roberta Ann, you better get up and get a move on!" Mrs. Minnows called from outside the door.

Robbie bolted upright. "I'm awake, Mom. Don't come in! I'm not dressed!"

"Roberta, I used to change your diapers, young lady!"

"Mom, I'm not a baby anymore! I need my privacy!"

"All right, but get a move on; breakfast is getting cold," her mother responded with a patient sigh.

"Be right there," she called and turned to Xavier. "You'd better go! If our parents find out..."

"You don't have to tell me," he remarked, standing and rushing to her window. Then, with a grin, he turned back to her and added, "It was nice sleeping with you."

"Xavier Wells! What a wicked thing to say!" she laughed, throwing a pillow at him, but missed for he had already teleported out of her room.

Xavier found himself swaying unsteadily on the edge of the patio wall very close to plunging off the third floor.

Swinging his arms wildly, he managed to regain his balance. Then he hopped down from the patio wall and crept cautiously into his father's room. His father was not in bed, in fact it was already made, nor did it appear he was in the shower or shaving. He hurried out of the room and down the walkway, finding the reception room empty. The palace was quiet. Relieved that he was having a bit of good luck, he opened his bedroom door and ducked inside.

"WHERE IN THE HELL HAVE YOU BEEN?" his father boomed, standing next to the bed.

"Ah...I...was...I was downstairs getting a drink."

"Don't lie to me, boy!" he barked.

"I'm not..." he shifted under his father's glare for several excruciating minutes. Finally, he muttered, "I...I was at Robbie's."

"What in God's name were you doing at Robbie's at this early hour?" he asked.

"I had to talk to her, and I couldn't sleep until I did. I didn't mean to be there all night. I fell asleep. I couldn't help it," he explained in a rush.

"What?" his father roared stomping toward him. "You spent the night there?"

"God, don't go crazy, Dad! I only went to apologize for dunking her in the lake! We were just talking!" he yelled defensively.

"I don't give a damn what you were doing! You were told not to go to Robbie's! You had no business being there!" his father hollered. "As the Prince of Warwood, your behavior and actions must be the epitome of honor and respect."

He huffed indignantly as he stomped across the room, sat on the bed, and began pulling off his shoes. "I was honorable. I was apologizing. You should try it sometime, *King Wells*," he spat before stomping toward the bathroom.

His father nearly came unglued, and his face flushed with anger. "Xavier Wells! Stop this instant!"

With his own temper teetering, he spun to face the fiery man. "No, Dad, you stop! No one is going to know I accidently fell asleep at Robbie's. You're being stupid about this and about Lana! Just because you and Lana aren't..."

The king's murderous glare silenced the boy instantly. After a long, tense moment, he growled, "You're grounded to the palace for a month, boy."

"What? No! That's not fair! You can't make me! God, why are you being such a jackass?" he spat out.

Before he could blink, his father tore across the room, grabbed him roughly, hoisted him off his feet, and pinned him against the wall. His eyes were wild and manic. "Do NOT speak to me like that EVER again, boy! And, believe me when I tell you, I CAN make you. It could prove painful for you if I do. Now, if you wish to continue to give me cheek, I may be inclined to show you a bit of that pain now!"

Xavier felt a shiver of fear sweep through him and he froze in his father's hard, painful clutches.

"Dad?" he squeaked. "Dad, you're hurting me..."

"Jeremiah Wells!" Mrs. Sommers snapped from the door and stomped into the room with fury flaming in her eyes. "Release that boy at once!"

Jeremiah's head snapped to Mrs. Sommers before looking back at Xavier with shock. Gently, his father lowered him to the floor and released him.

"Xavier? Breakfast is ready. Go downstairs; your father will join you shortly."

"Yes, ma'am," he whispered and scurried from the room.

Mrs. Sommers entered the dining hall fifteen minutes later.

"Did you get him straightened out?" he blurted indignantly and was met by a stern glare.

"Yes and now it's your turn, young man!" she scolded. "First, you have absolutely no business staying out all night! Why were you out that late?"

He shrugged.

"Don't shrug at me, Jeremiah Xavier Wells; answer the question! What were you doing at Miss Minnow's late last night?"

"I only went there to apologize to her for something that I did. I didn't mean to fall asleep."

"As noble as that is, Xavier, you had no business sneaking out at that late hour. Your father was frantic when he didn't find you in your bed this morning."

"Worried? Yeah, right," he spat sarcastically. "He just likes to have control over everything and everyone around him, especially me! Lucy's right. Dad's a bully."

"Xavier Wells! I cannot believe you! You have a knack for getting yourself in dire situations that your father has to rescue you from, and you have the nerve to call your father a bully and belittle his feelings? Shame on you!"

He tucked his head to Mrs. Sommers' reprimands.

"Sorry. I'm just mad at him. He wouldn't even listen to me! I hadn't meant to be gone all night. I only wanted to apologize to Robbie. That's all! He just got so...so bent out of shape."

His governess sighed and patted his shoulder before sitting next to him. "Honey, I'm not excusing your father's behavior at all, but you've got to understand that he's been under a great deal of stress lately. He's rebuilding the kingdom, he's preparing our shattered kingdom for a war that could come at any moment, he grieves and feels guilty about the lives lost during the invasion, and he's beginning to realize he ruined things with Lana. But the biggest and most overwhelming responsibility weighing on his shoulders is raising a willful, stubborn son who will someday be the King of Warwood and, more importantly, the savior of mankind. He struggles every day not to become the father he had, but when his stress level increases and when you challenge his authority again and again, the more difficult it is for him to overcome it. He lost that struggle this morning when he grabbed you the way he did. He feels horrible about it."

"Was Grandfather that...mean?" Xavier asked.

"Yes, he was. Lord knows he loved his sons. He just didn't know how to show it in the way they needed, not like the way your father shows you. Your grandfather wouldn't do anything with his sons unless it could serve as some kind of lesson or test on becoming a strong ruler. He never played rugby with them, he never took them fishing or on a picnic, he wouldn't wrestle around with them, and he never hugged or consoled them when they had nightmares or a bad day. He believed that by showing any kind of affection it would make them soft, and since your father was the heir to the throne, he received more severe discipline, sterner words, and harsher lessons and tests than Michael. This difference in treatment put a wedge between them and King Wells Senior used their rivalry against them, deepening their resentment for each other. Your grandfather flirted between the line of harsh discipline and abuse."

"Jeez, he sounds like a nightmare to me. I'm glad I didn't know him," he muttered.

Mrs. Sommers nodded. "Yes, he could be but, honey, you have to understand your grandfather was only doing the best he knew how. I grew up with your grandfather. As a boy, he wasn't much different than you or your father at that age. The throne brings enormous responsibility and power and that can change a person. Only your father has attempted to break the cycle of harsh parenting. So when he comes down for breakfast, you will apologize for worrying him and for your cheek. Is that clear?"

"Yes, ma'am," he muttered.

Ten minutes later, his father entered the dining hall as Xavier ate his waffles and fruit.

"I'll get your breakfast, Your Highness," Mrs. Sommers announced sweetly and left the room.

He settled in his seat with a nod and cleared his throat. "Son? I'm sorry for...well, for my behavior. I had no right to grab you the way I did."

"It's okay," he muttered. "I'm sorry too, Dad. I shouldn't have talked to you like I did, and I'm sorry I worried you when you found my bed empty this morning. I really didn't mean to be gone long. I only wanted to apologize to her."

"I know," his father replied softly, "but I told you not to go last night. Didn't I?"

"Yes, sir. You did," he mumbled.

"Therefore, you're grounded to the palace for the rest of the week. If you choose to defy me on this punishment, then I will put you over my knee and spank you." Jeremiah spoke softly, but his voice held a commanding finality so that Xavier found his mutinous thoughts evaporating and nodded.

"Good. Now, we have trials this morning. So when you're finished with your breakfast, get cleaned up. Mrs. Sommers laid out your clothes for today."

"She doesn't have to do that. I can find something to wear on my own."

"It's her job, son. Besides, you'll need to wear a suit, your royalty sash, and robe. A king's attire must reflect his authority on occasions like the proceedings we're dealing with today."

"Oh," he muttered, frowning. "But a suit?"

His father grinned. "I'm afraid so."

Chapter 6

Trials

Thirty minutes later, Xavier descended the steps into the reception room wearing a black pin-stripe suit, his gold royalty sash, and blue cloak. He felt a bit pretentious dressed as he was, and he fidgeted self-consciously as he approached his father, who was smiling broadly.

"Well, look at you! You look smart."

"Thanks, but I need help with my tie."

He handed the blue tie to his father who knotted it neatly at his neck in seconds.

"Okay, let's go. The hearings for the children are being held at the academy," his father announced, leading him out of the residence.

Loren joined them, looking uncharacteristically somber as they made their way out of the palace and into an awaiting limo. Within minutes, the limo pulled to a halt in front of the school, and Xavier followed Loren and his father out of the vehicle. As they strode into the building, he looked at his school with renewed eyes. All signs of the battle school the Dark Army had created were gone. Most classrooms had been refurnished with desks, tables, and chairs. It was as if the school had never been altered.

"The Council has set up in the cafeteria for the hearings," Loren told them, opening the cafeteria door for the king and prince.

The moment they stepped into the room, the High Council stood and bowed. Three new faces were among the council now. Governor Bracus and Marcus, a pinch-faced, middle-aged man with rectangular glasses, still held positions, but the other members were new.

"Hello, my kings!" Governor Bracus announced joyfully as he straightened and approached them with an extended hand.

"Hello, Simon!" his father greeted him with a smile and shook the older man's hand.

"Hello, Xavier! How have you been, little king?" the governor asked, turning to him and shaking his hand.

"I've been good."

"I'm glad to hear it! Have you been staying out of trouble?" he asked, his large eyes twinkling with humor.

"I've been trying, sir, but it's a lot harder than it sounds."

"Yes, I guess it is." The thin man chuckled. "I'll tell you what I told Garrett. No one expects you to go through life without making a few mistakes, but the important thing is that you learn from them. So? What have you learned?" he asked with an arched brow. On another man, this expression would have come across as stern and reproving, but on Garrett's grandfather, it looked amiable and warm.

Xavier faltered. "Ah, well, which time, sir?" he questioned bashfully.

Surprisingly, the governor coughed out a deep-throated, bellowing laugh. "Touché, Your Highness."

"Sire? The first child is waiting in the hall when you're ready to begin," the king's secretary, announced from the door.

"Thank you, Alexandra. Give us five minutes and then send him in," he told her before looking down at his son.

"Come. Let's get to our seats."

He followed his father to the table where the other council members sat waiting.

"How are you, Judge Stull?" the king greeted, nodding to a heavy-set man sitting at the end of the table.

"Good morning, King Wells," he responded in a deep gravelly voice.

Jeremiah turned back to Xavier. "As you can see, we have a few new members on the Council. This is Jack Stull. He's a high-level judge here in the kingdom. He resides over highly public trials or severe first degree crimes."

"Nice to meet you, Judge Stull," Xavier greeted the man.

"It's an honor, young prince," the judge replied. He had a friendly smile and gentle eyes. Xavier decided immediately that he liked him.

"Margaret! You're looking beautiful today," Jeremiah called jovially, winking at the woman seated next to the judge.

"Oh, sire," she giggled, waving at him dismissively. "You need glasses!"

"Son, this is Ms. Margaret Wilks. She is the new governor for the Wellington District."

"Hello, Governor Wilks. It's a pleasure to meet you, ma'am," he intoned sweetly.

She smiled. "Likewise, your highness."

"Good morning, Marcus," Jeremiah nodded to the familiar man with rectangular glasses sitting next to Governor Wilks. Marcus responded with a polite nod. "Son, I don't think you've ever been introduced to Mr. Anderson. Mr. Anderson is a long-time member of the Council."

He smiled at the man sitting stiffly in his chair. Mr. Anderson had been fair at his father's trial after he used the King's Key illegally in order to save Xavier's life. He respected the man's integrity. "How do you do, Mr. Anderson? It's good to meet you," he greeted, extending his hand.

Marcus Anderson smiled at the young prince and shook his hand. "You as well, young sire."

As they settled in two empty seats in the center of the table, his father nodded to the final new member. "Lastly, the man next to you is the latest member, but I'm sure introductions aren't necessary. How's business, Jon? "

"It's as busy as ever, Sire. Many families have a lot to replace since regaining their homes. I'm back-ordered on several things. Hello, Prince Wells. You've grown a bit since last fall. I suspect I'll be seeing you in my shop for alterations and new uniforms soon."

Xavier smiled at the man who owned and operated the only tailor shop in the kingdom. "Yes, sir. I guess you will."

"Okay, gentlemen, and lady," Governor Bracus announced from his seat at the end of the table. "The files for today's hearings are in front of each of you. The first child is waiting in the hall. Please take a moment to review his file before we begin."

Xavier jolted at the name on the top folder: Daniel Fine. He flipped open the file and feverishly skimmed through its contents, finding a picture of Daniel. The first boy on trial was none other than the little Daniel who had helped him when he returned to Warwood to confront William LeMasters. Why was Daniel on trial? He was just a little kid! LeMasters' men didn't even find him worthy of training. He was treated as nothing more than a servant; he wasn't a soldier. He turned to tell his father this, but before he could, the cafeteria door opened and the small, timid boy entered the room. Daniel looked terrified as he studied each adult sitting behind the long table, and when his eyes settled on King Wells, they nearly bulged out of his skull. Immediately, he sank to a knee and bowed.

"K...King Wells! It's an honor, sire," he squeaked.

"Stand up, child, and come closer," Jeremiah instructed firmly.

He rose and shuffled an inch at a time toward the king, looking totally petrified. Then his eyes settled on Xavier and he grinned.

"Prince Xavier!" he exclaimed and raced excitedly toward the table.

A royal guard swooped in to intercept the boy.

"No! Don't touch him!" Xavier blurted at the guard, jumping to his feet and scurrying over the table to Daniel, who immediately latched himself onto the prince like an eager puppy. "He's not going to hurt anyone," he told the guard, wrapping a protective arm around the smaller boy.

Without a word, the king nodded to the guard, who drifted back to his post at the end of the table.

Daniel looked up at Xavier, wide-eyed. "You're okay! When Master took you, I thought you were a goner for sure!" Then, he saw Xavier's bandaged hand and whispered, "Did he do that?"

He lifted his hand and flexed it. "Yeah, but it'll be as good as new in a couple weeks. Are they treating you okay in here?"

"Yeah! We get lots of food and we don't have to worry about being beaten anymore."

"Son? How do you know this boy?" Jeremiah asked, leaning forward and studying the smaller boy.

"Dad, this is the kid I was telling you about. Daniel helped me to get around without being recognized when I returned to Warwood. He's not a soldier! He wasn't even trained in combat. He shouldn't be on trial!" he explained eagerly.

The king studied the small boy in silence for several long seconds. Finally he intoned, "Well, young man it seems that I owe you an enormous debt for helping my son. Thank you! "

Daniel beamed.

"But I'm afraid I need to ask you a couple questions," he continued gently.

"Yes, sire. I'll answer any of your questions," Daniel replied, more confidently with Xavier beside him.

The king's eyes narrowed on the boy as he studied him more intently.

Xavier feared the worse and blurted out, "Dad, really! From everything I saw, he wasn't being trained at all! He wasn't one of the kids who attacked our kingdom. I know it!"

His father held up a hand silencing him as he continued to examine Daniel. Xavier huffed irritably but after a hard glance from his father, he went silent and waited.

Finally, the king asked, "How old are you, boy?"

"Nine and three quarters, sire. I'll turn ten in October," Daniel responded quietly. He could feel the king's energy growing more intense, and it made him nervous.

Jeremiah's eyes widened slightly and he asked in a rush, "What is your full name?"

The boy shifted nervously next to Xavier before responding, "Daniel Michael Spencer Fine, sir."

Xavier stiffened as his father leaped to his feet, his penetrating stare boring into small child. *Michael Spencer!* Xavier thought with a sudden understanding. He followed his father's wide, shell-shocked eyes to Daniel, who had cowered slightly at the king's sudden movement. He studied the younger boy's features with renewed interest.

"Who are your parents, boy?" Jeremiah continued.

"I never knew my dad, but my mom's name was Natalie

51

Fine," he answered quietly. His lower lip protruded and tears swelled in his eyes as he continued, "But...she's...she's dead. Master kidnapped us, and one day he took her out of our room, and she never came back." Tears poured over his cheek and a low sob escaped him. "She told me we'd escape someday and find my dad... that he'd protect us." His entire body shuddered as he tried to keep from sobbing. "But w...we never did. *He* k...killed her!" Then, he buried his face in his hands, turning into Xavier's chest, sobbing.

He hugged the smaller boy. "It's okay, Daniel. It's going to be okay. I know what you're going through. He killed my mom too."

He sniffed miserably. "He did?"

"Yeah, after Dad rescued me from the Institute, LeMasters kidnapped my mom and killed her," he told him.

"You were at the Institute?" he asked with wide, watery eyes. "That was a really bad place. Only the kids who wouldn't do what LeMasters said ended up there. None of them came back either!"

"Daniel?" Jeremiah called gently. "I must ask you one more question. I need to hear it from you. Did you participate in the attack on Warwood?"

Daniel's eyes widened to the size of saucers. "No, sire! Master didn't think my abilities were strong enough to help. Even if they had been, I wouldn't have done it! You're...the good guys! Why would I attack the good guys?"

"Why would LeMasters keep a child of no real value to him?" Marcus asked the king.

"Don't you see it, Marcus?" Governor Bracus hissed. Then, after a glance at Daniel, he whispered meaningfully, "The boy's name is Daniel *Michael Spencer* Fine! It doesn't take a genius to put two and two together."

Jeremiah looked at Alexandra. "Can investigators verify

this boy's claim?"

"Yes, sire. Lieutenant Henrick Davies interviewed the other child soldiers as well as the Royal Guard survivors. None of them remember a boy of Daniel's size and description on the battlefield. What the boy says is true," she responded.

The king nodded and turned to the Council. "I call to dismiss all charges and suspicion against Daniel Fine and ask for his immediate release."

The group voted unanimously for the king's motion.

The small boy looked at Xavier. "What does that mean?"

He grinned. "It means you're free."

Daniel returned the grin.

"I need a brief recess. I have a pressing matter that needs my attention," his father announced, moving around the table to Xavier and Daniel. He led the boys into the hall. "Xavier, take Daniel back to the palace. I will be home in a few hours."

"Dad, is Daniel..."

"Xavier!" his father's voice thrust into his thoughts, silencing his words. *"There are other people who need to be involved in this, son! Please, don't say anything until I've informed your uncle."*

"Yes, sir," he replied with a nod and turned to the boy. "Come on, Daniel. I'll show you my room."

"Uh, ok," he replied hesitantly, eying the king suspiciously. His expression resembling one he'd seen just a few days ago on Michael Spencer.

The boys exited the academy with Loren at their heels. "Daniel, this is Loren Jefferson. He's one of my father's closest friends and a general in the Premier Royal Guard."

"Hello, Mr. Jefferson," he greeted, extending his hand to Loren.

"*Mr.* Jefferson! Wow, I'm not used to that kind of respect, but really, kiddo, you can call me Loren," he replied enthusiastically, shaking the smaller boy's hand.

He grinned up at the enormous man beside him.

"Don't let him fool you, Daniel. He's the biggest troublemaker in the kingdom, but his daughter, Erica, is giving him a run for his money in that department," Xavier teased.

"I'm the troublemaker?" Loren roared and lunged at the prince, scooping him off his feet and carrying him over his shoulder like a sack. "You know something, Daniel. This little twerp has caused more mischief than my daughter and I combined!"

"Liar!" Xavier laughed.

"Hey, I'm talking to Danny here. So, hush up, Little Prince!" Loren retorted, smacking Xavier's rump.

"Ow!"

Daniel giggled.

"I hear you've decided to take over my job," Loren told the boy.

"What? N...no, sir. I didn't," he squeaked.

"That's not what I understand. I heard you did everything you could to keep Prince Wells here out of trouble," he explained, smacking Xavier again.

"Ow, Loren! Put me down!"

"Hush, Junior. We're trying to talk shop," he retorted dismissively.

"I only helped him a little. I didn't do much, really," Daniel protested, but Xavier could tell by the tone in his voice he was pleased with the compliment.

"I guess I better watch my back or I'll be out of a job," Loren answered with a wink.

"You WILL be out of a job if you don't put me down!" Xavier shouted, trying not to laugh.

"Princes! They can get so cranky when they don't get their way," he commented as he lowered Xavier to the ground.

Xavier chased the general around the limo several times trying to pummel him.

When they arrived at the palace, Xavier hopped out of the limo and led the smaller boy into the building. As they entered the antechamber they found Court kneeling on the stone floor reassembling his remote control helicopter.

"Hey Court! What's up?"

"I'm trying to fix this bloody thing! Caleb was messing with it and crashed it into Dennis's head. I had to superglue the propeller back on. It better work or I'm going to break Caleb's face." Court looked up and saw Daniel.

Xavier grinned. "This is Daniel. Daniel this is one of my best friends, Courtney Hardcastle. His dad, Ephraim Hardcastle, is another general in the Premier Royal Guard. Dad and Ephraim were friends growing up, too."

"Nice to meet you, Courtney," Daniel greeted, extending his hand to the other boy.

"Hey, good to meet you, but you can just call me Court." He shook the smaller boy's hand before turning back to Xavier. "Xavier, we've got to talk. The guys know the girls were still at the lake when we got out of the water. We need to figure out what we're going to do about it and come up with a plan for revenge. Mac and Beck are coming over later so we can come up with something. We could use your help."

"I can't. I'm grounded," he muttered.

"Grounded? How can you be grounded already?" Court asked.

"Do you even need to ask?" Loren teased as he entered the room. "He's Xavier Wells, son of King Wells. Of course he's managed to get himself grounded within the few short hours since you saw him last! Trouble is a Wells genetic trait."

Xavier punched Loren in the gut and laughed as Loren doubled over and mocked great pain. Daniel snickered at the big man.

"Seriously, Xavier, why are you grounded?" Court interrupted.

Xavier looked back at his friend and answered sheepishly, "Well, I transported to Robbie's last night and like an idiot, I fell asleep and didn't teleport home until 6:30 this morning. Dad was waiting for me in my room."

"Whoa! No way! You spent the night? What happened?"

"Nothing! I just fell asleep! We didn't even kiss!" Xavier hissed.

"Yeah, well, wait until Beck finds out!" Court remarked with a wicked grin.

"No, Court! Don't tell anyone! Dad will just come unglued again! Please!" he pleaded.

"Yeah, okay, Xavier. You know you can trust me," Court replied.

Chapter 7

Prince Daniel

When the king finally returned from the hearings, it was nearly dinnertime, and Xavier was lounging on the couch in the receiving room reading a rugby magazine. Jeremiah entered the residence in a rush with Loren and Ephraim behind him.

"Where's Daniel?" he asked, crossing the room.

"He's in my bed, asleep," Xavier answered, closing the magazine and setting it aside. "Is Daniel Uncle Mike's son?"

Jeremiah's gaze darted to the bedroom door before settling on Xavier. "Yes, I believe he is."

"It sure explains a lot!" Ephraim commented. "It explains why you lost touch with Natalie and why you couldn't find her or the boy. Speaking of which, I assume you've contacted Mike?"

He nodded.

"When do you expect him back?" Ephraim asked.

"I asked him to contact me when he was in a secluded place and we'd teleport him home," he stated.

"Where is he?" Ephraim asked.

"Boston," Jeremiah answered. "I need to wait on the patio so he can contact me. He won't be able to get through to me as long as I'm inside the palace."

"Should I wake up Daniel?" Xavier called after his father as he ascended the stairs to their bedrooms with Ephraim close behind him.

"No, let the boy sleep. From what I've been hearing, he needs it," he responded without breaking his stride.

Xavier looked at Loren as he flopped on the sofa next to him. "How did the rest of the hearings go?"

"Well, I'm afraid Daniel was the only child cleared of charges today. The other five children weren't as innocent. One boy was quite scary, in fact. I think he truly believes in the Dark Army's cause," he answered.

He nodded. "Yeah, I imagine years of torture and brainwashing could do that, but it's not their fault, Loren. The Council doesn't understand what it's like to be held captive and forced to do things you don't want to do, but I do. They're just kids!"

"I understand that, Xavier. I was there, remember. I saw what LeMasters and his evil concubine put those kids through. But let me ask you this: is that any comfort to the families of the people they killed? Would you have killed innocent people at LeMasters' command?" he asked gently.

"No, I wouldn't."

Loren nodded and the two sat in silence for a moment. Finally, Loren asked, "So, how do you feel about having a cousin?"

"I think it's brilliant. He's a cool little guy," he replied, grinning. "Do you think Uncle Mike will be happy to see him? I don't want Daniel hurt. He was really good to me, protecting me. It's my chance to return the favor."

Loren didn't have time to answer as a door on the floor above opened and closed.

Daniel shuffled out of Xavier's room with puffy, sleepy eyes.

"Hey, Daniel. We're down here," Xavier called, and the

younger boy scuttled down the steps yawning.

"I'm hungry," he bleated, sounding pathetically small, as he cuddled up against Xavier on the sofa.

"Well, there's an hour yet before dinner, but I'm sure Mrs. Sommers would give you a nice healthy snack. She's always been big on those. When we were kids, King Wells always wanted to come to my house after school. I had all the good junk food," Loren explained with a good-natured wink before patting Daniel's head, standing, and starting toward the kitchen. The large man froze when the king's bedroom door opened and three men appeared on the walkway, whispering feverishly.

"Sire?" Loren called up at the men. "The boy's here in the receiving room."

Michael's eyes darted to the sofa where Xavier and the smaller boy sat. For a moment, he seemed incapable of moving.

Jeremiah nudged his brother toward the stairs and whispered, "Come on, Mike. Let me introduce you to your son."

Xavier stood to face the men as they entered the room.

Daniel looked up at Xavier, bewildered. Then, he followed the older boy's eyes to the men walking toward them. The king approached with another man at his side, a dark-haired man with grey eyes. Daniel's stare widened with surprise and he jumped to his feet, unable to take his huge, grey eyes off of the approaching man.

"Y...You. I know you. My mom had a photo of you in her purse," he whispered.

Michael stepped forward with a watery smile. "She did, did she?" he asked, his voice hoarse with emotion.

He nodded fervently.

"What did she tell you about me?" he asked.

"She..." Daniel studied Michael with an expression that

was a spitting image of him. "She said that...that you're my dad."

"That's right," he responded quietly.

The small boy's eyes grew enormous and plump tears flooded them. "It's really true, then? You're really my dad?"

Michael knelt in front of him, running a thumb over the boy's wet cheeks as he nodded. "Yes, Daniel. I am your father."

The boy launched himself into Michael's arms. "Daddy! Oh, Daddy. Mommy said we'd try to find you one day. She said we'd escape from Master and we'd find you. She said you'd protect us because you loved us."

"She was right, Daniel. I won't let anything bad happen to you ever again," he whispered, his voice breaking. "And I love you with all that I am, Daniel. I love you with all that I am."

"Xavier? Let's leave them to talk," Jeremiah called softly, waving his son over to him.

He went to his father, who hugged him tightly to his side as he called, "Mike, we'll be in the dining hall. Would you and your son stay for dinner?"

He nodded without a word as he sat on the sofa with Daniel in his arms.

Xavier, Jeremiah, Loren, and Ephraim entered the dining hall and sat around the table in silence for several long minutes. Finally, Loren whistled softly. "Lord, what a day!"

The rest of the group nodded mutely.

Mrs. Sommers entered the room and stared down at the group in surprise.

"Oh, I'm sorry, sire. Did you want an early dinner? It won't be ready to serve for another thirty minutes..."

"No, Mrs. Sommers. We're just giving Mike some privacy," Jeremiah stated.

"Michael's meeting his son?" she gasped, hurrying toward the door and peeking out into the receiving room.

When the men looked at her dumbfounded, the governess gave them an impatient sigh. "Oh, really, Jeremiah! You sent the boy home with Xavier! One would only need to look at the boy to know that he's Michael's. He's the spitting image of him at that age."

"Yes, I know. That's what got me too. It was like looking at Mike all those years ago," Jeremiah added.

"So, how many for dinner?" she asked, surveying the men.

Jeremiah looked at his generals; both shook their heads. "Four. Michael and Daniel will be eating with us this evening."

"Oh, wonderful!" she chirped, clapping her hands together.

Twenty minutes later, Michael and Daniel entered the dining hall smiling.

"Xavier!" Daniel announced. "This is my dad!"

"Yeah, I know. Your dad is my uncle," he told him with a grin. "We're cousins, Daniel."

His eyes nearly bulged out of his head. "I...I'm Prince Wells' cousin?"

Jeremiah and Michael chuckled.

"Yes, Daniel. Your dad is my brother. So, you are Xavier's cousin, my nephew, and one of the heirs to the throne. You are *Prince* Daniel Spencer," Jeremiah explained, snickering as Daniel's jaw dropped.

"Dinner will be served in five minutes," Mrs. Sommers announced as she entered the room. "Michael! Oh, it's so good to finally see you over for dinner. You stay away too much," she scolded, hugging him.

"Hello, Mrs. Sommers," he muttered with genuine affection. "I'd like you to meet my son, Daniel. Daniel, this is Mrs. Sommers. She has been the palace's governess since before I was born."

"Yes, I've known your daddy all his life," Mrs. Sommers agreed with a teary smile. "Hello, Daniel. It's so wonderful to meet you, dear."

"It's very nice to meet you, ma'am," Daniel replied, extending his hand.

"A hand shake? No, no, no. Around here, we hug!" she announced, trapping the small boy in a breath-stealing embrace.

"Daniel, you can sit next to me," Xavier called, pulling out a chair.

With a grin and still blushing from Mrs. Sommers' attention, he shuffled to the chair next to Xavier.

"You'll get used to Mrs. Sommers. But words to the wise, when she hugs you, tilt your head to the side so you won't suffocate. I nearly passed out the first time she hugged me," he explained, grinning up at the governess.

"Oh, hush, you!" she tittered, swatting him with her towel. "You'd be an embarrassment to the throne if I didn't press your clothes and wash your dirty underwear."

"Mrs. Sommers!" he gasped, blushing, and the rest of the group burst into laughter at his expense.

"Well, now that I've thoroughly embarrassed Prince Xavier, I'll go and check on your dinner." She laughed.

"I'll see you in the morning, Sire," Loren announced.

"Thanks, gentlemen. Have a good night," Jeremiah called, nodding at the generals as they left the residence.

"Wow, I can't believe we're cousins!" Daniel whispered when their fathers had settled into a conversation on how the kingdom's repairs were going.

"Yeah, it's cool, isn't it?"

"Really cool!" Daniel agreed. "You must know my dad really well."

Xavier recognized the prompt. He had done the same thing with Loren and Ephraim when he first met his father. "Yeah, I guess I do. I've only been living with my dad in Warwood for about a year, but your dad is the headmaster at Wells Academy and taught my telepathy class. So I've spent a lot of time around him."

The smaller boy glanced at Michael, who was in deep conversation with the king, before looking imploringly at Xavier. "What's he like, Xavier? Is he as nice as he seems?"

"Oh, yeah. He and my dad are a lot alike. Though, Uncle Mike is a little more serious than my dad. My dad will tease and goof around with me. I always thought it was kind of odd that your dad is the serious one when my dad is the king. You'd think it would be the other way around. Uncle Mike is really nice though. I don't know if he's as strict as my dad. I did something one time and it really made Uncle Mike mad. I thought he was going to spank me, but he gave me a second chance. He still yelled at me and made me feel like crap, but if it had been my dad, my butt would have been sore."

Daniel smirked. "What did you do?"

He glanced at his father, making sure he was preoccupied before answering. "Garrett and I got caught destroying these mining carts at King's Mountain, the mountain we hid in after LeMasters invaded Warwood. And Uncle Mike happened to be the adult on duty for the children's dorms. He decided to punish us with extra chores. I had a moment of stupidity and challenged him, back talked. Man, his look was deadly. I still shudder thinking about." Xavier chuckled dryly. "Anyways, he was yanking off his belt ready to beat my butt into oblivion when I finally wised up. I begged and pleaded for him to forgive me, and thank God, he did."

Daniel snickered. "Wow. I bet it would have hurt a lot

too. He looks really strong!"

"Yeah, it doesn't tickle," he noted with a shy smile.

He looked at his father and frowned suddenly.

"What? Got another question about your dad? Ask. I'll tell you everything I know about him."

"Well, yeah. I was wondering...what happened to his leg? He limps."

Xavier glanced over at the men, who had gone quiet at the question. Daniel followed his gaze.

Michael smiled at Daniel. "I was badly injured in the attack on Warwood. If it hadn't been for Xavier, I would have died."

Daniel's eyes grew turbulent. "The Dark Army attacked you? Who? Who did it? Was it one of the other kids?"

"No, son. It was William LeMasters," Michael answered.

Daniel slumped back in his chair with a scowl. "I hate him! I'm glad he's dead. He killed my mother, he nearly killed you, and...and..." The scowl was replaced by a pained expression and tears began to swell in his eyes.

When the small boy buried his face in his hands, Michael was at his side in seconds, lifting him into his lap. Daniel wrapped his arms around his neck. "Daniel?" Michael whispered with great tenderness hugging his son against him.

Xavier looked at his father watching the exchange and knew even without abilities that his father was reminiscing of a similar occurrence between the two of them.

Chapter 8

Celebration

The kingdom was fully operational by the weekend and as a reward, the king called for a day of rest and an evening of celebrating in the rebuilt Center Square. The entire kingdom buzzed with excitement over the celebration planned for later that night. Even the king had taken the day off and had been seen in Nottingham's getting a new pair of slacks and shirt for the occasion. Many believed that it would be the party of the century!

Xavier and his friends spent the day in the royal residence playing video games, hanging out, and eating contraband junk food Beck and Garrett snuck in past Mrs. Sommers. Later that evening after everyone had left to get ready for the celebration, Xavier stood with a towel wrapped around his waist rummaging in his closet for something to wear. He had asked Robbie to walk with him to the celebration and was excited to spend some time with her. Between working to rebuild the kingdom, the trials, and his grounding, he'd seen very little of her the last week. He missed her and longed to kiss her. It had been weeks since he had done that. He smiled at the thought as he pulled a light green shirt from the closet and tossed it on his bed. There was a knock at his door and Mrs. Sommers peeked into the room.

"Xavier? Robbie is here. She's waiting for you in the receiving room," she announced.

"Okay, thanks, Mrs. Sommers," he answered, pulling out a pair of khaki cargo pants. "I'll be right there."

Ten minutes later, he bounced down the stairs and into the receiving room to where Robbie waited. He nearly stumbled as his eyes raked down her body. She was wearing a very short skirt and a snug blouse that made it very apparent that she had grown...womanly. She was...hot!

Robbie shifted her weight under his gaping stare, fidgeting with the hem of her skirt. "Do I look alright?" she whispered, unsure.

"Yeah. You...you look awesome."

She beamed. "Thanks! You do too."

But when the king entered the room and saw Robbie, he was anything but impressed. He paused at the sight of her and surveyed her clothes disapprovingly before speaking. "Hello, Roberta. How are you this evening?"

"Fine, sire," she answered, still smiling from Xavier's compliment.

"Good. Did your mother happen to see what you chose to wear tonight?" he asked finally.

"Uh, no, sire. She wasn't home when I left. She had to run an errand," she replied unconvincingly, her smile vanishing.

Jeremiah nodded thoughtfully. "Well, in that case, I'm going to have to ask you to go home and change out of that provocative outfit."

"Provocative? It's not provocative...it's sexy," she responded.

"For a thirteen-year-old, provocative and sexy are the same things. Neither is appropriate," he told her.

"I don't want to change. I like how I look," she retorted.

"I know you do as would most boys over the age of ten, but you will change into something more appropriate."

"What if I refuse?" she questioned stubbornly.

"Then one of two things will happen. First, I could help you by picking out a suitable outfit, which I am certain will not meet with your approval," he stated firmly. "Or you will not be permitted to attend the celebration."

The rebellious girl stared mutinously up at the king as Xavier held his breath.

"Fine, I'll change," she muttered finally and stomped toward the door.

"Wait! I'll walk over with you, and then we can go straight to the celebration afterwards," Xavier called, hurrying to catch up with her. After opening the door for her, he called over his shoulder, "See ya over there, Dad."

Once outside the palace, they began to make their way back to Robbie's house when she muttered bitterly, "Your dad is such a meddlesome, controlling, bossy, old-fashioned prat!"

He stifled a laugh and answered as evenly as he could. "Yeah, I know! I live with him, remember?"

"I don't understand why he feels it's *his* responsibility to hover over me all the time. I mean, what business is it of his if I wear this or not!" she growled.

"I think you look beautiful, Robbie."

She grinned. "I could just grab a sweater to wear whenever your dad's around."

"I don't know, Robbie," he cautioned. "You could get into trouble."

She frowned. "You like my outfit; don't you?"

"Well, yeah..."

"It's settled then," she replied with finality.

After a brief pit stop at Robbie's house so she could grab a sweater, they strolled toward Center Square. They heard the party long before they could see it. Once they were within a block of Center Square, voices flooded through the cobblestone streets of Warwood. Music drifted in the air, and a rhythmic beat vibrated the ground under their feet. Xavier turned to Robbie with a grin, took her hand in his, and hurried toward the sounds. The party was well underway and people were dancing around an enormous bonfire. Colorful Chinese sky lanterns floated and swayed in the air above the crowd. On the dais behind the dance area, there were several kegs and all sorts of adult beverages. Henrick Davies was supervising the table and shooed three teenage boys away from the beer as he handed a drink to Lucy Jefferson. Below the dais stood an elongated table filled with every kind of snack imaginable, and on either end of the table sat five large tubs of bottled drinks.

"Wow," Xavier muttered before turning to Robbie. "What do you want to do first?"

"Let's dance," she suggested, tugging him toward the fire and throwing her sweater over a chair.

As they made their way to the dance floor, Xavier became very aware of the jeering looks, smirks, and whispers Robbie's attire was receiving from several teenage boys and it bothered him a lot.

"What are you looking at?" he spat at Jonas, who was brazenly ogling Robbie.

Jonas smirked and gave him a wink as he taunted, "*Nice*, very nice, Pipsqueak! But why she chose to come with a *little* boy and not a man beats me. That chick is so hot she could have any guy here on her arm!"

He advanced on Jonas, but Drew beat him to it. "Hey, mate! That's my cousin you're talking about! Watch it!"

Jonas immediately backed down.

"Xavier! Come on!" Robbie called from the dance floor,

oblivious to the brief confrontation.

After a murderous glare at Jonas, he joined Robbie.

Soon, a slow rhythm filled the air around them and Xavier stared awkwardly at the couples around them moving into each other's arms. Finally, he looked at Robbie. The last time he had danced with Robbie was at his birthday party. So he found the idea of being close to her, swaying to a slow beat very intoxicating. Smiling he held his arms open to her in a silent invitation. With a small grin that sent goose bumps over his body, she moved into his arms and he shuddered. He could hardly breathe as they began to move in time with the music. When the song finally ended, he was light-headed and sweating.

Robbie giggled. "Xavier? How can you possibly be hot? It's only 50 degrees!"

He shrugged, desperately trying to regain his composure. Then he murmured with an ornery grin, "I guess being this close to your hot body did it to me."

She laughed and swatted him. "Xavier Wells! That was a perfectly wicked thing to say!" And, when she hugged him, his body felt like it might ignite from the heated sensations coursing through him. Then, she pulled away and giggled, "I liked it."

He grinned back at her. "Come on. I need a cold drink to cool me down." He pulled her toward the snack and soda table.

"Roberta Ann! What are you wearing, young lady?" Mrs. Minnows' voice came from behind them and they spun to face her.

Robbie looked stricken at first, but soon she had a haughty expression in place as she muttered cheekily, "Clothes, Mother. What does it look like?"

"I can see that, missy. However, these *clothes* leave little to the imagination. I want you to go home and change this instant!" She ordered, ignoring her daughter's attitude.

"God, Mother! Other girls wear stuff like this. It's not *that* bad. Xavier likes the way I'm dressed; don't you, Xavier?" she asked, turning to him.

Oh, God. He *loved* the way she was dressed, but he could see why his father and Mrs. Minnows did not. "Ah...I," he stammered, not sure he liked being dragged into the argument between mother and daughter.

"Roberta! It doesn't matter if my son likes the way you're dressed or not. No red-blooded male in his right mind wouldn't like that outfit, but the point is, as I explained to you earlier when I told you to change, it's inappropriate!" Jeremiah interrupted, stepping up beside Mrs. Minnows.

"Geez! I don't know why it's any of your business to tell me what to wear or what not to wear, *sire*," she blared angrily.

Xavier gulped as his father's eyes went fiery.

"Roberta Ann!" Mrs. Minnows bellowed. "You have no business talking to King Wells in that tone of voice!"

"Tamarah, I'll take care of this," Jeremiah whispered. "Please go and enjoy yourself. I'll see to it that she changes her clothes and the attitude."

Mrs. Minnows looked between the king and her daughter and nodded before turning and accepting a dance from a man waiting a few feet away.

His father looked down at Robbie. "Let's go, Roberta."

She glared up at him, and for a moment, Xavier thought she'd refuse. Finally, with an indignant huff, she turned on her heel and marched out of the crowd toward the king's limo.

"Hey, X!" Court bellowed as he fought his way toward him. "Where's Robbie going?"

"Dad is making her change her clothes. Too bad, though, she looked great," he replied with a grin.

"Yeah, I heard. Most of the boys are talking about it!" Court grinned before adding, "You better watch your back. You may have some competition building."

He looked blankly at his friend. *Competition? Competition for Robbie?* He studied the crowd around him, looking for his competitors.

His friend laughed at his reaction. "Come on. The guys are hanging out over by the kegs. Beck's hoping he'll be able to sneak a cup when Henrick isn't looking, but personally, I think it's a lost cause." Court led him toward the group.

"Beckley Wilcox! If you pick up that tap one more time, I'll chop your hand off!" Henrick bellowed, stopping Beck's hand in mid-movement toward the keg's nozzle.

"Geez, Henrick! Do you have eyes in the back of your head or something?" Beck whined.

Henrick turned toward the boys, shook a bottle of soda water, and sprayed the group. Giggling and laughing, the boys darted out of range of Henrick's attack.

"Beck, are you ever going to give up on bettering Henrick? There's no way you'll win!" Court asked laughing at Beck's drenched hair and shirt.

"Never!" he retorted with a grin and then his eyes settled on Xavier. "Hey, X! Where's Robbie?"

"She had to go home to change her clothes," Court answered for him.

"Yeah, I heard her outfit was smoking and could make any man instantly combust if he got too close," Beck noted, triggering whistles and laughter from the rest of the group.

Xavier shrugged uncomfortably. Suddenly, he shared his father's opinion about the outfit and was relieved that Robbie was changing. He didn't want to spend the evening defending her honor from the onslaught of looks and snide comments.

The boys temporarily gave up on their quest against Henrick and focused on getting a dance with a pretty girl.

When Court spotted Erica, he muttered, "See you gits later," and approached her.

Xavier joined in with the rest of the boys with catcalls and hoots of appreciation. One by one the group dispersed, pairing up with a dancing partner. Beck and Melissa Dorne had paired up and stood off to the side talking.

Xavier settled in a chair and watched his friends trying their best to impress girls. He couldn't help snickering at them. Did he look that awkward around Robbie? He probably did. He was beginning to feel antsy and self-conscious without her with him. When the king's limo finally pulled up, he hopped eagerly to his feet and hurried over to the vehicle. His father slowly climbed out of the back and spoke softly to the driver before turning to him.

"Where's Robbie?"

"She's in the limo. She's a bit upset. She could use a bit of comforting," he answered telepathically.

Xavier nodded and made his way to the vehicle. Cautiously, he knocked on the window. "Robbie? Hey, Robbie, can I come in?"

In answer, the car door opened, and he climbed inside and found Robbie in tears, dressed in a modest skirt and sweater.

"What's the matter?" he asked softly, closing the door.

She didn't seem capable of answering as her sobs increased, racking her body harshly.

"Robbie, you're kind of worrying me. Please talk to me."

She shook her head, burying her face in her hands.

"Well, can...can I read your mind?"

Still weeping uncontrollably, she nodded.

Gently, he took her hand in his and squeezed it lightly. Then, after a couple of slow, deep breaths, he emptied his thoughts of everything but connecting with her mind. Slowly, the white haze in his mind dissolved to reveal a brooding Robbie and his father leaning toward her in the back of the limo.

"Roberta, I'm sorry you don't see that your mother and I are trying to protect you. We don't want others to get the wrong idea about you. And when you become queen of our great kingdom someday, you, like Xavier, need to hold yourselves to a higher ideal," his father explained softly.

"Queen? How...how...?" she stammered.

He smiled weakly and responded, *"How did I know? I know a lot of things."*

"Well, you're not my father," she muttered begrudgingly.

"No, I'm not. But your father bestowed on me the task of watching out for you, your mother, and your sister. So it is by his insistence that I am, at the moment, your surrogate father. Now, I want you to think long and hard about something. If your father was alive today and you spoke to him like you did me, what would he have done?" his father questioned.

Robbie's defiant face slipped and for a moment she looked vulnerable, hurt. After a moment, she looked up at the king, her eyes flooding with tears as she whispered, *"He'd...he'd probably spank me."*

This admission seemed to be what his father had been waiting for and his face softened as he pulled the girl into his arms.

She simply broke down. *"I'm sorry, King Wells. I am. I just...I don't know why I dressed like this. Daddy wouldn't...have let me. I...I miss him. I really miss him,"* she cried into his father's chest.

"I know, sweetie. I miss him too," Jeremiah told her, holding her close and rubbing her back, soothing the sobs that came out in heaves.

Slowly the white haze began to descend on the scene and Xavier opened his eyes. Robbie was watching him and hiccupping quietly, but she was no longer crying.

"Is it true?" she whispered weakly.

"Is what true?"

"Did Daddy ask your dad to look out for my mom, my sister, and me?"

"Yeah, he did. I was there. He asked Dad to do him a favor and look out for his girls," he answered, caught for a moment in that overwhelming memory.

She nodded, her eyes threatening to overflow with tears again. Unable to stand seeing her cry anymore, he did the first thing he could think to do and pulled her into his arms and held her. He felt her hiccup against his body, but no more tears fell. Her body was pressed snuggly, warmly against him. She nuzzled her face into his neck, and he groaned as every hair stood on end. She looked up at him with a watery smile.

"Why did you do that?" she asked.

"Do what?"

"Groan."

He blushed. "Why do you think?"

"I don't know. Why?" she asked, smiling.

"Jeez...you know why! Having you this close makes me want to do more than just hold you."

Robbie's grin grew enormous. "Like what?"

He squirmed. "Oh, God, Robbie! I don't know. Stuff!"

"Do you want to kiss me?" she asked.

"God, yes!" he hissed.

"Well? What are you waiting for? Kiss me!"

In his eagerness, Xavier accidentally butted his forehead against hers and they immediately separated, rubbing their heads.

"Ouch! Take it easy before you knock us both unconscious!" she giggled.

"Sorry," he muttered, smiling, "I'll do better."

Then he grasped her chin, tilting her lips to meet his. The moment their lips met, a spark ignited from Xavier, and Robbie gasped with surprise before succumbing to uncontrollable giggles.

"Jeez, I wish you'd stop laughing at me! It doesn't do much for my ego to have you laugh at me when I kiss you," he grumbled, trying not to smile. It was good to see and hear her laugh because when she cried, he wanted to cry with her.

"Sorry. It just...it tickled," she told him.

"Tickled? Tickled? You like being tickled, huh?" he bellowed playfully, pinning her to the seat cushion and tickling her mercilessly.

Robbie's laugh was infectious and he couldn't help but laugh with her. Her squeals only egged him on, and he excitedly tortured her into an uncontrollable bout of laughter.

"XAAAAAAAVIER!!" she cried. "I...CAN'T ....BREEEEEEATHE!"

He sat back on his heels and laughed at her as she desperately gasped for air.

"Okay, you two. Think you should rejoin the party, now," Jeremiah chuckled from outside the car door.

"Yes, sir," the young teens chimed as they poured out of the vehicle, still laughing.

Shaking his head, the king closed the limo door behind them. When he turned, Robbie launched herself at him and clung to him in a tight embrace. Stunned, his arms slowly encircled the girl, rubbing her back soothingly.

"Thanks, King Wells," she murmured against him before pulling him down to her by his tie, standing on tip-toe, and kissing his cheek.

"No need for thanks, sweetheart. Your dad was one of the greatest men I had the privilege to call my friend. I'm just happy I could help him find peace," he whispered and kissed the girl's forehead before releasing her and leaving her in Xavier's company.

Chapter 9

Moving Heaven and Earth

The party was still going strong at midnight and Xavier and Robbie were sitting with Court and Erica at a folding table a few feet away from the fire where a group of rambunctious adults were dancing. Most families with small children had left a half an hour earlier when several members of the Royal Guard, clearly inebriated, took off their shirts and began belly dancing, horribly. The king and his generals simply stood back and watched, occasionally egging the men on.

"I think it would be hilarious to see our fathers cut loose like that," Xavier noted.

Court laughed. "Don't hold your breath, mate. I can't see our dads ever doing anything like that. As for Erica's dad... well, you know what he's like. Our dads aren't the trouble-makers like Loren and his mini-me daughter!"

"Hey!" Erica exclaimed. "Just so you know, my dad has told me loads of stories about the trouble your dads got into over the years, and they didn't need much coaxing from Daddy either." She laughed before continuing, "Wow, you know what? That's an area where you guys aren't anything like your fathers. You can find trouble without any help from me!"

"Hey! Take that back! We don't cause nearly as much

trouble as you do," Court growled, poking her in the side. But Erica refused to take it back and he tackled her to the ground, tickling her until she was gasping for breath.

He paused in his torture and stared down at her triumphantly. "Are you ready to take it back?"

"Never," she hissed.

"Your funeral," he declared and tickled her with more vigor.

It didn't take long for Erica to finally choke out, "Okay...okay...I...take it...back!"

Grinning, Court stood and helped her to her feet only to get punched in the gut. He doubled over with a grunt as she ran off giggling.

He slowly stood upright and looked at Xavier. "Excuse me. I've got to teach that wench who's the boss."

Xavier and Robbie burst out laughing.

"You don't have to teach her anything, Court. She already knows she's the boss!" Xavier blurted at his friend's back as he tore off after Erica.

"Robbie, it's time to go, honey," Mrs. Minnows beckoned.

"Okay, Mom. I'm coming," she called and turned to Xavier. "Will you call me tomorrow?"

"By phone or telepathy?" he boasted with a grin.

"I don't care." She laughed and kissed him fully on the mouth. "Bye," she whispered and jogged after her mother.

"Uh...yeah...bye," he stammered softly, watching her go until she disappeared into the darkness.

With a sigh, he turned and continued to watch the rowdy group of men dancing near the fire. When the music changed from an upbeat, celebratory melody to a love ballad, the partying men drifted toward the kegs, making room for couples to fill the dance floor. Then he saw them. Lana entered the celebration on another man's arm.

"Oh, shit," he muttered to himself and quickly searched the crowd for his father.

The king stood next to the refreshment table talking and joking with Loren, Ephraim, and Henrick. Something, telepathy, instinct, or simply a hunch, *something* drew his gaze directly to the couple. His entire body grew taut, attracting the attention of his generals. When Lana and the gentleman moved into each other's arms and began dancing, his face grew dark with fury and his right hand twitched as though he was reaching for his sword.

"Steady, Jer. They're just dancing," Ephraim muttered, but he no more than spoke the words when the gentleman holding Lana pulled her closer and whispered something in her ear.

She pushed the man at arm's length and laughed anxiously. "Mitch, stop."

Mitch laughed at her dismissively, pulling her against him and planting a long sloppy kiss on her mouth.

"Sire, no!" Ephraim hollered as the king barreled into the dancing crowd, jostling dancers aside as he went.

Lana saw him coming and pulled away from Mitch to point accusingly at the king. "Don't you dare, Jeremiah Wells! Stop right there."

He stopped a few feet from her, huffing and barely controlling the obvious urge to pummel Mitch into the ground. "What are you doing, Lana?" he hissed.

"What does it look like? I'm dancing," she replied firmly.

"You must have a broader definition of the word dancing than I do. Why are you with *him*? He's...he's..."

"A better man than you, *Jeremy*," Mitch finished facetiously, stepping aggressively forward, and the king bristled.

"That's King Wells to you, Mitchie!" Loren spat out.

Mitch smirked at Loren before turning back to Jeremiah. "I don't pretend to know what happened between you and Lana, but if I had to wager a guess, I'd say you just couldn't satisfy her."

Loren and Ephraim grabbed Jeremiah as he lunged toward the other man.

"Sire, don't," Ephraim hissed.

"Yes, *Jeremy*. You don't want to get caned again, do you? Though I must admit, I rather enjoyed watching your generals beat you to a pulp. I only wish I could have had a go at you. You know, it reminded me of the time when we were kids and you used empowerments against Lucy. Remember? When your father found out, he came storming into the academy and whipped you into the infirmary, and Lucy refused to date you again," Mitch noted gleefully.

As one, Loren and Ephraim released the enraged king. The man's smug, self-serving grin disappeared as Jeremiah tackled him to the ground. Xavier raced toward the commotion, determined to help teach this yahoo a lesson when Henrick grabbed him. But, it appeared his father didn't need any help. He held Mitch to the ground and repeatedly punched him until the generals finally intervened and hauled him off the battered man.

"Okay, okay, Sire. I think *Itchie Mitchie* has had enough," Loren muttered, grinning.

"I'll have you brought up on charges, King Wells! I'll see to it that I get to cane you myself this time!" he spouted between cuss words.

"It doesn't work like that, Mitchie. A king still has the right to defend himself when a person threatens to do him physical harm, and I believe you just announced in front of multiple witnesses that you wish to have a go at the king! Be grateful that we aren't hauling your butt to a jail cell for it," Loren announced firmly as he motioned to two nearby guards. "Help this piece of crap home."

The men watched with smirks as the guards hauled Mitch away before clapping the king on the shoulder.

"Well done. I bet that felt good," Loren commented grinning broadly.

It had felt good, but looking at Lana's livid face he wasn't so sure it was worth it.

"Yes, King Wells, *well done*! You've only proven that you're nothing more than a big brute! Are you happy now? Are you? No man will want to cross you to date me! I'll be alone for the rest of my life! Is that what you wanted? Is it? God! I hate you, Jeremiah Wells! I hate you! Now, will you kindly leave me alone and never talk to me again?"

She turned abruptly on her heel and stormed away.

"Lana!" He called, jogging after her. "Lana, wait!" He grabbed her arm and spun her to face him.

Her hand came without warning and a loud crack resounded back to the small crowd watching the confrontation.

"Ouch," Loren whistled as he sidled up beside Xavier. "Man, that woman is a wild cat!"

The king grabbed her wrists and growled, "Will you just listen to me?"

"No! I won't! Let go of me this instant!"

"Lana, please! You know why I pushed you away...you know that I only did it to protect you...you know that I'm sorry for hurting you."

"Yes, *sire*. I know all of that. We've been through all of this before, but I refuse to be with a man who treats me like a subject!"

"I have never treated you..."

"Yes you have! You decided how best to handle me and the danger I was in by being close to you without talking to me like an equal. You assumed that as king only you had the right answers, only you knew what was best. That, sire, is treating me like an ignorant subject not worth consulting!" she blared, pulling her arms free and stomping away from him.

"Lana! Lana stop!" he pleaded, but she continued to march away without a single glance back. He couldn't let it end this way. He knew what he had to do. An air of supremacy vibrated from him as he straightened and commanded forcefully, "Lana Applegate, as the King of Warwood, I order you to stop right there!"

She jumped at his hard, demanding tone and froze.

"Turn around," he ordered, moving to her in several long, powerful strides.

She turned to him, her face set with anger.

"Oh, you're so good at ordering people around, aren't you? Well, *Sire*, you may rule this kingdom, you may rule on the Premier Court, but you do not rule me! Not anymore," she hissed.

The king's expression stiffened at her words but his shoulders drooped. For a moment, they simply stared at one another. Finally, he sighed and whispered, "You're right. You're right about all of it. I didn't treat you as an equal partner in our relationship, and I've acted like a complete brute. I was wrong, Lana. I'm sorry. I'm so sorry. But, Lana, my sweet, you're wrong about one thing. I never thought that I ruled you. Darling, it's you who rules me."

Suddenly, he dropped to his knees in front of her and took her hands in his. There a brief murmur of uneasiness from the crowd. It was apparent that they had never seen their king voluntarily kneel before a citizen, and many found the act shocking. Xavier looked up at Loren standing beside him and found the man grinning.

He looked down at him, gave him a wink, and

whispered, "I think he's ready to move heaven and Earth now. He has her."

He turned and focused on his father kneeling like a beggar in front of the speechless woman.

"You rule me: body, mind, and soul. I am only half a man without you...I am a substandard king without you. God, woman, I don't know how to breathe without you near me. Please, please, I beg you...forgive me, save me. Please, save me from myself and come back to me."

When Xavier looked at Lana to see her response, he realized that Loren had been right. It was clear by her expression and her tear-soaked face that his father had her in the palm of his hand.

"Oh, Jeremy. Yes. Yes!" she managed between sobs.

Jeremiah jumped to his feet and took her into his arms, covering her mouth with his. The crowd who had watched the entire exchange burst into loud cheers, whistles, and applause.

"Yes!" Xavier whooped, jumping into the air.

"High five, little sire," Loren cheered, grinning and holding up his hand.

Xavier slapped it and looked back at his father and Lana.

"Well, I don't know about the rest of you, but I've had more than enough excitement for one night. I think I'll round up my boys and head home," Ephraim announced.

"Ah...Sire Wells? God forbid, you should come up for air, but should I take the boy home?" Loren called to the embracing couple.

"He's coming home with me, Loren," Ephraim called, snickering and draping an arm around the young prince.

"Is it okay with Dad?" Xavier asked.

The general smiled knowingly. "Who do you think suggested it?"

He looked back at his father and Lana, who had separated enough to talk.

"Come on, Xavier. They have a lot to work out, yet. Help me find my boys," he concluded.

Chapter 10

Ephraim's Temper

Xavier made his way with the Hardcastles back to the palace on foot. Ephraim and Rebecca trailed behind their rambunctious sons, holding hands and talking softly. Drew kept teasing Court about a kiss he had given Erica.

"You should have seen it, Xavier. It was hysterical! He missed and kissed Erica's nose! She was laughing so hard that she couldn't even stand let alone let him try again," Drew told him, chuckling.

"Shut up, Drew, or I'll tell Xavier about the time you got caught spying on girls in the lavatory at King's Mountain," Court blared.

"Hey, I'm proud of that!" he insisted.

"Yeah, well, would Cynthia be proud of you?" the younger brother challenged.

Drew's carefree attitude faltered and he walked ahead, leaving the younger boys alone.

"What did he do?" Xavier asked.

Court grinned. "About two weeks before we returned from the mountain, Dad caught him spying on Cynthia and her friends through a peep hole he made in the girls' shower."

"Seriously? And Cynthia doesn't know?"

He shook his head. "Nope. I have to admit, I've had a great time taking the Mickey out of him about it. She's great ammunition against him when he starts giving me a hard time."

"Taking the Mickey?"

"Sorry, one of Dad's sayings...teasing him," he explained.

As they approached the palace gates, Xavier couldn't resist the urge to rib his friend. "So, how in the world did you miss Erica's mouth?"

"Shut up!" he growled, grinning and giving him a playful shove.

When the group finally arrived at the palace, it was nearly one o'clock in the morning.

"All right, I want you all in bed in fifteen minutes. Court, give Xavier a spare pair of pajamas. He can sleep in Caleb's bed, and Caleb will take Dennis' bunk since he's spending the night with Terry," Ephraim announced.

"What? I don't want that bed-wetter in the bunk above me!" Drew bellowed.

"I don't wet the bed, Andrew!" Caleb yelled, punching at his brother.

Drew effortlessly held his smallest brother at arm's length. "Dad?"

"Andrew, Dennis's bunk bed is the only spare bed in the house," Ephraim replied.

"Fine, then let Xavier sleep in it," he suggested.

"Andrew, this isn't a debate! I told you how it's to be. No more complaining."

"Yes, *sir*," he spat condescendingly and saluting his father.

Ephraim's hand came quick and before any of them knew it, he had Drew pinned against the wall. "Watch your attitude with me, laddie. Sixteen or not, I can still take you over my knee."

The group tensely watched father and son. Finally,

Drew muttered, "Sorry, Father."

Slowly, Ephraim released his oldest son and Drew stormed past the group and into the Hardcastle residence.

Within ten minutes, Court and Xavier had changed into pajamas, brushed their teeth, and climbed into opposite beds.

"Man, your dad is a badass!" Court blurted. "Did you see Mitch's face when he was done with him?"

He laughed. "Yeah, I kind of felt sorry for him."

"Don't. Mitch is a complete jerk! He completely set up my dad once and nearly got him banished by your granddad."

Xavier sat up and studied his friend. "What? How? What happened?"

"I don't know all the details exactly, but Mitch accused my dad of stealing. It wasn't true of course, but Mitch's father was on the High Council and good friends with the king whereas my dad was a lowly merchant and wasn't seen as a true citizen because he wasn't born here. He was born in Ireland, the Cahir Kingdom. Anyways, the king believed Mitch. If it hadn't been for your dad and Loren catching the real thief, Dad would have been whipped and banned from the kingdom."

"Whoa. I didn't know about any of that," he gasped. "Okay, screw Itchie Mitchie!"

The boys burst into laughter just as Ephraim opened the door wearing pajama bottoms and a t-shirt.

"Lights out, boys," he ordered hoarsely.

"Yes, sir," the boys chimed together.

Ephraim strolled over to Court, ruffled his hair, and kissed his forehead. "Goodnight, son."

"Goodnight, Dad," Court muttered, settling under his covers.

Ephraim turned to Xavier and rubbed his head

affectionately. "Goodnight, my prince."

"Goodnight, sir."

Ephraim turned out the light and left the room.

The boys lay silently in bed for several minutes before Court asked, "Xavier? Are you happy about your father and Lana?"

"Yeah! I think it's great!" he whispered.

"Well, you know that they'll probably get married someday."

"What makes you say that?" he questioned, trying not to sound too hopeful.

"Well, Dad thinks so. I overheard him and Mum talking about it. He said if your dad ever made up with Lana, that he wouldn't be surprised if they got married within a few months. He said that he's never seen your dad that happy since your mum," he whispered.

"Really?" Xavier replied with a grin.

After a brief pause, Court asked with a snicker, "Hey? Do you think he's *glowing* tonight?"

He laughed. "God, I don't know. I don't really want to talk about my dad's love life."

"What? Don't you find it interesting that your dad glows pink when he's all hot and bothered?" he asked between giggles.

"Eww, gross! Knock it off," Xavier groaned, trying not to laugh.

"I don't get it, though. Why does a bad-ass like your dad glow pink? Pink! Blimey!"

The boys burst into uncontrollable giggles.

"Boys! Go to sleep," Ephraim's voice called from his bedroom.

"Yes, sir," the boys chimed innocently together before giggling again.

"Courtney Aaron, I mean it! Don't make me come in

there," his father yelled.

"Oops," he hissed. "Dad's getting grumpy."

After a long silent moment, Xavier whispered, "Court?"

"Hmm?"

"How could you possibly miss Erica's mouth?" He chortled before clamping his hand over his mouth in an attempt to muffle the noise.

"Shut up!"

Xavier felt a pillow strike his head and threw it back at the other boy, but a loud crash followed.

"What the hell?" Ephraim's voice blared moments before his heavy footsteps stormed into the room and he flicked on the light. "What in bloody hell are you two doing in here?"

In the light, Xavier saw that he had knocked over a bedside lamp and a vase of some sort. Both were shattered next to Court's bed.

"Sorry, Dad. I...I must have bumped the lamp," Court lied.

"Just how did you manage that, Courtney? The lamp is out of your reach. How could you possibly knock it over?"

"I...I was...I"

"I did it, Mr. Hardcastle. I threw a pillow at Court and...missed," Xavier muttered.

Ephraim sighed, entered the room, and gingerly began to pick up the glass. "Boys, it's very late. I am not in the mood to put up with your shenanigans. I'm warning you now, if I come back in this room before morning, I will bare your bottoms and beat them until they glow."

"Yes, sir," the boys intoned solemnly.

"Good. Now, go to sleep," he ordered and left the room, turning off the light behind him.

The boys listened as Ephraim threw the glass away in a waste bin and returned to his bedroom down the hall.

Court released a loud sigh.

Xavier snickered. "Court? Will your dad really bare our..."

"If he says it, he means it," he responded seriously.

"Ouch." he laughed.

"Xavier, God. I'm telling you, he's serious. Be quiet before you get us both in trouble."

"Sorry," he whispered. But he wasn't sleepy. He was wired and excited. Lana was back in his father's life, back in his life! He lay in bed listening to the silence of the residence, grinning and wondering what his father and Lana were doing. Then he thought of Court kissing Erica on the nose, and he giggled.

"Shh," Court hissed.

"Sorry, but I just pictured you trying to kiss Erica and missing! I bet she'll avoid your kisses like the plague now," he blurted.

"Oh, yeah? I'll have you know that she enjoyed every minute of it. She was putty in my hands," his friend bragged.

He scoffed. "Don't you mean snot in your mouth."

"You're disgusting!"

"Yeah? Well, at least I know how to kiss a girl!"

"Really, now? Then why did Robbie say you kiss like a fish!"

"She didn't mean that!"

"Yeah, yeah. Of course, you'd say that..."

"No, no...really..."

"Whatever you say, Prince Guppy."

"Prince Guppy?" he blared playfully, charging across the darkened room and pouncing on Court.

There was a loud grunt. "God, Xavier! I think you just ruptured my kidney."

"Really? Sorry about that," he retorted mockingly as he

jumped up and down on the other boy.

"Ouch! Ow! Okay, okay, I take it back. You're not Prince Guppy," Court recanted.

"Good," he replied with smug satisfaction and made his way back to his bed in the darkness. He had just settled under the covers when Court whispered, "No, a better name for you would be Prince Tadpole."

"All right, you're dead," he exclaimed, jumping from his bed back onto Court.

"Ow!"

"BOYS!"

"Oh, no! Dad! Get off! Get off!" Court hissed as a door down the hall slammed open.

"I can't! You're lying on my shirt tail. No, not that way!" Xavier cried out as he slammed to the floor with a loud thump. Suddenly, the door banged open and light poured down on them from the overhead lamp as Ephraim stomped into the room, looking extremely grumpy.

"Get up off the floor, boy," he spat at Xavier.

Quickly, he scrambled to stand as the angry general stormed toward his son.

"Dad...Dad...please...not in front of Xavier," Court pleaded, shrinking away from his father.

"It won't matter if I spank you in front of Xavier or not because he's next," he growled, lifting the boy off the bed like he weighed no more than a feather and pinning him against his hip.

Court hadn't been lying when he said his father meant what he said. Ephraim did just as he said he would, and when he was finished, both boys were sniffling and rubbing their stinging behinds.

"Now, I don't want to hear another peep from this bloody room or this will all seem like a patty cake game. Understand?" he growled.

"Yes, sir," the boys whimpered.

"Good," he spat, stomped to the door, turned out the light, and left the room.

The boys didn't say another word to one another for the remainder of the night.

When Xavier awoke the next morning, Courtney was still sleeping soundly in the bed next to his. Still sleepy, he wanted nothing more than to go back to sleep, but he had to pee so badly, his eyeballs felt like they were floating. Begrudgingly, he staggered out of the warm bed and into the hall.

Ephraim's light laughter drew his attention to the kitchen where the general and his wife sat sipping tea. "Henrick said that he and Lana left the celebration soon after we did."

"I'm so relieved they worked things out," Rebecca whispered back. "Jeremy needs her. It's about time he got past that ego of his to admit it to her."

Ephraim chuckled. "I agree. He's been a bloody toss-pot to nearly everyone since they broke up. Lana is one of few people who's able to call him on it and keep his ego in check. She's a strong woman despite all she's lost."

"No, sweetheart," Rebecca interrupted softly. "She's a strong woman because of all she's lost."

It was nearly one in the afternoon when Xavier returned to the royal residence.

"Good afternoon, honey," Mrs. Sommers greeted him the moment he stepped through the door. "Are you hungry?"

"No, ma'am. I had a late breakfast at the Hardcastles'. Where's Dad?"

"He's still in bed. He was out quite late," she told him. "You can go and wake him. He shouldn't sleep much longer or he'll never sleep tonight."

"Okay. Thanks, Mrs. Sommers," he chirped, bounding up the steps to his father's room.

Slowly, he opened the door and tip-toed into the room. His father was sprawled across the width of the bed, and the clothes he had worn last night had been thrown haphazardly on top of his dresser. He crept closer and looked down at the sleeping king.

"Dad?" he whispered, shaking him. "Dad?"

His father stirred, rolling over and yawning. Finally, he opened his eyes. "Hey," he muttered, smiling broadly.

"Good afternoon." Xavier grinned. "Mrs. Sommers said you didn't get home until really late."

"Yeah, it was nearly four in the morning when I got home," his father muttered with a grin. "Lana and I had a lot to talk about."

"Really? The only talking I saw you two doing when I left the celebration was the kind that had your lips attached," he teased, smacking kisses at his father.

Jeremiah laughed and pulled him onto the bed next to him. Giggling, Xavier snuggled against him and sighed as his father began stroking his hair.

"Are you going to marry Lana?" he blurted in a whisper.

"What!" his father choked. "It's too early to talk about that, son. We've decided it's better if we take things slowly."

"Oh, come on, Dad. Haven't you even thought about it?"

He sighed. "Yes, I've thought about it. Would it be okay with you if someday in the distant future, I asked her to marry me?"

Xavier grinned. "Sure, as long as it's not too far into the distant future."

His father laughed. "Okay, point taken. I invited Lana for dinner tomorrow. So be on your best behavior."

"Of course I will, Father," he chirped innocently.

"So, how was the sleepover at the Hardcastles'?"

"Fine...mostly," he muttered, avoiding his father's eyes. "So, when will the academy start up again?" he asked, trying to change the subject. Why had he asked about school? Stupid, stupid, stupid! There's no way his father wouldn't know something was up now.

"Okay. What happened at Ephraim's?" he asked, tipping Xavier's chin so that he met his eyes.

"Nothing."

"Nothing? You know I will find out. Just tell me, son."

He inhaled deeply. His father wouldn't be happy that he blatantly disobeyed Ephraim, but he tried to minimize it. "Ah..., well...Court and I kinda got into a little trouble with Ephraim," he replied nonchalantly.

"I see. Explain your definition of a little trouble?"

"Well, he told us to go to sleep...and we didn't right away."

Sighing heavily, his father announced, "Lord, boy! Getting information out of you is like pulling teeth. What were you doing instead of sleeping?"

"Ah... just...talking."

"Just talking, eh? Nothing else?"

"I...well, maybe we were goofing around a little."

"And how many times did Ephraim tell you to stop goofing around?"

"Um, a few," Xavier muttered, blushing.

"Xavier..." his father sighed exasperatedly.

"I know, I know. I just couldn't seem to unwind after you and Lana made up...I'm sorry," he pleaded.

"I understand that, son. I'm just a little disappointed," Jeremiah stated, exhaling. "But, knowing Ephraim, I'm sure he handled it so you'll be more mindful of him in the future."

"Yes, sir. He sure did!" he mumbled sincerely.

Chapter 11

Dating

Two days following the celebration, Jeremiah had the first of his "take-it-slow" dates. Five minutes before Lana was due to arrive at the palace for dinner, he galloped down the stairs and into the receiving room wearing a dark green pin-stripe suit.

Xavier looked up from his magazine and muffled a snicker as the king studied his reflection in a polished silver vase on the mantle above the fireplace.

"Well? What do you think? How do I look?"

He tried to keep a straight face as he answered, "Ah... you look...good, I guess."

His father turned to him with a wide grin. "Yeah? Does this tie look okay with the suit?" He turned back to his reflection and combed his fingers through his hair before studying the tie.

Xavier burst out laughing. "Jeez, Dad, I don't know. Ask Mrs. Sommers if you're worried about the tie. But, hey, if you're going for the overgrown leprechaun look, I think you've nailed it."

His father was too nervous and wrapped up in his reflection to hear the rib. "Naw," he muttered to himself as he smoothed the tie down his chest. "It's fine; just wanted a second opinion."

When the doorbell rang, the king all but lunged for the door. "I'll get it!"

"Yeah, no duh," Xavier teased, slumping back across the couch. "I wasn't planning on answering it. I value my hands, arms, legs...my life really."

Ignoring him, his father reached for the door, took a deep breath, and yanked it open. Lana didn't have a chance to even breathe before he pulled her into his arms and kissed her.

As the kiss grew awkwardly long, heat crept across Xavier's cheeks and he snickered uncomfortably. "Hey, old people! *Excuse* me, but there's a minor present!"

The king waved him away and continued kissing the woman in his arms.

Shaking his head, he scurried from the room and into the dining hall where Mrs. Sommers was putting the final touches on the table. It looked beautiful with the floral arrangement in the center and a rose bud in each wine glass in front of the place settings.

"Hello, dear," she called cheerfully. "Has Lana arrived?"

"Yes, ma'am. She and Dad are...still saying hello," he answered with an enormous grin.

She returned his smile before tears filled her eyes.

"Mrs. Sommers?" he questioned apprehensively, moving toward her.

She shooed him away. "I'm all right, sweetie. I'm just so pleased for your father. He deserves this happiness. Lord knows he hasn't had a lot of it." She blotted her cheeks with her apron before returning to her business-as-usual attitude. "I've got too much to do today to get weepy. Go on and sit at your place, honey. When your father and Lana are ready, they'll join you. I'll prepare the soup for serving."

"Yes, ma'am," he replied and sat next to the head of the table as she disappeared into the kitchen.

"Hello, Xavier," Lana's honey-smooth voice announced their presence.

He jumped to his feet and turned to greet her. "Hi, Lana! I would have said hello earlier if Dad hadn't attacked you the moment you walked in," he teased, giving her a hug.

She giggled and gave him a quick, tight hug.

"Hey, you better keep your smart aleck remarks to yourself before I attack you!" his father reprimanded as he worked to keep a straight face.

Xavier gave him a fake horrified look. "Ew, Dad! Don't you dare attack me like you did Lana! She might put up with it, but I'd barf on you!"

His father lunged at him and smacked his bottom before he could even think about dodging him. "Let that be a lesson to you," he announced smugly.

He choked out a laugh. "A lesson? What kind of lesson? That my father hits like a girl?"

"All right, you two! Is this how the whole night is going to be? Settle down!" Lana laughed, smacking both father and son.

Laughing together, the three sat at the table just as Mrs. Sommers reemerged with a large serving pot.

"Hello, Miss Applegate. It's wonderful to finally see you at the palace for dinner," the governess announced, ladling soup in their bowls.

"Thank you, Mrs. Sommers," she responded sweetly. "The cream of mushroom soup looks delicious."

She gave an appreciative nod and returned to the kitchen.

"Lana, I know we haven't talked about it, but...if you'd like your job back at the Governing Hall..."

"No, Jeremiah. I don't want the job back. I have a new job..."

"Lana, don't be silly. It would be no trouble to give you the job back. Surely, you only resigned out of anger..."

"Jeremiah Wells!" she interrupted, her back stiffening. "I didn't resign out of spite! I resigned due to a conflict of interest! And, unless you're not the intelligent man I've taken you for, you'd realize that I *still* have a conflict of interest!"

"Okay, okay. Take it easy!" he chastised, holding up his hands in surrender.

"Don't talk to me like that! Don't talk to me as if this was all my doing. *You're* the one..."

"Lana, please, stop. I'm sorry. Lord Almighty! I didn't mean to rub you the wrong way. Please, forget I ever mentioned it. I just thought it would be nice working with you again. I'm sorry if I offended you. Really!" he gushed sincerely.

She stared at her bowl for a long moment before finally nodding. His father expelled a breath he had been holding and turned to Xavier with a "that was close" look.

By the end of the meal, the couple appeared to have completely forgotten about their brief tiff as they snuggled on the sofa. But, when the air of intimacy between them grew more intense, Xavier squirmed and fidgeted with a magazine, trying not to watch the couple. Finally, the discomfort became too unbearable, and he excused himself and fled up the stairs to his room. He ventured one last glance at his father in the receiving room below, holding the woman he loved in his arms. With a stroke of a finger against Lana's cheek, his father coaxed her to look at him before kissing her. It was a soft, tender kiss full of love, and within seconds the king was glowing.

Xavier smiled. He had no doubt that his father would marry Lana. With any luck, it would be soon.

The king and Lana continued to see a lot of one another over the next few weeks, but they never went out alone together. Xavier guessed that this had something to do with his father's "take-it-slow" dating plan. Whenever the couple went out for dinner or dancing, they always had a small entourage with them.

The movie theatre was another one of these "take it slow" dates, if you could call an outing with eight boys and another couple in tow a date. Xavier sat between Court and Beck in the dark movie theater, chomping on salty popcorn and watching the film. His father sat next to Lana in the row in front of them, a few seats down.

His father didn't seem too interested in the movie. The woman next to him ensnared the majority of his attention, and he went out of his way to find reasons to touch her. When a loose strand of hair fell into her face, he stroked it away from her eyes. More than once he intentionally brushed against her hand while groping for more popcorn from the bowl in her lap. Then, at one point, he playfully licked the butter off her fingers while she giggled and half-heartedly pushed him away. Xavier watched, snickering as his father slyly slid his arm around Lana's shoulders and coaxed her to cuddle against his shoulder.

"What'cha' laughing at?" Court asked with a grin.

"Dad," he whispered, nodding toward where the king sat, now stroking Lana's cheek and jaw with his forefinger.

"Crikey, I think he's moving in to snog her," Beck noted in awe. "The king sure doesn't waste time, does he?"

Xavier snickered. "Yeah, what do you say I make it more of a challenge for him?"

Both boys nodded with a grin.

Scooping up a handful of popcorn, he turned back to his father and Lana, who were no longer watching the movie but staring at one another. Then just as they drifted toward one another to kiss, he tossed the popcorn at them. It worked. Lana jerked away and Jeremiah turned and hissed, "Hey, cool it!"

"Me?" he asked innocently. "I'm not the one who needs to cool it, *Dad*."

Snickering, the boys turned back to the movie. The film was a typical scenario. The hero finds a damsel in distress and helps her. They fall in love and live happily ever after. After a series of spectacular explosions and stunts, the hero and the damsel, realizing they were in love with one another, began to kiss. As the romantic scene unfolded on the screen, the boys squirmed uncomfortably and groaned.

"Man! Enough lovey-dovey stuff! Blow something up!" Beck called out, sending the other boys into hysterical giggles.

"Yeah, blow *him* up," Caleb called out, but was interrupted by loud guffaws and laughter. He didn't fully understand why the older boys were beside themselves with laughter, but he joined them.

"Cut it out, boys!" Ephraim hissed, and the boys' laughter was cut silent. The group remained silent for all of thirty seconds when Court began making exaggerated kissing noises as the characters in the movie continued to kiss. Beck and Xavier burst out laughing again. After another glare from Ephraim, they attempted in earnest to stifle their giggles.

Following another brief moment of silence, Beck quietly imitated the female character on the screen with a high-pitched voice, "Oh, James. I was so scared when all those bad, bad men blew up the building. Please, hold meeeee!"

Xavier caught on and imitated the hero in the lowest voice he could muster. "It's all right, sweetheart. I'll protect you. I'm the hero after all."

"Oh, Jaaaames!" Beck squealed, and the boys made

smacking and smooching sounds again.

Both Ephraim and Jeremiah turned.

"Boys!" Jeremiah called, glaring at them. "Knock it off."

The laughter instantly stopped.

"Sorry, sire," Beck muttered meekly.

The boys sat quietly as the romantic scene continued on screen. As Xavier watched a brilliantly bad idea came to mind, and before he could think it through, he whispered, "Hey guys, watch this."

With a small flick of his finger, a loud whistling sound filled the theater moments before a loud crack and a shower of fireworks exploded above the movie screen. The boys' laughter caught horridly in their throats as a continuous stream of fireworks whirled, whistled, and exploded above the movie screen, which erupted into flames. The people around them screamed and scrambled out of the theater in a mob.

"Rebecca, Lana, get the kids out of here!" Jeremiah ordered as he and Ephraim hopped over rows of chairs and raced to the front of the room.

"Boys! Come with us," Rebecca called, leading them to the back of the auditorium.

Xavier watched, shell-shocked, as his father and Ephraim fought to gain control over the fire using their empowerments. When he felt a hand on his shoulder, he looked up at Lana.

"Come on, Xavier. Your father and Ephraim will get the fire under control," she called softly and led him out into the lobby with the rest of the group.

Filled with regret, he dropped his head and avoided his friends' eyes. What had he done? God, what he wouldn't give to keep his father from finding out that he was responsible for the fire. Desperately, he began clearing his mind and replaced his guilt with fear and puzzlement of how the fire started.

Several pain-staking moments later, his father and Ephraim exited the theater and approached the group.

"Is everyone okay?" the king asked.

Xavier could feel his father's eyes on him, and he worked to keep his thoughts innocent.

"Yes, sire. We're all fine. Any idea what happened?" Rebecca asked.

He and Ephraim looked at one another before speaking.

"It was the strangest thing," Ephraim began. "We'd get the fire put out in one area only to have it flare up again in another..."

"So that means someone in our group is responsible," Rebecca concluded.

The king nodded. "Yes, it does. Now, if you would all excuse me, I need to speak to the owner and see if we can settle this thing without the local police becoming involved."

Jeremiah strolled to the concessions booth and interrupted the manager, who was already on the phone. The man slowly hung up the phone, his face unmasked with awe. Suddenly, he knelt at Jeremiah's feet.

"Sir, please. There's no need for that. Please stand. I just wanted to apologize profusely for the damages, and I am more than happy to pay for it and help you acquire new equipment. One of the boys in my group must have brought fireworks into the theater and got the stupid idea of setting them off. I promise I'll find out which one is responsible and he will volunteer his services for the next two months."

"Of course, sire. That sounds fair...Lord! I can't believe I'm meeting you. I've heard a lot about you. You're a very powerful king, they say."

"Thank you, Mr. O'Donnell..."

"All right, you lot. Who's *brilliant* idea of a joke was this?" Ephraim hissed, snapping Xavier's attention away from his father and the cinema owner.

But, the group remained silent and shuffled their feet.

"Come on now. Surely you know by now we'll uncover who the culprit is and he will be punished. Let's skip this childish act of innocence. Be a man and take responsibility for your actions." Ephraim's stare bore into each boy, but to no avail.

The king returned from his talk with the owner and looked at the boys who stared at the floor in front of their toes.

"Okay, boys. Mr. O'Donnell has agreed not to press charges. Now, who's responsible for this stupid, dangerous stunt?" he questioned.

Again no one answered.

"Boys? If I must, I'll invade your thoughts to learn the truth."

"Xavier did it," Jonas spat out.

"I did not!" Xavier blared, glaring accusingly at Jonas.

"You did too. I heard you..."

"Shut up! That's a lie!"

"Xavier, that's enough," his father instructed firmly.

"I'm not lying, pipsqueak, and you know ..."

"Don't call me pipsqueak, you big stupid ..."

"Xavier!" Jeremiah thundered, intercepting Xavier as he started toward Jonas with his hands in fists. "THAT'S ENOUGH!"

He froze in his father's grasp, but continued glaring at Jonas.

"Excuse us," Jeremiah declared shortly to the group as he pulled Xavier to the side. Jonas waved mockingly and mouthed the word, "Busted" at him.

"Jonas, eat shh..."

"Xavier!" his father hissed, cutting him short. "Calm down and watch your language, boy. Now, I want the truth. Did you create those pyrotechnics and start that fire?"

"No!" he shouted.

"Do not yell at me, son," his father cautioned.

"But I didn't do it!" he protested, a bit calmer, but not much. "It was Jonas, not me!"

"Xavier, don't accuse innocent people of something this serious, and stop lying to me," he insisted, his temper very close to the surface.

"I'm not lying!"

"Xavier!"

"I'm not lying! Jonas is the liar. He probably started it all. He always was a show off..."

Xavier yelped with surprise when his father spun him and struck his backside with two sharp smacks. His gaze flickered to the group waiting quietly a few feet away and was mortified to find all of them watching.

"Are you done with your tantrum?"

He nodded. "But, I'm telling the truth..." he muttered unconvincingly.

"Son, I don't need telepathy to know that you're lying to me. When you lie to me, you don't look me in the eye and you fidget like a man with Parkinson's. So even though your head is full of believable thoughts and feelings, I know they're lies." The boy gulped as he continued, "Now, I'm going to give you one more chance to take responsibility and make this right. If you lie to me again, I'll break through your feeble blocking techniques and get the truth from you anyway. Did you start those fireworks?"

Xavier ducked his head submissively. "Yes, sir."

"I see." The disappointment in his father's voice hurt more than the smacks, and he winced. "We'll discuss this more at home. Right now, you and I need to work out arrangements with Mr. O'Donnell. Come with me."

He led him over to the enamored manager. "Mr. O'Donnell..."

"Oh, my!" Mr. O'Donnell exclaimed, his eyes widening with surprise as he studied Xavier. "Oh, my! This...this is your son, isn't it? Oh, young sire, it's so nice to meet you. It's an honor." The gushing man grabbed Xavier's hand and shook it vigorously.

"Mr. O'Donnell, my son is the one responsible for the fire," Jeremiah announced.

Mr. O'Donnell's face fell, and he looked down at him with hurt-filled eyes. Guilt gnawed inside Xavier and his gaze dropped to stare at the man's feet.

His father reached into his hip pocket and withdrew a billfold. "First, here's some money to get started on the repairs." He pulled out a check and hastily filled it in. Xavier's eyes widened at the amount. "And, here's my phone number and fax number. Please send me an estimate for the repairs," he requested as he handed the man a small rectangular business card.

"Oh, th...thank you, sire. You're too kind," the manager bumbled.

"No, Mr. O'Donnell. You're the one who's kind. We are very grateful that you've been generous enough to work this out and allow us to make amends. In that spirit, my son will volunteer his services for the next two months to do whatever you need done. I do not want him to receive any special treatment or favoritism. Whatever tasks your current employees dislike doing the most, I want Xavier to do them. He's very lucky that you were gracious enough not to call the police. We want to make this right."

"Thank you, sire. I have every confidence that you will. And I'd be more than happy to have the boy's help on the weekends. It's our busiest time and there's plenty around here that needs to be done like sweeping and mopping out the theater, emptying waste bins, cleaning and mopping the lavatories..."

"Ew! You've got to be joking," Xavier muttered. "I'm not cleaning toilets and urinals."

"Yes, son, you will," Jeremiah growled.

"But, Dad! That's not fa..."

"Fair? Please tell me that you weren't about to tell me that this arrangement isn't fair, boy. What's not fair is that this man will be out of business for weeks because of the damages you caused with that idiotic stunt!" he boomed.

Again, Xavier felt every eye on him, and he ducked his head at the attention. He didn't say another word as his father made arrangements for his community service at the theater.

Chapter 12

Punishment

On the way home, Xavier sat in the back seat of the car with Beck. His father was furious with him. Anger radiated off the king in waves and the passengers sat in tense silence. Beck threw sympathetic glances toward Xavier that did little to relieve the thick, hard lump in his throat. In no time, the car pulled through the kingdom's gatehouse and the king drove the short distance to Beck's house in the Merchant Area of Warwood.

"Thanks for taking me, King Wells. It was...well, thanks."

"Anytime, Beck. Tell your mother and father I said hello."

"I will, sire." he turned to Xavier with another look of sympathy. "Good luck, X."

"Thanks. I think I'm going to need it," he mumbled.

"You definitely will," his father whispered savagely from the front seat.

Xavier met a pair of enraged, seething eyes in the rear view mirror and knew he had not only crossed the line today but pulverized it. He hadn't seen his father this angry since the time he had used his empowerments against Drew in a fight. His father had taken a belt to him for it. He gulped and stared down at his lap, tears flooding his eyes.

Beck shifted uncomfortably beside him. "Ah, well, goodnight, Ms. Applegate."

"Goodnight, Beckley. See you soon," Lana replied sweetly.

Beck opened the door, hopped out, and galloped into his house.

The car lunged forward, and they continued toward the palace. In that moment, Xavier would have given anything to be Beck, untroubled and carefree.

"Dad," he whispered shakily. "Please..."

"Not now, Xavier. I'm dropping off Lana and then, you and I will head home..."

"No, Jeremiah. Take me to the palace with you. I'd like to have that nightcap you promised me, and we need to talk," she insisted firmly.

"Fine," he muttered as he squealed the tires, taking the turn through the palace gates a little too fast.

The car jerked to a stop in front of the palace, and Loren trotted over with a grin. His father jumped out, leaving the car running.

"Loren, park the car," he ordered hastily.

Loren gave him a puzzled look before responding, "Yes, sire."

Jeremiah wrenched the back door open and growled, "Get out."

"Dad...I..."

"Get out of the car, son," he ordered with such authority that Xavier obeyed without further argument.

As he stepped from the vehicle, his father's large hand clamped onto his arm and marched him into the palace. The guards seemed to sense their king was in a foul mood and quickly cleared out of his path with solemn faces. Once inside the royal residence, his father released him and nudged him toward the steps leading to the bedrooms.

"Go to your room," he muttered, unbuckling his belt.

"Dad...Please! Listen to me. Let me explain."

"Explain? You used your empowerments in a common village and endangered the lives of everyone there! Then you lied about having done it! What is there to explain?"

"I'm sorry, Dad!" Xavier pleaded, crying.

"Not nearly as sorry as you're going to be," he announced, pulling his belt free from his waist.

"Jeremiah stop!" Lana ordered grabbing his arm. "You're not punishing him tonight. You're too angry!"

"Lana..."

"No, Jeremiah. Not tonight! You'll regret it if you do!"

"Lana, he nearly burnt the movie theater to the ground, and then he lied about..."

"Yes," Lana replied, anger spiking her tone, "and everyone in that theater knows how you handled his lying. You humiliated him in front of his friends and perfect strangers by spanking him right there in the middle of the lobby!"

"You can't be serious!" his father growled, turning to her. "You can't possibly think he didn't deserve it!"

"That's not what I said! Yes, he probably did, but you sure as hell didn't handle yourself maturely. You were too angry and you allowed your temper to get the better of you. Jeremy, can't you see it? When you allow your anger to rule how you punish Xavier, you're treating him just like your father treated you!"

He opened his mouth in protest, but said nothing and simply stared at her. Finally, he nodded his assent.

Lana turned to Xavier. "Xavier, it's late. Go to your room and get ready for bed. We'll be up in a few minutes to say goodnight," she told him.

"Yes, ma'am. Ah...th...thanks," he answered with a small smile.

"Don't thank me yet, young man. Though I deeply care for you, I happen to agree with your father on a number of things. Releasing a pyrotechnic force in a movie theater was a stupid thing to do, and you deserve to be punished. However, I think it's wise to revisit this when we all have cooler heads," she told him sternly.

His smile dropped, and he stared at her uneasily.

"Now, go to your room Xavier," Lana repeated.

"Yes, ma'am," he muttered before turning and trudging to his room.

Fire! The wood was ablaze! He could feel the infernal heat searing his back as he raced through the wood, his hand tightly clamping Robbie's.

"Robbie!" he shouted when she stumbled and frantically pulled her to her feet.

"X...Xavier," she coughed. "I can't...I can't breathe. The smoke is too...thick."

"Come on, Robbie. We must keep..."

Suddenly there was a flash and the trees just feet from them exploded into consuming flames. A blood-curdling scream jerked him awake. His sheets were twisted around him like pythons, and his body was clammy with perspiration. With a shuddering sigh, he ran his fingers through his hair, untangled himself, and stood.

Music lulled into his room through his bedroom door. Curious, he crept onto the landing and peered down into the room below.

Lana and his father were dancing in time to the music, slowly swaying next to the low-burning hearth. The fire cast long shadows throughout the room, but provided enough light that Xavier could see the couple quite clearly. As they swept across the floor, their eyes never left one another. Finally, his father whispered something to Lana.

She smiled and whispered her answer. The king pulled her against him and kissed her. It was quite a kiss, and soon, his father's pink glow filled the room. Xavier blushed in the darkness, but his curiosity wouldn't allow him to look away from the happy couple.

It appeared that his father's take-it-slow dating plan had just moved into full-fledged dating. He liked Lana. She was fair, kind, and beautiful. She didn't take any crap from his dad either, and she could get through to him when he was being a complete jerk too. He couldn't wait until they made it official and got married. He couldn't wait to have her as his new mother, but these thoughts made him feel a bit traitorous towards his mother.

"Xavier, go back to bed," the king's voice startled him, and he jumped. He looked down at his father who had stopped dancing. Both he and Lana were staring up at him. "It's late, son. You should be in bed."

"I...I tried. I had a bad dream, and then I heard the music. I was just ...Oh, never mind. Night." He sighed and returned to his room.

He climbed into bed, knowing that sleep wouldn't come easily. It wasn't just the dream that would keep him awake. It was the fire at the theater. Yes, he had intentionally sent *one* force over the screen, but the finale of explosions had not been deliberate, and he certainly hadn't meant to start a fire. How had he lost control of his power like that? Was it a freak incident? Trying to swallow past the lump in his throat, he knew it wasn't. He had experienced too many similar incidences lately for any of it to be a coincidence. For some reason, his abilities were going haywire. In the last couple of weeks, he had lost control of his telekinesis and nearly crushed a man to death, he had accidentally summoned Robbie and her friends into the lake, his telepathic abilities went silent, and now, his pyrotechnic force had become hypersensitive. The trouble with his powers seemed to be getting worse! What ability would go rogue next? How unruly would his powers become? Why was this happening now?

Maybe he should tell his dad. Maybe if he knew about the trouble he was having controlling his abilities, he wouldn't belt him. The thought of being hit with his father's belt again sent him into a panic and for the first time since he had come to live with his father, he contemplated running away.

He was so self-absorbed that when the door opened with a soft click he jumped. The king's large frame filled in the doorway.

"Lana has gone home," he whispered. "So if you wanted to sleep in my bed tonight, I'm going to bed now."

Grinning in the darkness, he hopped out of bed and followed his father into his room. As his father flicked on the light and set about getting ready for bed, Xavier threw the decorative pillows on the bed to the floor and scurried under the covers. A couple moments later, his father joined him and turned out the light.

"So, what was the dream about?"

He stiffened at the question, frightened that the word fire might send his father into another temper-driven rant, and he briefly considered lying. But, lying would only make things worse so he told the truth.

His father didn't get mad at all; he simply pulled him close and murmured, "It was only a dream. Everything is all right. The fire today didn't do any lasting damage and nobody got hurt. Though I'd like to know why you did it."

"Well, I was just trying to be funny...you know...like when people in love kiss in cartoons, they always have fireworks going off above their heads," he explained.

"I see," his father responded neutrally.

He thought he heard a smile in his father's voice, but in the cloak of darkness, he couldn't be sure. So he quietly added, "Dad, I'm really sorry about the fire. I never intended for it to happen."

"I know," he replied, pulling him close. "Get some rest, son. We'll talk about it in the morning."

When Xavier opened his eyes the next morning, he found his father sitting up in bed beside him, reading the morning paper and drinking a cup of coffee. The king's hair stood up on end and stubble covered his face. He took a long drink from the steaming mug before looking down at him.

"Morning," he murmured huskily.

"Morning, Dad," Xavier whispered, stretching and yawning.

"Did you sleep all right?"

"Yeah. Once I fell asleep."

His father chuckled. "I'll say. You sure like to spread out. I've got the bruises on my shins to prove it."

He smiled meekly. "Sorry."

"No worries. I'm sure I won't have any permanent damage." He folded his paper and set it and the coffee mug on the bedside table before patting Xavier's leg, standing, and heading into the bathroom. "We need to talk about last night," he called over his shoulder.

At these words, any grogginess fogging Xavier's mind evaporated and he was wide-awake. His stomach burned with dread as he silently waited for his father to finish using the bathroom and render the verdict. When his father emerged from the bathroom, he scratched his head and stopped at the foot of the bed. He studied the nervous boy before moving and sitting next to him on the edge of the bed.

"I've been thinking about it, and since you used your empowerments without the intention to do harm, I will not whip you," he explained quietly.

Xavier expelled a great sigh of relief. "Thank you, Father. Thank you."

"Now, hold on. I'm not saying you won't be punished."

"Yes, sir. I know, sir," he answered, trying to keep the enormous relief from his voice.

"You will be on restriction. For the next month, you are grounded to the royal residence. When you're not fulfilling your duties here at the kingdom or at the theater on weekends, you are confined to the palace. No playing rugby, no playing with friends, no camp outs, and no swimming at the lake. Do you understand?"

"The entire month? But, Dad, by the time I'm no longer grounded, it will be time for school to be back in session. The guys were planning a huge camp out the weekend before school starts," he pleaded.

"I'm sorry about that but the punishment stands!" he replied. "Son, you know what happens to a king when he endangers others with his powers, intentionally or not."

He nodded solemnly. "Yes, sir. He can be caned for it."

"Yes, so intentional or not, the next time you use your empowerments that endangers or hurts any living soul, you will be caned. Do you understand?"

He gulped. "Y...Yes, sir."

Chapter 13

Little Boy Prince

With a reduced sentence for good behavior, Xavier's restriction came to an end two days before the start of the new school term. He missed the huge back-to-school campout at the lake so he was anxious to meet up with the guys and see how it went. Determined to spend at least one of his last days of freedom hanging out with his friends, he sprang from bed, showered, dressed, and sat at the dining table eating breakfast when his father entered the room.

"Well, well, well. Look who's up! It's strange how I had to drag your butt out of bed during your grounding to do your chores yet here on your first day off of restriction, you're up with the birds!" he stated, shaking his head.

"What can I say? Freedom agrees with me," he noted through a mouthful of oatmeal.

His father chuckled. "Well, I'm sorry to say that I will require your company this afternoon from one to two-thirty."

He gave his father an exasperated look. "What? You're kidding, right? What for?"

"Your uniforms need altering. You've grown a bit since last year," his father replied, forking eggs into his mouth.

"Great! Just great!" he mumbled moodily. "Why do I have to go this afternoon? Why can't I do it this morning?"

"I have a meeting this morning, son," he answered patiently.

"So? I can go by myself, Dad. I don't need my daddy holding my hand to get sized for uniforms!" he protested.

His father looked at him impassively, but something close to hurt flickered in his eyes before he smiled. "All right then, I'll call Nottingham's and let Jon know you'll be there at nine. Okay?"

Xavier grinned. "Yeah. Thanks, Dad."

"Will you be home for lunch?" Jeremiah asked, continuing with his breakfast.

"Ah, well, I wanted to talk to you about that. I was...hoping that I could take Robbie to King's Cafe for lunch so I was wondering, can I borrow some money?" he asked hopefully.

Jeremiah gave his son a knowing grin. "Really now?"

"*Daaad*! Don't start!" he griped trying not to laugh at his father's teasing. "Can I have the money or not?"

He laughed. "You don't need money."

"Yes, I do! How can I pay for it?"

"Son, you don't need money in Warwood. Merchants will just bill me," his father stated before whispering jovially, "For some reason, they believe I'm good for it."

"Oh, yeah. Right," Xavier snickered. "Okay."

On his way to Nottingham's, Xavier called out to his friends using his telepathy ability and made arrangements to meet them at the Coliseum at ten-thirty to play rugby. Beck suggested that they could go to the lake and cook hotdogs over an open fire for lunch afterwards. Everyone was eager and willing, except Xavier.

"*Sure, but you'll have to count Robbie and me out,*" he told them.

"*Why?*" Robbie's voice crowded into his thoughts.

"Well...I'd like to take you out."

"Ew, God! If this is going to get mushy, Xavier, please do the rest of us the courtesy of disconnecting with us," Erica's dry, mocking voice interrupted.

Beck began making kissing noises and the group laughed.

"Shut up, you guys," he spat, feeling himself turning red. *"Geez. How about Robbie and I meet you guys at the lake after lunch. We can all go swimming!"*

The group answered at once, their enthusiastic agreement blasting painfully into Xavier's mind. *"Ouch! You don't have to shout! Man that hurt! All right, see you guys at ten-thirty."*

"Oi, X? Glad you're finally paroled. It's been boring without you," Garrett added.

"Thanks, but there was no way you were as bored as I was. See you later," he responded before disconnecting with his friends.

When Xavier entered Nottingham's, he found several Wells Academy students with their parents shopping and being fitted for new uniforms for the new school year, but the moment the owner, Jon Nottingham, saw Xavier, he immediately stopped what he was doing and hurried toward him.

"Good morning, young sire," he greeted happily. "Your father said you'd be by this morning. Right this way and I'll get your new measurements."

The man led him past staring customers to the rear of the store where racks upon racks of school blazers, slacks, and shirts hung. He set a stool in front of the young prince and Xavier quickly mounted it, hoping the measurements wouldn't take long. He felt uncomfortable being measured while twenty people gawked at him. It wouldn't have been as bad if he hadn't been facing the other customers, but as it was, he was extremely self-conscious as every inch of his body was measured. His face combusted with heat as Mr. Nottingham measured his inseam, running the tape measure from his ankle to his groin. Two girls started giggling unmercifully before their mothers hushed them.

"All right, Prince Wells, that's the last of the measurements. I'll alter your slacks and jackets and make arrangements with the palace to have them picked up before the end of the day," Mr. Nottingham told him.

"Okay. Thanks Mr. Nottingham," he responded and shook the man's hand before rushing out of the store.

The rugby match with the guys was an absolute blast, and after a brief scuffle between Beck and Garrett, the group decided that playing rugby against one another was asinine and defused the argument by ribbing Beck over an incident involving Melissa Dorne.

"Yeah, it's a shame you were grounded, Xavier! You missed a classic!" Court laughed.

"What happened?" he asked with a grin.

"Well at campout," Court began, dragging out the story with dramatic flair. "Beck and Melissa snuck behind the rocks for some *alone* time, and Beck...well, let's just say he discovered a new ability!"

"What?" he asked eagerly.

The entire group looked at the blushing Beck before bursting into laughter. Beck glanced meekly at Melissa before finishing, "We...kinda got stuck together."

"Stuck together?" Xavier prompted.

"Yeah! They were snogging, and Beck's glaciator ability suddenly manifested itself and froze their lips together!" Court blurted before succumbing to uncontrollable laughter, with Xavier joining in. "Man! You should have seen them! They had to walk sideways through the woods, along the streets of the kingdom, and through the palace gate to get to the infirmary so that a healer could unfreeze them. You should have seen the guards' faces along the way. It was hysterical!"

"Damn! I would have killed to have been there to see that!" Xavier laughed.

"Okay, okay! Are we doing this picnic thing or not?" Beck spat grumpily, eying Xavier irritably. "See you and Robbie later, *loverboy*," Beck muttered and stomped toward the woods.

"You kids have fun," Erica chirped.

"Yeah, don't do anything I wouldn't do." Court chuckled, elbowing Xavier.

"Better yet, *do* something Hardcastle wouldn't do. It's the only way you'd have any fun," Erica ribbed and was chased from the Coliseum by Court, who was spouting threats of revenge.

Xavier and Robbie laughed as they watched the group leave. Then Xavier turned to Robbie, suddenly nervous. "Ready?"

Robbie nodded eagerly, smiled, and slipped her hand into his.

He felt a rush of heat course through him and his heart skipped in his chest. His legs felt like weights and didn't seem to work properly as he led Robbie from the Coliseum. As they exited the arched doorway, Xavier's feet tangled with each other, and he stumbled into Robbie. The pair collapsed into a heap onto the grassy earth. Xavier was devastated.

"Oh, God! Robbie...I...I'm so, so sorry," he blubbered, carefully rolling off of her and detangling their legs.

But Robbie wasn't angry or hurt. She shook in barely suppressed hysteria, and the moment she saw his concerned face, laughter erupted from her.

"I'm sorry...I...can't... stop! It's... just... I keep seeing...

what we must have... looked like..." She was unable to continue as laughter swallowed the last of her words.

Xavier tried to imagine what they would have looked like falling, and he chuckled half-heartedly with her. When her laughter finally died away, Xavier looked at Robbie lying on the ground next to him. She was panting to regain her breath and his eyes dropped to her chest.

"Xavier Wells!" she snapped and playfully slapped him.

He jerked his gaze to her flushed, moist face. God! She was pretty. "What?" he muttered guiltily.

She giggled. "What? What? I'll tell you what! You just keep your eyes and your mind out of the gutter, *sire*!"

"Hey! My mind wasn't in the gutter!" he retorted indignantly.

"Oh, yes it was! I saw where you were looking!" she blurted and pinched him playfully on the side.

"Ouch! Hey!" he laughed, pinching her back.

Suddenly, Robbie lunged at him and pinned him to the ground.

"Ah, come on, Robbie. Get off!" he complained, squirming under her weight. "This is embarrassing! My girlfriend shouldn't be able to out-muscle me! I'm a man after all!"

"A man?" a voice guffawed above them.

Robbie and Xavier jerked upright to find Sara Jefferson grinning down at them. They quickly stood. Though Sara was only a little over a year older, she was tall and had developed much of her womanly shape. She looked much older than fourteen. But what annoyed Xavier no end was that she often talked to and treated him like a little kid.

"Now, Prince Wells. Don't be in such a rush to grow up. You have plenty of time to grow into a man. Just enjoy being the cute little boy that you are," Sara remarked in a sticky sweet voice.

He drew himself up to stand as straight and tall as he could and met the older girl's eyes unwaveringly.

"Thank you for the compliment, Miss Jefferson," he remarked, doing his best imitation of his father. "Now, is there something Roberta and I could do for you?"

Sara's confidence and maturity slipped and she gave Xavier a searching look before she responded, "Ah, yes. Daddy is looking for Erica. If either of you see her, tell her that Daddy got a call from Angus McCrady, the manager of Wellington Bookstore."

"Uh, oh," Robbie muttered. "Thanks, Sara. We'll warn her. Is Loren very angry?"

Sara's smugness was back in full force. "Oh, yes! Erica won't be able to charm her way out of trouble this time, and I think it's about time Daddy punished her. She's always getting away..."

"Yes, Miss Jefferson. We understand the message. Is there anything else?" Xavier interrupted with superiority.

Sara faltered and looked hesitantly at him. "No. No, that's all. Have a good day, kids," she added before turning and making her way to the secret passage in the palace's wall.

"*Miss Jefferson*?" Robbie hissed with a snicker.

"Well, I'm sick of her talking down to us like babies! She acts like she's *so* much older than us when she's just fourteen and a half, for crying out loud!" he blared.

She studied his irritated face a moment, nibbling on her bottom lip. "Xavier? You don't *like* her, do you?"

"What? No way! She's too bossy and conceited for me!" he gasped indignantly. "Besides," he added with a rueful smile, "I've got a complete hottie for a girlfriend."

She beamed. "Good answer," she replied, kissing him.

He felt a kick in his gut and his face flooded with heat, but as he reached for her to lengthen and deepen the kiss, she bounced out of reach, giggling. He felt a wave of irritation and reached for her again, scowling.

Again, she leaped out of reach, giggling, "You're gonna have to be faster than that, Prince Wells."

He lunged toward her only to grope air as she danced away. He dove at her again but tumbled to the ground empty-handed. Suddenly, a loud reporting crack pierced the sky above them and lightning blazed a path to the ground only a few yards from Robbie. With a scream, she fell to the ground and cowered into a tight ball.

"Robbie!" he shouted, clambering to her. "Robbie? God! Are you all right?"

Slowly, she unwound herself and looked at him with large frightened eyes. Without a word, her eyes glanced to the screaming blue, clear sky before looking accusingly at him.

"Why did you do that?"

"What?" he asked shakily, but he knew what she meant. He had done it again. He had lost control of his abilities and nearly killed the one person he held most dear. He looked away from her large, pain-filled eyes, unable to bear the guilt they stirred in him.

"Xavier, why did you conjure an electro force?"

He squirmed before finally dragging his eyes back to her, and his guilt turned into annoyance. It would have never happened if she hadn't been teasing him and messing around with his emotions.

"Well, *you* shouldn't have teased me and made me mad!" he sputtered indignantly.

"*You* were mad at *me*? What on Earth for? I was just playing!" she replied, her voice rising with apprehension.

"You're kidding, right? You can't possibly be that...Look, it's not all that comforting for a guy to know that his girlfriend is taller, quicker, and stronger. It's embarrassing and humiliating!"

"What? You mean you did it on purpose? You did it because I got the better of you?"

"No..yes...I mean no! You're twisting my words up!"

"Which is it then, *your highness*?" she spat condescendingly.

He released a weighted breath. "No, I didn't do it on purpose. I'd never try to hurt you. I just...my power just happened, like before. I was embarrassed and it just got away from me is all."

She stared at him.

Guilt gnawed at him. "Look, Robbie, it was an accident," he coaxed as he rubbed her shoulders gently. "I didn't mean to do it. Please, just...just don't tell my dad. Please? He'd cane me if he found out. Please!"

She shrugged his hands off of her shoulders, stood, and glared down at him. "Tell me something, *sire*. Are you more concerned that you nearly killed me, or that I might tell King Wells?" she spat.

"How can you ask that?" he questioned indignantly, getting to his feet.

"Well, it sounds to me that you're scared to death that Daddy will find out and you'll be punished. You know what? Sara was right. You *are* a little boy. A man wouldn't be worried that his girlfriend might tattle on him. A *real* man wouldn't be embarrassed because his girlfriend has some advantages over him. A real man would say he was sorry when he did something wrong and not try to blame someone else! It's always someone else's fault! You never think you have anything do with anything! Well, I'm done putting up with it. I'm going home!" With her insults said, Robbie turned and marched toward the secret passage.

"So, I guess this means the date is off?" he called sarcastically after her before turning and stomping into the woods.

Chapter 14

Dealing with Daddy

As he trekked to the lake, Xavier chastised himself over how he had handled the situation with Robbie. He should have never mentioned his father. He shouldn't have lost his temper when she was playing around with him. He should have told her he was sorry. He should have ... oh, what was the use of that now? Robbie was ticked, and she would probably tell his father everything. He tried not to imagine what would happen to him when the king found out. With a heavy sigh, he pushed through the last barrier of vegetation and into the clearing of the lake. His friends had built a small fire, and Frankie, Court, and Garrett were roasting hot dogs over the flame while the others splashed riotously in the lake.

"What are you doing here? I figured you'd be off snogging your number one groupie," Beck taunted.

"What happened, mate?" Court asked.

Xavier glared darkly at Beck before mumbling, "Well...uh...Robbie remembered she had to go home."

"That means, they had a huge fight and Robbie stood him up." Erica snickered.

"Yeah, well, speaking of fights, Jefferson," Xavier retorted testily, "your dad's looking for you. Mr. McCrady called him, and according to your sister, he's pissed."

Her haughty expression flickered, but she quickly recovered. "Oh, well. Daddy's been mad before, but I've always been able to smooth things over."

Xavier shook his head. "I don't think so this time. Sara doesn't think you'll be able to charm your way out of it." He flashed a grin at her stricken face.

Erica stammered, "Ah...w...well, I'm sure Sara was exaggerating."

"Yeah, right!" Garrett hissed.

"You're dreaming, Jefferson. After what you pulled in the bookstore, Loren will bust your butt and you know it." Beck laughed. "And I'm betting he wallops a good punch behind his whippings. I mean, the bloke's biceps are as big around as Garrett! Xavier could tell you. I think every member of the Royal Guard has had a go at his butt!"

"Shut up, Beck!" Xavier growled. "It hasn't been the entire Royal Guard...just...Loren and Ephraim..."

"And Sir Spencer, and Lieutenant Davies, and Sir Blaire, and Sir Underwood..." Beck added snidely.

The group snickered.

"Seriously, mate," Court commented, "you seem to have a fascination with Xavier's butt. What's up with that?"

The children burst into riotous laughter and several began heckling Beck. Xavier looked at his best friend and nodded his thanks.

"Shut up! The lot of you! I'm telling you I can handle my father. Besides, he's never hit me in my entire life," Erica boasted.

"He just might, love. I think you pushed it too far this time," Court commented.

"What exactly did you do, Erica?" Xavier asked.

She gave him the most devil-may-care smile he'd ever seen. "Well, it was old Mr. McCrady's fault! He was being a huge prat! Yesterday, I was in Wellington Bookstore browsing with Melissa and Robbie, and he started yelling at me that if I wasn't there to buy anything, to leave. I mean, how rude is that?"

"Well, Erica, you *were* being kind of loud and obnoxious. You seemed to offend the other customers a bit. Especially Ms. Williams! Your comment about her being wider than the aisle probably had something to do with it," Melissa noted with a snicker.

"That's beside the point!" she waved away Melissa's comment before continuing gleefully, "Anyway, this morning, I bought three bottles of bursting bubbles from Gregor's Novelties and dumped one down each toilet in the Wellington Bookstore bathroom. In hindsight, I probably shouldn't have used an entire bottle. I guess the pressure from the bubbles proved too much for the pipes because the toilets blew up, literally. It shook the entire building."

"Whoa!" Xavier gasped, and she grinned at him proudly.

"That's not all," Melissa stated. "After the toilets exploded, sewage came gushing out of the bathroom like a tsunami, ruining a lot of books and stuff."

"God, Erica! I'd have to agree with everyone else. Your butt's toast!" Xavier concluded as the rest of the group groaned their agreement.

"Oh, stop it you guys! It's nothing! I'm telling you I can handle my father," she retorted smugly.

"Can you now?" a deep voice grumbled from the edge of the clearing. "Then, you better start handling him."

The group turned and found Loren Jefferson standing stiffly with his massive hands on his hips. He looked livid, and Xavier shuddered at the cold, icy glare he saw in the green depths of the general's eyes. Erica stopped knee-deep in the lake, frozen at the sound of her father's stern tone.

It took her a moment to find her voice. "Ah, hi, Daddy," she called timidly. "I thought you were working this afternoon."

"I was supposed to, but I received a very disturbing call from Angus McCrady," he hissed.

"R...really? How's Mr. McCrady?" she asked breathily.

"You know damn well how he is since you single-handedly destroyed his store," he spat.

It wasn't looking good for Erica. Loren only swore when his temper was near the boiling point.

She changed ploys and her head dropped. "Yes, Daddy. I know. I really didn't mean for that to happen. It's just, I remembered that story you told me about you and King Wells using bursting bubbles in the palace's toilet, and well, I just wanted to be like you, Daddy."

Xavier had to hand it to Erica. She really knew how to sweet talk her way out of trouble, but it appeared that her father wasn't buying it this time.

"Really? And do you remember what happened to the king and me as a result of that little indiscretion?" her father asked. But, he didn't wait for a response as he continued, "King Wells' the senior whipped the pair of us until we couldn't sit."

Erica looked flustered. "Oh, I forgot that part."

"How convenient!" he growled. "I think I have a solution for your lapse of memory, my daughter. A swift, memorable punishment will fit the bill."

She opened her mouth to rebut, but Loren waved away the unspoken complaints with his hand.

"I don't want to hear any more excuses, Erica. Now, as I said before, it's time to start dealing with your father. Come on."

Erica looked pleadingly at Court, who simply shrugged. Deflated, she waded out of the water and slunk over to her father, who took her by the arm and led her away from the lake.

The group stared after them in complete silence for several long seconds when suddenly Court stood and raced into the wood.

"Court? Where are you going?" Xavier called.

"Where else?" he answered and disappeared into the woods after Loren and Erica.

"Crikey, he's right! This is a once-in-a-lifetime moment, and I for one don't want to miss it," Beck hissed.

Almost in unison, the group sprinted into the forest after Court. But when they entered the palace, there was no sign of Court, Erica, or Loren.

"What are you lot up to?" Ephraim asked from the dais next to the royal residence.

"We're looking for Court. Have you seen him?" Xavier asked.

"No, I haven't. I thought he was with you," Ephraim stated.

"He was, but he went tearing off," Garrett answered.

"Sorry, I can't help you but, Xavier, your father's looking for you," Ephraim called.

He felt his stomach drop. "He is? Did he say what he wanted?"

"No, he didn't, but he's in the residence now if you want to ask him." Ephraim suggested.

"Naw, we were just about to cook hot dogs at the lake. Tell him I'll check in with him later," he blurted and raced down the hall with the rest of the group following.

"How come you don't want to see your dad? Are you in trouble too?" Garrett asked.

"I don't know. I might be," he grumbled as they walked back out into the sunshine.

"What's that supposed to mean? How do you not know

if you've done something wrong?" Beck snorted with laughter.

Fed up with his snide comments, Xavier turned on the other boy and growled, "You know, I'm getting sick of your put-downs, Beck. Shut the hell up before I punch you!"

Beck held his hands up and snickered nervously. "Okay, okay! Geesh, I was only teasing!"

"Hey, there's Court!" Harry interrupted, pointing toward the stables. "Hey, Hardcastle! Over here!"

Court waved and jogged over to them. "Hey. What are you guys doing here? Why aren't you at the lake?"

"Why do you think?" Beck asked. "Where else would we be on a historical day like this? We wanted to witness Erica getting pummeled by her old man. Lord knows, she's managed to land all of us into major trouble at one time or another when she's always gotten off lightly."

Court grimaced and shook his head pitifully. "She didn't this time."

"You mean it's already happened?"

He nodded.

"How do you know?" Melissa asked. "You weren't even in the palace."

"Yeah, I was. Well, sort of. I snuck into the secret passage that runs to Erica's room."

"So, you saw?" Beck asked.

He nodded. "Yeah, but, guys, I don't think she needs to be ribbed about it..."

"What? Not rib Erica? Why on Earth not! She always teases us about our punishments...calling us babies..." Beck spat.

"No, Wilson!" Court stated firmly. "I'm not asking. Not a word about it. Got it?"

"Come on, Court. If we're not allowed to rib her, at least tell us what happened," Beck pleaded.

"You know what, Beck? You're a right foul git sometimes, you know that?" he spat. "No, I'm not telling you a bloody thing, and if you rib Erica, I'll pound you into the earth! Got it?"

With a groan, the group turned and made their way to the rear of the palace to return to the Wood. Court and Xavier lagged behind just out of hearing of the others.

"Is she okay?" Xavier asked.

"Yeah...but I have never seen Loren that angry or actually hit anyone before."

"I have," he muttered.

Court studied his friend. "Yeah. It's kinda disturbing to see him like that, huh?"

He nodded.

"Well, Loren was definitely right; Erica will remember that punishment. Heck, *I'll* remember that punishment. I've never seen her cry before." His voice faded. With a small jerk, he continued, "Anyways, I don't think we'll be seeing much of her for the next few weeks. She has to work every day after school at Wellington Bookstore to help pay for damages."

"Wonder how long that will take," Xavier thought aloud.

He shrugged. Then, for no other reason than to change the subject, he asked, "So? What's up with you and Robbie? Why is she ticked?"

"Ah..." He grabbed Court, pulling him to a halt and watching the others slip into the shrubs to the secret door before continuing. "Look, I'll tell you, but Court, you have to promise me first not to tell anyone, especially my dad. Okay?"

He gave him a wary look, but nodded. "All right, I promise. Now what's going on?"

"Well, I've been having trouble controlling my abilities

lately."

"Trouble controlling your abilities? How do you mean?"

"Well, remember the camp out when I threw the girls into the water?"

Court nodded and grinned. "Yeah, that was fantastic!"

"Well, I didn't mean for it to happen. I just couldn't turn off my powers. Afterwards, my abilities, all my abilities went silent. I couldn't have conjured a single thing even if my life had depended on it. That's why I didn't know that the girls were still hiding in the bushes, spying on us when we got out of the lake," he explained.

Court stared at him with alarm. "What? Wait a second! Is that what happened at the movie theater too?"

He nodded. "Yeah, and it happened again today with Robbie. She was teasing me and I got angry. Then, before I knew what was happening, an electro force the size of a bolt of lightning flashed out of the sky and struck the ground beside her. It nearly hit her! So, now she's pissed at me, and I don't blame her."

"Tell King Wells, Xavier! You have to! You might be sick! It may have something to do with how you took LeMasters' powers. Maybe it affected yours! Tell him!"

"NO! I'm not telling him and neither are you! You promised, Court!" he blared at his friend's apprehensive face. "If you tell him...I...I'll give you a beating that will make Loren look like a sissy!"

"Doubt that," he muttered dryly.

"If you tell...I'll tell Erica you spied on her and saw her dad spank her."

"Geez, Xavier! That's a low blow."

"Yeah, maybe, but I'll still do it."

"But, X, if you're having trouble controlling your powers, nothing you've done is your fault! Why don't you want to tell him?" he asked exasperatedly.

"Because...because it's embarrassing! I'm the future King of Warwood; I'm the Chosen for crying out loud! I'm not supposed to be weak...I'm not supposed to have fading or uncontrollable powers!" he hissed. "Besides, it's probably only temporary. Are you going to keep your promise or not?"

Court didn't look convinced as he muttered, "Aye, I'll keep my promise, but I'm telling you, you're being stupid by not telling the king."

Xavier didn't see Robbie for the remainder of the day. Sure that she'd told his father about the earlier incident, he sat down to dinner that evening with trepidation and anxiously awaited the king's wrath.

"Your new school uniforms arrived this afternoon. Emma put them in your closet. Did you get new socks? What about shoes? I doubt your old ones would fit anymore," his father began as he forked at his salmon and scooped a bite into his mouth.

"Ah...no. I didn't think about that," he murmured, confused that his father would want to talk about trivial things when he'd broken the Codes of Warwood. Maybe he was waiting for him to confess.

"Well, we'll take care of that tomorrow when we go out to get your school books," the king continued. "It appears we'll need to get your books from the used bookstore this term. Wellington Bookstore was vandalized and much of the store and its books were damaged."

"Yeah, I heard," he muttered.

"Erica's lucky her father was able to talk Angus McCrady into not filing charges against her. I don't know what Loren said to Angus to work that out, but I'm sure his daughter will think twice before pulling a stupid stunt like that again."

"Yeah, I guess she will." What was up with all this chit-chat? It was driving him insane. He wished his father would just get to the point and start yelling at him.

"Oh, and I won't be home Friday night. Lana and I have a business trip. We leave for New York Friday, but we should be back sometime Saturday evening. I want you to mind Mrs. Sommers while I'm gone. If you have any problems, both Ephraim and Loren are just down stairs," he continued.

Enough! He couldn't take it anymore! "Dad? What did you want to talk to me about?"

His father gave him a blank look.

"Ephraim said earlier that you wanted to see me."

"Oh, that! I just told you. Lana and I are going out of town on a business trip next weekend."

So, he didn't know. Robbie hadn't told him. The tension melted from his body and a strong sense of giddiness wiggled into its place. He grinned at his father.

"What's the grin for?"

"So, you and Lana have a *business* trip, huh?" he questioned, knowingly.

His father's face went crimson.

It wasn't until the next day at Sunday mass that he saw Robbie again. She sat in a pew next to Erica, whispering feverishly. Bits and pieces of the girls' conversation managed to pierce into his thoughts without any effort on his part.

"He nearly hit me with his electro force...he blamed me...he wouldn't even say he was sorry..."

Sighing, Xavier shuffled toward the girls. Erica saw him first and nudged Robbie.

"Hey, Robbie," he greeted tentatively, but she didn't answer and turned away.

"Guess you're still mad at me," he commented, crowding into her thoughts.

"Get out of my head, Xavier Wells!" her voice snapped so loudly that he clutched his head with a grimace.

The exchange didn't go unnoticed by the king. "Are you and Robbie having trouble, son?" he asked as they settled into the front pew to wait for the sermon to begin.

"I...well...we kind of had a fight yesterday," he muttered, grumpily.

"Do you want to talk about it?" Lana asked. "Maybe we could help?"

"No!" he barked before continuing more calmly. "I mean, no thank you, Lana."

His father's brow rose at his anxious response.

Eager to keep his father from prying into his memories and thoughts, he blurted the first thing that came to mind, "Dad? How big were you at my age?"

He glanced at Lana with a smile before turning to him. "I probably wasn't much bigger than you. Does this have something to do with the fight you had with Robbie?"

He nodded. "All my friends are taller, bigger, and stronger than me! Aside from Garrett, I'm the runt! Even Robbie is taller," he grumbled. "It's embarrassing when your girlfriend can kick your butt. It should be the other way around!"

Jeremiah did his best not to laugh. "Xavier, I know it's hard to be small for your age, but you won't always be. You'll have a growth spurt..."

"When? When will I have a growth spurt, Dad? When I'm ninety?" he spat.

"Xavier, these things usually run in families. Most likely, your growth spurt will occur around the time your father's did," Lana responded as she leaned across Jeremiah's lap to give his hand a squeeze. "Don't worry,

134

sweetheart. You're going to be tall and strong just like your father."

"Yeah? Well, I just wish it wasn't taking so long," he muttered.

His father snickered, earning an elbow in his side from Lana.

Xavier looked at him. "When did you have your growth spurt?"

"Well, let me think," he began, leaning back in the pew trying to remember. "I believe it was between year two and year three in school, so I would have been about fourteen. I grew close to six inches in eight months. My father had to buy me new uniforms three times that school year. He complained about it, but I could tell he was pleased that I was growing tall."

"Why would he care if you were tall or not?"

His father sighed, "I guess he thought I'd have a more powerful aura as king if I was tall, large, and imposing. He wanted citizens to quaver and cower at my feet. He wanted men to respect me and children to fear me."

"Mrs. Sommers told me a little about him. He sounds like a jerk to me," Xavier muttered.

"I guess he could be, but he did the best he could with the enormous task of raising a future king. It takes a strong man to rule a kingdom, to instill loyalty in his subjects, and when necessary, to command obedience. However, your grandfather and I had different opinions on how to achieve that. He believed in physical prowess, fear, and steadfastness. I believe in truthfulness, compassion, and communication. A kingdom is no more powerful than its lowliest peasant. Warwood is stronger when its citizens have a voice in what goes on at the executive level of their government, including what bills become laws. I believe citizens are more loyal and have more confidence in my rule if they have a legal means to challenge me without fear that I'd have them beheaded."

"Beheaded? Really?" he snorted.

His father nodded. "It was still a law up until ten years ago."

"So, the High Council?"

He nodded again. "Yes. The High Council provides citizens with a say in what I do and gives them a means of questioning me, legally."

His father's eyes trailed to the pulpit where Father Reinhart stood ready to begin his sermon. The new priest was a much better preacher than his predecessor. He didn't scream at the congregation the way Father O'Brien had. He was more involved with the community and wasn't afraid to do his fair share of hard work. He had eagerly pitched in with cleaning and rebuilding the kingdom.

As Father Reinhart began his sermon, Xavier's mind wandered to his father's philosophy on being a king. Being king meant being truthful and communicating with people. He looked at Robbie, who sat deep in thought. She was right. He never really said he was sorry. He had selfishly worried that she would tell his father about his rogue powers. God, he acted like a complete jerk! She deserved better. She deserved an apology.

After services, he spotted her sitting on the low wall separating the church from the street. He walked over to where she sat, rehearsing his apology in his head. He had never felt this nervous to speak to Robbie before in his entire life.

He stopped behind her and took a deep breath.

"Robbie?"

She visibly stiffened and started to stand.

"No, don't go. Please, just hear me out. I hate it when you're mad at me. I know I deserve it. I know I was a jerk.

I'm really, really sorry. I...I'll do anything to make it up to you. It was an accident! I'd never, ever intentionally hurt you. I'd *die* before I'd let anything happen to you."

Slowly, Robbie turned, looked at him, and sighed. "I'm not mad anymore. I would have forgiven you yesterday if you had just said you were sorry instead of jumping down my throat like it was my fault."

"I know. I was a jerk," he muttered, sitting next to her so that their legs brushed against one another. "To be truthful, it scared the hell out of me when the electro force came so close to you, and I felt guilty. Then I got angry, but I wasn't really angry at you. I was angry with myself for losing control of my powers and nearly killing you. I acted like a complete idiot. I am so, so sorry."

She gave him a feeble smile. "It's okay, but I'll take you up on your offer."

He frowned at her. "What offer?"

"God, Xavier! Not five seconds ago, you pledged that you'd do *anything* to make it up to me!" She laughed.

He laughed with her. "All right. I think I might regret this, but what can I do for you, Miss Minnows?"

"Oh, my! So many choices!" she teased. "Well, first I think you should start by giving me a kiss, Xavier Wells."

"Man, I like your thinking." He laughed and kissed her just as a flood of people spilled from the church.

"Hey, you two! This is consecrated ground! Watch that you don't incite the wrath of God," Loren joked from the door, his hand clutched firmly on Erica's shoulder. It looked as though Loren intended to keep a short rein on his trouble-seeking daughter.

Xavier laughed and squirmed uncomfortably before turning back to Robbie. "I guess we'll have to make up later. Can you meet me at the lake after lunch?"

"Sorry, Xavier. I can't. I have to get my books for school

and Mom is taking Brit and me into New York City to shop," she told him.

"Oh, well, that sounds like... fun. When will you be back?" he asked.

"Not until kind of late, I think," she responded.

"Well, I could *drop* in," he suggested with a snicker.

Robbie laughed. "Don't you dare! Mom nearly had a heart attack when King Wells called and told her you spent the night in my room. I had to sit through a very long, long, *long* lecture on the birds and the bees, and now she makes surprise visits to my room just to make sure I'm alone!"

"He called your mom?" he gasped.

"Yes, what did you expect he'd do?"

He shrugged. He hadn't thought much about the incident aside from his own punishment, but he wasn't surprised that his father had called Mrs. Minnows. It was exactly what his father *would* do.

"Well, I guess we'll just have to get together after school tomorrow, then. Maybe I can take you to King's Cafe for a milkshake," he stated.

"It's a date!" she grinned.

Chapter 15

Powerful Headache

Early the next morning, Xavier awoke with a start, bolting upright in bed. Panting he looked around the room as though the threats from his dream waited for him here, but his room was still and quiet. Almost immediately, he dropped back into his pillows and rubbed his head with a groan. It didn't hurt exactly; it just felt...strange. An intense throbbing pressure was building behind his eyes as if an invisible force pushed to get out. He rubbed his face vigorously and looked around the room once again. Moonlight slipped through the crack in his curtains. It was either very late or very early. He glanced at the clock on his bedside table and confirmed it was just after four in the morning.

At that moment the pressure behind his eyes intensified and his head began to tingle and crawl as though thousands of tiny critters were scurrying across his head. He leaped from the bed, ignored the thumping tension in his temples, and rushed into the bathroom. Frantically he searched through his hair but found no bugs in his long, white locks. Exhaling in relief, he splashed cool water over his face attempting to soothe the overwhelming pressure but to no avail. He turned and flicked on the shower. Hoping a long hot shower would do the trick, he stripped, stepped into the frosted-glass enclosure, and submerged his head under the steaming spray. The water seemed to ease the sensation somewhat so he stood under the water for nearly an hour before finally stepping from the shower and toweling dry. He wrapped the towel around his waist, wandered out of the bathroom, and flopped on the bed. The relief was short-lived and within seconds the throbbing returned with a vengeance.

Two hours later, when Mrs. Sommers came bustling into the room and threw back his curtains, Xavier hadn't moved. Turning, she spotted him lying halfway on his bed with his legs dangling over the edge.

"Well! I guess someone must be a bit anxious to start his day," she chirped.

"I guess so," he moaned, not offering to move. The strange sensation had lessened considerably, but it was still there, nagging at him.

"Well, sweetie," she continued as she walked to his closet and pulled out his school uniform, "you better get a move on. You'll want to be early for your first day back so that you can get your new class schedule and find your classes."

Slowly he sat up and watched her fling his clothes on to the foot of his bed. "I see you've already had your shower," she continued rambling as she disappeared into the bathroom and returned with his pajama bottoms. "For heaven's sake, Xavier Wells! Would it hurt you to pick up after yourself and not leave your clothes on the bathroom floor? Your pajamas are soaking wet!" She gave him a stern tut-tut and frowned, but she wasn't fooling him. She basked in the idea that he still needed her to pick up after him. "Well, I'll leave you to get dressed, dear. No dawdling! Your father is already dressed and will be having his breakfast soon."

"Yes, ma'am," he replied, finally standing.

"Lord, it's been over a year and those scars are still visible. Poor dear, he's been through so much, too much," she commented.

"What?" he questioned, turning to Mrs. Sommers, but she had left the room. Odder still, her voice continued as clear as if she was standing next to him.

"This family has been through hell. It's a relief that the evil monster that caused it all is now dead. Maybe the boys can finally find some peace and happiness. Lord knows, they deserve it."

He shook his head trying to disconnect from his governess' thoughts, but they clung to him.

"Especially little Xavier. No child should ever have to deal with the evilness he's had to face. That poor, poor baby boy," her thoughts continued.

He gave his head another hard shake before the governess' thoughts were finally forced out of his mind. He sank onto his bed with a shaky breath and a light headache. What had just happened?

Fifteen minutes later, he entered the dining hall fighting a growing headache.

"Morning, son!" his father bellowed jovially, making him cringe.

"Morning, Dad," he grumbled.

"Your books are in my study on the table. After you eat, get your books and pack up for school."

"Yes, sir." He rubbed his temple vigorously.

"He looks a bit peaky." His father's voice crowded into his mind before he asked aloud, "Are you feeling alright?"

He nodded. "Yeah. I'm just a little tired. I guess I'm not used to the school routine," he lied.

"Why are you lying to me, son."

"God, Dad! I'm not lying! I'm just tired. That's all!" he spat, dropping his silverware loudly on the table.

Stunned by his outburst, the king lowered his newspaper to study his son. "Why are you reading my thoughts?"

"Why are you calling me a liar?" he retorted.

"Xavier, I'm your father, and as I've told you before, I know when you're not being completely honest with me. Now, answer the question, why are you reading my thoughts?" he repeated with as much patience as he could muster.

Xavier floundered. There was no way he wanted his father to know he had unintentionally connected with him. So, he did the only thing he could think to do. He went on the defensive.

"I'M NOT LYING!" he bellowed, standing and stomping from the room.

"Xavier!" his father barked, and before Xavier could reach the steps, he seized him and spun him around. "Do not raise your voice at me!"

"Oh! I'm *soooo* sorry, Your Highness. I forgot how you like to have everyone bowing down to you and kissing your ass!" he spat.

What the heck was he saying? His father would kill him and from the expression on his face, it appeared he was about to do just that. With a jerk, he found himself pinned against his father's hip. He held his breath as the stinging smacks found their mark on his backside. It didn't matter how he prepared for it, his father's spankings always sent tears to his eyes.

Then, with another jerk, his father held him at arm's length and growled furiously, "If you ever speak to me like that again, your backside will be too sore to sit! Do you understand?"

He nodded, not trusting his voice.

"And, that little indiscretion has earned you a night indoors. You will come straight home after school. There will be no hanging out with friends, no playing rugby, and no swimming in the lake."

"I don't care," he murmured under his breath.

"Excuse me?"

"Nothing."

His father studied him for a moment before releasing him. "Go get your books and pack. We're leaving in ten minutes."

"Yes, sir," he grumbled as he shuffled toward the dining hall and his father's study.

Twenty minutes later, the limo pulled up in front of Wells Academy. Children in identical uniforms swarmed around the front of the building. Michael Spencer stood imposingly at the top of the stairs twirling his cane. Daniel stood anxiously beside him, fidgeting with his Academy uniform.

Xavier climbed from the vehicle, doing his best to push away the insistent pressure still building in his head. He could feel every eye on them as he and his father climbed the steps to where Spencer stood.

"Hey, Xavier!" Daniel chirped, his voice flooding with relief.

"Hey. What's up?" he asked as the smaller boy bounded down the steps to meet him.

"Daddy is letting me attend the Academy since my electro force ability has gotten stronger over the summer. Watch!" Daniel chattered, lifting his hands.

"Daniel," Michael warned quietly. "What did I tell you about that?"

"But I was only going to show Xavier," the smaller boy protested.

"I said no. You haven't had enough training or supervised practice with your electro force. You could hurt someone," he told him firmly.

"Yes, sir," he muttered, his shoulders slumping dejectedly.

"There's a good boy," Spencer added with a smile before turning to Xavier. "So, Your Highness, ready to start a new school year?"

"Yes, sir," he responded.

"I have your schedule here. We had to do some last-minute re-arranging with your classes since your father is only available after lunch," Michael told him.

"Why would my father need to be available?"

"I'm teaching your telepathy lessons now, remember?" Jeremiah reminded him.

"Oh. Yeah. I forgot," he mumbled, taking the schedule from Michael's outstretched hand.

"Oi! Xavier! Over here!" Court bellowed from a small grassy knoll where he stood with Beck, Garrett, and Mac.

He waved at his friends. "Well, I guess I'll see ya after lunch, Dad," he remarked before moving toward the group.

"Hey, Xavier? Can I come and hang out with you and your friends?" Daniel asked hopefully.

"Sure, come on," he responded nonchalantly.

The boy grinned and ran to fall into step with the prince as they approached his friends.

The two men watched the boys join the group, who all smiled and began thumping Daniel on the back like a long-lost buddy. Spencer snickered.

"It appears that Xavier has a surrogate little brother. I hope he'll be mindful of how fragile Daniel is right now. He desperately wants to fit in. I don't want him hurt."

"No father wants that, Michael. Unfortunately, pain is a fact of life, but don't worry. I'll have a talk with Xavier about watching out for Daniel. After all, that's what families do. They look out for one another," Jeremiah replied meaningfully.

Michael eyed his brother before calmly responding, "Yes they do. But sometimes they overstep their boundaries. Jeremiah, I'm thankful you found Daniel, but I can't just forget what you did! If you hadn't interfered, Daniel would have never been taken by that madman. If you hadn't interfered, Natalie would still be alive."

The king looked everywhere but at his brother. He was right. He should have never interfered. Even with all the posturing and excuses he claimed to have for sending Natalie away, he was ashamed of how he had gone about it. He had been distraught, angry, and even jealous to discover Michael had found love and happiness when he had nothing. He had just sent Julia and his infant son away for their own safety, and the burden of the throne weighed heavily on him. He resented being king. He was jealous that Michael could run away and begin a carefree life without the strains of kingship. When he discovered his brother's location, he immediately went after him. He remembered that day well, too well.

Michael and Natalie had found a quaint, little apartment in Cleveland. He still remembered the surprised look on his brother's face seeing him at his door.

"Hello, Michael."

"Jeremiah! How did you...what are you doing here?"

"I've come to get you. The kingdom needs you."

"Bullshit! It never needed me, not with the heir of Warwood running it."

"Those are father's words not mine. I need you!" He fought the tears that pooled in his eyes. "I sent Julia and Xavier to the Menes's. They're gone."

The hardness in Michael's face dropped and he sighed.

"I'm sorry Jeremy. That sucks. Come in."

The conversation that followed had been cordial. Michael agreed to return to Warwood while Natalie packed up their things and made arrangements to store the things they didn't need. Jeremiah had promised to send transportation for her in two days, but he came instead. The guilt clawed at him as he remembered the wounded look in her eyes when he told her she would not be joining Michael.

"He's too young to start a serious relationship! He needs time to straighten out his life before he can share it with anyone! He's only nineteen for God's sake!"

"He loves me, and I love him!" she protested.

"Love has nothing to do with it! It's a matter of duty and honor. If he stays with you he will not stay in Warwood, and he must stay. It is his responsibility, his duty to return. Do you really want to be the reason he shirks his heritage and responsibilities?"

"But, I can live there! He doesn't have to leave his people to be with me!"

Jeremiah shook his head. "You cannot stay in Warwood. There is a lot of turmoil and it's not safe to outsiders right now. Some of my people are very distrustful of outsiders, and I fear you would be in danger from the growing resistance in the kingdom. If you were injured, Michael wouldn't hesitate to leave to protect you. He will not stay in Warwood without you, but Warwood needs him. I need him. I need him to help me resolve the threats to our way of life."

Natalie understood. He could see it in her face as she paled.

"What do you want me to do?"

"Write a letter to him. Tell him he must stay in Warwood and that you will not be coming. Say whatever you must to ensure he does what is best for him and his people."

Nodding, she sat at the small kitchen table with a pen and paper. He had offered her a sizeable amount of money to help her get started somewhere where Michael couldn't find her, but she had refused the money. She earned his respect for that action. He hadn't known she was pregnant at the time, but even if he had known, it wouldn't have changed how he dealt with the situation. He had been young and head-strong. He had believed that LeMasters wasn't aware of Michael's relationship with Natalie and therefore sending her away was the safest thing to do for her and Michael. Yes, at the time, he thought separating the couple was best for everyone involved. He had been wrong, deadly wrong.

"You're right, Michael," he commented quietly. "I handled it poorly. I thought Natalie would be better off away from Warwood and away from William's radar. I misjudged the situation. If I'd known William knew about her... I didn't think he would go after her if she wasn't around you or Warwood. I assumed she'd be safe as long as she stayed away. I was mistaken, but I swear to you, I didn't know about the baby. I didn't know about Daniel until the hearings! I'm sorry, Michael. I'm so very, very sorry for my actions. The only excuse I have is that I was devastated after sending Julia and Xavier away, and I wasn't in my right mind. I hope someday you'll be able to forgive me."

"Someday I might," Mike answered before looking over at his son, who was tugging on Xavier's sleeve for his attention. It had been years since he had been a young boy tugging on his big brother's arm, and he knew he would never see Jeremiah with the same reverence again. But maybe that was the natural course of things. Boys grew to be men and outgrew their childhood heroes.

Xavier's first class was history, and he was pleased to discover that all his friends would be in the same class. So as one loud, boisterous crowd, they made their way into the classroom and waited for the teacher to arrive. Just before the bell, Lana Applegate entered the room with an armful of papers.

"Lana?" Xavier blurted and stood. "What are you doing here?"

"It's Madam Applegate at school, Xavier. I'm teaching now. Didn't your father tell you?" she asked with a smile.

"No, he didn't," he said, "but I think it's great."

"Well, I am glad you approve. Now, will you find your seat so I can begin?"

"Yes, ma'am," he responded, sitting and digging in his bag for his textbook.

Ten minutes into the lesson, the throbbing pressure in Xavier's head had intensified, and by the next class period, he began to hear voices; a lot of voices. In fact, every thought from every student in the classroom assaulted his mind. Needless to say, by third period, his head was hurting so badly from the influx of thoughts that he was beginning to feel nauseous.

He submerged his head under the water fountain hoping that it would help ease the pain when Robbie's voice fought its way through the mob of thoughts in his mind.

"Hey, Xavier? Want to walk with me to Latin class, since we have it together?"

Slowly, he pulled his head out from under the cold oasis and met Robbie's eyes vacantly. "Ah...I can't...I...I feel like crap. I think I'm just going to go home..." he answered weakly, turning toward the Academy's doors.

"But, Xavier, you need the headmaster's permission and he's teaching our next class!" she called after him, but he couldn't hear her past the pain and noise in his head.

With his hands clamped over his ears, Xavier raced from the school and across the field to the secret door in the palace's wall. Out in the open, the bombardment of voices grew exponentially with not only the thoughts of the students and staff from the Academy, but with the thoughts from every living soul in the kingdom. He didn't make it to the secret passageway before he fell to his knees and began retching uncontrollably. The noise in his mind continued to intensify and he found himself crawling the remaining distance to the secret door. Once through the passage, the noise in his head was so disorienting that he got lost in the thick tangle of branches before finally collapsing to the ground.

Chapter 16

Found

Michael Spencer surveyed the students sitting quietly in his classroom and noted immediately that Xavier was not among them.

"Has anyone seen Prince Xavier?"

Robbie Minnows and Courtney Hardcastle exchanged uneasy looks. He stepped toward the two children.

"If you know where the prince is, you must tell me."

Robbie took a hesitant breath and answered in a quiet rush, "I told him he needed to see you first, but I guess he was too sick to hear me. He...he really did look horrible!"

"Easy, Robbie. Where precisely is Xavier?"

"Home. He said he was going home. He's not in trouble, is he, sir? He really was sick!"

"No, he's not in trouble. I'm just concerned about him. Don't worry, Robbie. I'm sure he went home like he said," Sir Spencer replied, patting her shoulder.

Maintaining a business-as-usual attitude, Michael distributed a pre-test to the groaning students.

"Yeah, yeah. I know. We all hate pre-tests, but I assure you they're an important tool used to determine where to begin your lessons. Do the best you can. It isn't for a grade."

"Then why do we have to do it?" Beck challenged,

earning a hard glare from the headmaster.

"I just explained that to you, Mr. Wilson, but if you're still unclear, I can explain it further after school in detention."

Beck stammered, "No, no, sir. It's fine. I understand."

Michael smirked at the boy as he slouched in his seat and began working. His gaze left Beck and swept the room. All the students were working quietly and diligently. Taking advantage of the orderly class, he silently sent a message to Sir Blaire to report to his classroom.

Within minutes, Blaire quietly entered the classroom. While most of the students didn't even look up, Robbie studied the men with a frown as they exchanged hushed words. Finally, Sir Spencer patted the other man's shoulder and exited the room. Although he was trying to hide it, it was clear Spencer was just as worried about Xavier as she was. It wasn't so much that Xavier had looked horrible, it was his peculiar behavior. He had been disoriented and flustered. He may have had every intention of going home, but in his state, Robbie worried that he may have gotten lost or done something stupid. That scared her more than anything, but at least the headmaster was doing something about it. He would find Xavier.

When Xavier came to, his head still throbbed but at least the noise had lessened. He wasn't sure how long he had been unconscious, but he had to get inside the palace before his telepathy powers got worse again. The branches scraped his arms and legs as he crawled out of the shrubbery before slowly standing. The sun hung low in the sky. It had to be near dinnertime or later! He had been unconscious for hours!

"Prince Wells!" a gruff voice called.

Xavier turned to see a Royal Guard hurriedly approaching him with a grim expression. *"Oh crud!"* he thought. *"It must be really late."*

"Prince Wells, you had better come with me. You have a good number of people out looking for you," the guard stated, grabbing his arm and leading him toward the front of the palace.

Loren stood at the palace's entrance and the moment he saw Xavier, relief flooded his face. He spoke into the walkie-talkie in his hand as he moved toward him. When Xavier was within a few feet of the general, Loren whistled softly.

"Christ Almighty, Xavier Wells, you better have a great explanation for your disappearing act, or I might be inclined to help your father by holding you down while he beats your butt into a pulp!"

He opened his mouth to respond when suddenly the pressure in his head exploded as hundreds of voices flooded into his mind. Biting his lip to keep from screaming, he dropped to his knees and cradled his head with a whimper.

"Xavier?" Loren gasped, dropping to a knee next to the boy. "What is it?"

"M...my head. God! It's killing me! I...I...going to throw up!" he uttered before vomiting.

He knew Loren was talking to him, but for the life of him he couldn't hear him past all the noise in his head. Even after the nausea waned, he continued to cower on the ground, crying. Then he felt himself being lifted and carried into the palace. The moment the outer door to the building closed behind them, the voices dropped off like a sudden calm in a storm and the only voice he heard was Loren's.

"I wonder where he's been all this time. The boy is

definitely sick. Lord, I hope it's not the Super Flu raising its ugly head again..." Loren thought as a sudden panic rose inside him, belying his cool, calm exterior. Then, his thoughts jumped to his daughters. Erica, it seemed, had a very special place in Loren's heart. He adored her. It had nearly killed him to punish her for the incident at Wellington Bookstore.

He carried Xavier into the royal residence, past a relieved Mrs. Sommers, up the stairs, and into his bedroom. He tore back the blankets and laid him on the bed.

"How are you doing, Tiger?" he asked softly, stroking back damp hair from Xavier's eyes.

"I feel better now that I've thrown up," he lied with a meek smile.

The general glanced at the governess, who had followed them into the room. "Mrs. Sommers, could you get me a cool wet cloth."

He pressed his hand to Xavier's forehead. "You seem to be running a fever. I'll call for a healer. Rest up little sire. Your dad will be here..."

"Xavier!" Jeremiah sighed as he rushed into the room.

"Right about now," Loren's thought finished the sentence with a silent chuckle as he scrambled out of the way as the king raced to his son's side.

"Are you all right?" he questioned, placing a hand on Xavier's forehead and looking at Loren. "Call a healer."

"Yes, sire. I was just about to do that," Loren responded and left the room.

Mrs. Sommers shooed his father's hand away from Xavier's head and replaced it with a damp cloth. The king busied himself by pulling Xavier's shoes and socks off, but Xavier could hear his panicking, fearful thoughts. Like Loren, his father feared that the Super Flu had returned.

"Where have you been? I've been worried out of my mind."

"When I left school, I tried to come home, but my headache got so bad...I threw up and passed out or something," he answered. He was starting to feel much better. The palace's lead-lined walls protected him against the chaotic thoughts of Warwood's people. The only thoughts that assaulted him now were his father's, the guards' and the servants'.

"When the healer gets here, I'll have him give you something for the pain," his father told him as he slowly helped Xavier to sit upright and peeled off his Academy blazer. When he moved to help him with his pants, Xavier stopped him.

"Dad! God, I'm sick not paralyzed! I can take my own pants off!" he spat indignantly, his gaze flickering toward Mrs. Sommers, who had picked up his shoes and blazer and moved toward his closet.

Jeremiah backed off, but his hurt feelings and memories bombarded Xavier's mind. When Uncle Mike had called his father and reported him missing, he had been terrified, and his thoughts had obsessed on the possibility that the Dark Army was somehow involved in his disappearance. Xavier felt his eyes tearing as he experienced his father's panic and fear first-hand.

"I'm sorry," he mumbled. "It's just my head...I just want to go to sleep. Maybe I'll feel better after I sleep for a bit."

"It's all right, son. I'm just relieved you're safe."

"I know," Xavier whispered.

"I'll step out so you can change, sweetie," Mrs. Sommers announced, setting clean pajamas next to him and kissing his cheek. She paused and rubbed Jeremiah's arm before leaving the room.

Xavier pulled the pajamas toward him and changed

into them while the king hovered over him like a mother hen, but he didn't have the heart to complain. Jeremiah picked up his discarded garments and pulled up the blankets around him.

Xavier closed his eyes and tried desperately to block out his father's worried thoughts. He sighed as another voice joined the crowd in his head. The healer had arrived. Maybe he could give him something to make him sleep. Lord knew, with all the voices blaring into his brain, there was no way sleep would happen otherwise.

When the healer entered the room, he froze at the sight of the king and cleared his throat.

Jeremiah turned. "Ah, you must be Healer Dorne."

The healer nodded stiffly.

Jeremiah stood and approached the smaller man. "Thank you for coming on such short notice," he noted, relief filling his body, thoughts, and voice as he shook Dorne's hand. "Prince Xavier is ill. He complains of a headache, nausea, and he lost consciousness on his way home from school today."

"Hm, well, let's have a look at him," Dorne replied with a reassuring smile, but Xavier could feel the man's anxiety. His thoughts punched into his mind, overcrowding and overpowering his father's.

"What if I can't help him? What if he dies? The king would have my head if I can't help his son! God! Why did I have to be on call this evening!"

Healer Dorne approached Xavier, sat on the edge of the bed, and set his medical bag on the bedside table. Then he shakily reached into the bag, pulled out a thermometer, and placed it in Xavier's mouth. As he waited for the thermometer's reading, he pulled out a stethoscope and placed the cold metal piece against the boy's chest and listened.

"He has a good, strong, steady heartbeat," he commented, removing the stethoscope. He returned it to the medical bag and extracted a small pen light. "Look straight ahead, young sire," he instructed with quiet authority.

He passed the light across Xavier's eyes and nodded with approval. Then he finally removed the thermometer and studied it.

"Hm. He has an elevated temperature, sire. It appears to be nothing more than the common cold. It's been going around, especially at the grammar school. See to it that he rests and drinks plenty of fluids." Dorne dropped the light and thermometer back into the bag and stood to leave.

"Wait!" Xavier blurted. "Could you give me something to help me fall asleep? I'm exhausted, but I don't think I'll be able to fall sleep."

The healer looked at King Wells, who nodded his consent, and within moments, Xavier was fast asleep.

Chapter 17

Bullied

Xavier didn't wake again until early the next morning. The pressure in his head was mostly gone and the voices were quiet.

"Thank God!" He sighed loudly, rubbing his face.

After a noisy yawn, he stood and padded into the bathroom to shower. Mrs. Sommers had not come in at her normal time to wake him, which could only mean that no one expected him to go to school today. Tempted to play hooky, Xavier stood in the middle of his room with a towel around his waist, contemplating it. No, if he wanted to see Robbie and take her to King's Cafe for a shake, he would have to go to school, that was if his dad would let him. He was supposed to have been grounded yesterday. Hadn't he served and abided by his grounding? Hadn't he come home and not gone off with his friends to play rugby? Did it really matter that he spent the evening in bed sick? Xavier tossed his towel aside and reached for his clothes when his bedroom door opened. His father froze at the sight of him as he scrambled for his towel, praying Mrs. Sommers wasn't behind him.

"God, Dad! I'm naked! Close the door! Is it too much to ask that you knock?" he blared.

Jeremiah stepped into the room and quickly closed the

door. "I'm sorry, son. Well, it looks like you're feeling better."

He gave his father an annoyed glare before responding, "Yeah, I feel like a million bucks!"

Ignoring the boy's attitude, the king smiled. "I'm glad to hear it, but you really should take another day to regain your strength."

"Thanks, but I can't. The teachers usually assign a lot of work on the second day. I don't want to fall behind," he replied, pulling on his underclothes.

"All right. If you're sure."

"Yeah, I am. Thanks though," he told him. "Ah...Dad? I know I was supposed to be grounded yesterday, and I was sick, but it still counts, doesn't it?"

His father gave him a devilish smile. "Yes, it counts. Why?"

He grinned. "I kinda have plans."

"Plans, huh? Would these *plans* be about five-foot-three with brown hair and brown eyes?" he asked, snickering.

"Maybe," Xavier answered with a grin.

After a quick breakfast where Mrs. Sommers tutted at him while he shoveled mouthfuls of oatmeal and fruit into his mouth, resembling a hording hamster, Xavier finally exited the royal residence and descended the steps. His father had wanted to drive him to school and it took a lot of arguing and protesting to convince the king otherwise. He was more than a little annoyed over his father's overprotective smothering, yet at the same time, he liked it too. After feeling how worried and scared his father had been to discover him missing and then ill, he understood why his father hovered. If being a father meant feeling all of that, Xavier wasn't sure he ever wanted kids.

"Morning, little sire," Loren greeted from his post next to the residence staircase. "My, you look worlds better than you did yesterday." He felt Xavier's forehead. "Are you sure you're all right to go to school?"

He shrugged off the general's hand. "Geez, Loren! Of course, I am. Dad's letting me go."

Loren looked unsure.

"Is Erica allowed to walk to school?" he asked.

The large man sighed and then grinned. "I guess so. I'll go and round her up," he answered, heading toward his own residence.

"Thanks," Xavier mumbled, turning toward the Hardcastle residence. Long before he rang the doorbell, he heard the uproar of activity from behind the closed door.

"Mom! Where're my shoes?" Court's voice bellowed from behind the door.

"I am not your maid, Courtney Aaron Hardcastle! Try looking where you took them off," came her annoyed answer.

"I am! I can't find them! What am I supposed to do? Go to school barefooted?" he blared.

"Boy! Watch your tone with your mother, or I'll take my hand to your backside!" Ephraim's voice thundered as he opened the door to the residence. Then he turned and saw Xavier in the doorway, and his brows rose with surprise. "Xavier! I didn't expect to see you here. Feeling better?"

"Yes, sir. Is Court about ready to go?"

"I imagine, once he finds his bloody shoes," Ephraim replied.

"I'll get him going, Mr. Hardcastle," Erica chirped, skipping up from behind Xavier.

Ephraim stepped aside to let Erica through as she bellowed, "Court Hardcastle! Get your butt in gear or you'll make all of us late!"

Five minutes later, after completely ransacking the Hardcastle residence in search of Court's shoes, which Andrew had hidden in Caleb's toy chest, the three children exited the palace and made their way to the secret passage.

"So? What happened to you yesterday, mate?" Court asked as they ducked into the row of pines along the wall.

"Well..." Xavier glanced at Erica, who ducked through the passage ahead of him. Then he whispered meaningfully, "It happened again."

Court's eyes bulged and he froze on the spot. "It...it happened *again?*"

He nodded solemnly. "Yeah. My telepathy powers went overboard this time. The thoughts of everyone in the kingdom came blasting into my brain. I thought my head would pop!"

"Is...is it better now? I mean, can you hear my thoughts?"

"Well, I get little snippets of thoughts from people now and again, but not enough to make anything out. So, yeah, it's a heck of a lot better," he answered.

"Oh, good." Court breathed, sounding relieved, but the expression on his face was anything but relief.

"God, you guys! What's taking so long in there? Are you snogging or something?" Erica teased.

"Shut it, Erica," Court hissed, not resorting to the usual carefree banter he normally gave Erica when she teased him.

The boys darted through the passage and the group made their way across the field to the enormous, dark-stoned school.

Xavier was relieved that he hadn't missed much in his classes, especially Latin, which wasn't his best subject. He didn't want to think about what his year would be like if he fell behind on the second day of school. Fortunately, all he had missed was a pretest reviewing last year's concepts and vocabulary. Sir Spencer spent the class period reviewing the test and focusing on concepts the class struggled with the most. Surprisingly, Xavier found that he knew most of what was being covered. Relieved that his day was going so well, he made his way to Advanced Mathematics. He had always been good in math, and as a result, he had been placed in an Advanced Algebra Concepts class.

When he entered the classroom, he was pleased to find Garrett there, waving enthusiastically at him from the far side of the room. As he made his way over to his friend, he collided with a large, beefy body.

"Well, well, well. If it isn't the Prince of Pipsqueaks!" Jonas sneered down at him.

"Back off, Jonas!" Xavier felt a rush of relief at Drew's voice behind him.

"Since when did you decide you were the keeper and protector of nose-miners, Drew?" Jonas chastised.

"Since now," Drew stated firmly.

"God, you're becoming a complete crown polisher, Hardcastle. Are you going to wipe his butt when he takes a crap too?" Jonas spat out.

"No, but if you keep it up, you'll be eating through yours!"

The boys stood glaring at one another until Jonas finally muttered, "Crotch sniffer." Then he turned and walked away.

Xavier looked up at Drew. "Thanks for that," he whispered.

"Anytime. Besides, it's my fault Jonas is targeting you." Drew shrugged. "Sorry about that."

"It's not your fault Jonas is a jackass. Forget about it."

The older boy snickered. "Well, just let me know if he bothers you anymore. You can sit next to me and Seth if you want."

"Is there room for Garrett?" Xavier asked.

"Sure," Drew agreed, waving Garrett over to them.

Following math class, Xavier wandered into the cafeteria with Drew, Seth, and Garrett and paused inside the doorway to search for the rest of his friends.

"Move it, Prince of Pissants," Jonas spat, shoving Xavier out of his way and he fell hard to the linoleum floor.

There was a blur of action as Drew turned, tackled Jonas to the floor, and repeatedly pounded him. One of Jonas' friends, a boy Xavier recognized from the Dark Army, started to pull Drew off of him, but Seth intercepted him.

"He's a big boy. Let him fight his own battles," he hissed, yanking the other boy away from Drew.

"What on Earth is going on?" Headmaster Spencer blared, moving quickly toward the ruckus. "Andrew Hardcastle! Jonas McKnight! Break it up!"

The boys didn't seem to hear him and continued to wrestle around on the floor until Michael bullied between them and tossed Andrew off of Jonas. Xavier was impressed by his uncle's strength, and the crowd of children watching the ruckus groaned with appreciation.

"I said, break it up!" Michael shouted loudly. "Now, what is going on here?"

"He started it, Headmaster!" Jonas spat. "Xavier fell over his own feet and Drew just attacked me!"

"That's bullshit!" Andrew shouted.

"Andrew! Watch your language!"

"Well, it is," Drew responded, his voice slightly calmer. "He put his slimy hands on the prince and knocked him to the floor for no reason other than to mess with him. Ask them!" Drew told him, gesturing to the others.

Michael looked at Xavier and Garrett expectantly.

"It's true, Headmaster Spencer. I saw Jonas do it," Garrett responded.

"Liar!" Jonas spat.

"All right! That's enough. Mr. McKnight, you will come with me to my office. Mr. Hardcastle, get some lunch, but I want to see you during break," Michael ordered.

"Yes, sir," Drew replied meekly.

Michael Spencer turned and with Jonas' arm clutched in his hand, led him out of the cafeteria.

"Thanks, Drew," Xavier whispered as they made their way to the growing lunch line. "I hope you don't get into too much trouble because of it."

"Don't worry about it. We're mates, right? I stick up for my friends," the older boy told him before moving into line with Seth.

"Xavier! Xavier! Wait up!"

He turned as Daniel fought his way toward him through the crowded cafeteria.

"Hey, Daniel."

"Did you see that?" he blurted in awe. "My dad tossed that big kid like he was a feather!"

"Yeah, I saw," Xavier noted, humoring the smaller boy.

"Boy, he's really strong!" Daniel continued, following Xavier into line for food.

"Yeah, he is," he answered.

"Dad said you were sick yesterday. Are you okay?"

"Yeah, I'm fine, Daniel," he responded, eying Garrett, who stifled a snicker.

Daniel's eyes settled on Garrett. "Oh, hi, Garrett."

"Hey, Daniel. How's it going?" he responded with a smile.

"Great!" Daniel chirped before turning his attention

back to Xavier. "Hey Xavier, whatcha doing after school today? Do you want to come to my house and play?" he asked eagerly.

Garrett didn't even attempt to smother his laughter this time and Xavier gave his friend a quick warning jab to the ribs. "Ah well, I can't. I sort of have plans with Robbie."

"Oh. What are you guys going to do? Can I come?"

"Not this time, Daniel. It's a...well... it's sort of a date," he told the smaller boy.

"Oh," he replied, looking like a wounded puppy.

"Sorry, cousin," he added patting the younger boy's shoulder. Feeling sorry for the little guy, he continued without thinking, "Maybe Robbie wouldn't mind stopping by afterwards though. Would that be okay?"

Daniel grinned, his entire face lighting up. "Yeah, that would be great! Thanks!"

Chapter 18

Special Treatment

Following lunch, Xavier walked with dread to his next class. After all the catastrophes involving his abilities in the past four weeks, he desperately wanted to avoid using his powers whenever and wherever possible, but this would be problematic in his afternoon empowerment classes, where he was not only expected to conjure his abilities, but also to control them.

Unfortunately, Xavier's first empowerment class would be telepathy with his father. He was scared to death to even think about what would happen if he conjured the ability after yesterday, but he didn't have much of a choice. He either had to summon his telepathy during the lesson, or he would face his father's wrath. Contemplating his choices, Xavier moseyed down the hall before finally concluding that refusing to use his abilities and facing a row with the king would be the lesser of two evils. With a shaky breath, he entered the small classroom that had been reserved for their lesson. His father was already there. He stood staring out the window at the flowering courtyard.

Without turning, Jeremiah called, "Hello, son."

"Hey," Xavier began grumpily.

Jeremiah turned and pinned him with a puzzled look.

"Why are you worried about doing this lesson, son?"

Xavier felt the coolness in his bones too late.

"Dad! God! Do we have to start the moment I walk through the door?" he spat.

"Do you think Fox LeMasters will give you time to prepare?"

"Of course not! I'm not an idiot! Geez! But this is only our third lesson, and you're my dad, not Fox! Don't be such a...a...tosser," he blurted. He wasn't sure what a tosser was, but he recalled Court calling Drew that once when he was bossing him around.

"If I didn't know better, I would think you're intentionally starting an argument with me. Now, why would you want to do something like that?" his father's face was calm and passive, but the edge in his voice contradicted his composed exterior.

"I don't know! Maybe it's because you're an irritating..."

"Do **NOT** finish that sentence, young man," the king barked. "Now, sit." He pointed to the chair in front of him.

Xavier immediately complied. He wasn't so sure he had it in him to intentionally start a fight with his father after yesterday.

"Why would you want to fight with me?" he asked.

"Shit!" Xavier thought bitterly. "Who says I wanted a..."

"You did, son. Okay, what's going on?" he asked, sitting across from him.

"Nothing," he mumbled.

"Xavier," Jeremiah warned.

"I just don't feel like having a telepathy lesson after spending all day with my head ready to explode. I'm not sure how well I'd do after that."

"You'll do the best you can, Xavier," his father told him patiently.

"But, Dad..." He knew that he had to give his father a bit

of truth in order to get out of the lesson. "I haven't been able to connect with my telepathy since my illness yesterday!"

"What?" Jeremiah hissed softly. "Are you sure?"

"Yes, sir. I'm sure it's just temporary like the last time I got sick, but I just can't do it right now," he told him.

After a long moment of studying him, the king gave him a small smile and nodded. "You're probably right. Let's cancel your lessons for today. Be ready to go tomorrow."

"Okay. Thanks, Dad," he sighed.

For the most part, the rest of the day went well. His empowerment teachers didn't expect much from him his first day back to class. So Xavier entered the last class of the day feeling pretty confident that he would make it through the entire day without having to conjure a single power. After all, he wouldn't be required to make use of his powers in fencing class, right?

"Good afternoon class!" Ephraim bellowed jovially. "I'm sorry our class had to be cancelled yesterday, but an emergency required my immediate attention."

Xavier's face ignited as he shifted uncomfortably. No one had to tell him that *he* had been Ephraim's emergency.

"So let me give you an idea of what my plans are for fencing class this term," he stated.

"Sir Hardcastle? Why are we still taking fencing lessons when William LeMasters is dead? Isn't the whole Dark King and Dark Army thing over with now?" a year five student asked.

"Well," Ephraim sighed as he hoisted himself up to sit on the end of a table. "Your parents may not want you to know this, but the coming war will not be fought just by your parents. You have a right to know. The Dark King is not dead! William LeMasters was never the Dark King. It has always been his son, Fox LeMasters."

There was a sudden burst of murmuring from the class. Ephraim held up his hand for silence.

"Now, Fox is only seventeen but he grows stronger each day, and one day, he will come for our kingdom. He will come for King Wells and Prince Xavier. We must be prepared to do our part to protect our kings, our kingdom, and our families," Ephraim stated, pausing to allow the news to sink in. "Now, are you ready to continue with your training?"

"Yes, sir!" the group chanted, and Ephraim smiled.

"But, sir. If the Dark King still exists, then where is the *Chosen*. I mean, *He's* the one who's supposed to stop the Dark King and save *us* from the dark rule. Is he a coward or something? Is that why we have to do all the work for him?" Jonas asked somewhat smugly.

Ephraim's eyes burrowed into the older boy. "Mr. McKnight, the Chosen could be a child and not ready to take on the burden of his destiny. So until he is properly trained and ready for the responsibilities of his role, he will remain anonymous."

"Wait, you mean, you know who the Chosen is, and he's a kid here at the Academy?"

"I didn't say I knew who he was, Jonas. I was simply giving you a hypothetical reason for your accusation. Even if I did know the identity of the Chosen, I couldn't answer your question." Ephraim turned to the rest of the class as he continued, "Besides, it's our duty as Warwoodians to do our part to protect the kingdom. Understand?"

The class nodded enthusiastically, several glaring at Jonas, clearly disgruntled.

"Now, during this term we will continue to perfect our fencing techniques and work on integrating empowerments during sword battles. With that said, before you leave here today, you must get a medical release form from me for your parents to sign."

"Medical release?" a girl asked, shaken. "Why do we need medical releases?"

The general smiled reassuringly. "It's nothing to fret over. It's just a precaution. Now, are you ready to get started?"

The group nodded again, less enthusiastically.

"Good. In today's lesson we'll be reviewing and practicing a skill we learned while at King's Mountain: using an electro force as part of a carefully orchestrated sword fight. So, everyone pair up and put on your protective gear."

As the group quickly paired up, Drew moved to stand next to Xavier. "Want to be partners?" he asked.

"Yeah..."

"Sorry, Andrew. You need to partner up with Jonas. I'm Xavier's partner. I have orders to train him personally," Ephraim told his son.

"Orders?" Xavier gasped.

He nodded. "Yes, young sire. As future king, you must have impeccable fighting techniques. You'll only learn that by training with a skilled, experienced swordsman." Ephraim smiled and bowed playfully.

"Great," Xavier thought with sudden panic. *"How can I possibly avoid using my powers if I'm partnered up with General Hardcastle?"*

As Xavier slipped on his padded vest and helmet, Ephraim turned to the rest of the class and announced, "Before you get started, I'd like everyone to watch as Prince Xavier and I demonstrate. Xavier has had some experience with using this technique in real combat, so I want you to watch what he does and critique it. What does he do that is successful? What can he improve upon? Does he at any time over-extend himself or open his body up for a mortal wound? Understand?"

"Yes, sir," the group chimed together and moved to form a circle around the general and the prince.

"Your sword, Your Highness," Ephraim called, dutifully presenting Xavier with a sword.

He took the sword with dread. He was going to make a fool of himself! He couldn't use his electro force, and without it, Ephraim would surely pulverize him in front of the entire class.

"En guarde!" Ephraim barked, getting into position.

Xavier flipped his mask down and assumed his fighting stance.

General Hardcastle immediately lunged, and Xavier stumbled backwards, off-balance.

"Watch your balance, boy!" he barked, straightening and backing off to allow Xavier to regain his composure before assuming his battle stance. "En guarde!"

Xavier inhaled deeply and prepared himself. Again, the general attacked first. He parried and countered the attack, but Ephraim batted away his sword as if it was nothing more than a chopstick.

"Come on, Prince Wells. Use your electro force to stun me," he hissed as he lunged again.

He barely managed to defend himself and stammered, "But...I...I'm not allowed. I'll get in trouble."

Ephraim withdrew from the attack and straightened, looking down at the boy, a bit confused.

"Xavier, this is your training. You're expected to use your powers."

"But what if I hurt someone?"

"You won't. I have blocking abilities. Now, give me a good fight worthy of a king, Your Highness!" the general finished sternly and readied himself to fight again.

He hesitated. Would he be able to control the force once he conjured it? Would it even present itself? It appeared he didn't have a choice but to try. Ephraim expected him to use it during their spar.

"That puny thing couldn't beat a flea in a wrestling match, let alone give General Hardcastle a *good* fight," Jonas chortled to the boy next to him, who burst into laughter.

Xavier felt hot anger surge through him and he turned back to Ephraim, determined to give him what he had asked for, "a good fight worthy of a king."

"Yes, sir," he whispered, and this time, he attacked Ephraim.

He initiated the attack with a simple lunge with his sword that Ephraim easily parried and countered. Xavier took a step backwards as the general came at him and managed to chop the general's sword aside. To his relief, the electro force materialized without effort, and he pelted it at Ephraim, sending him staggering backwards. Xavier took advantage of the general's loss of balance and swung his sword, but Ephraim was a superior swordsman. Before Xavier could complete his back swing, the general had his balance back, parried Xavier's attack, spun, and with a move that could only have come with years of training, countered with an attack of his own. In the blink of an eye, Xavier found himself on his back with a sword hovering over his heart.

Ephraim smiled and help him to his feet. "Not bad...but we've got a lot of work to do, Your Highness." He bowed his head slightly in respect before turning to the class. "What did you see?"

"A bloody awesome counter, sir," Drew responded in awe, and the class joined in with a similar sentiment.

Ephraim smiled and Xavier could tell he was pleased to

have impressed his oldest son, but he continued firmly, "Thanks, but I meant about the prince."

Jonas spoke up next. "Xavier is a shitty swordsman, and it's amazing he lived through his sword fight with William LeMasters."

There were a few snickers at this, but the majority of the class simply glared at Jonas.

"Mr. McKnight, can you reword your comment into something *constructive* so that we may have a specific area Prince Wells can work on?" the general asked stonily.

Jonas faltered. He hadn't intended on giving any real suggestions; he had only wanted to belittle Xavier. "Well..." he began, trying to come up with something, "well, he was off balance...at first."

"That's right, but I've already pointed that out to him. Is there something else?" He continued.

"I think he did bloody brilliant for a thirteen-year-old kid against a fully grown man," Drew commented, winking at Xavier.

"Yeah," Seth Brown agreed. "But he needs to be less hesitant in using his abilities in battle. If he hesitates in a battle, he could die."

"Yes, excellent insight, Mr. Brown," Ephraim responded. "Anyone else?"

Xavier timidly raised his hand and Ephraim looked down at him in surprise. "Yes?"

"I need to learn more fencing techniques. You're obviously bigger and stronger. I need to learn ways to fight people with finesse since I can't count on brute force," Xavier commented.

"Excellent suggestion, Xavier!" he stated with a grin and turned to the group. "All right, the rest of you get with your partner and give it a try. Remember to develop your blocking force before you begin, but keep in mind that in battle, conjuring a block isn't always possible nor is it always effective. Okay, get started." He turned back to Xavier. "All right sire. Let's go over a couple of techniques that might help when fighting a stronger, bigger opponent."

For the remaining period, Ephraim showed him the moves and had him practice them several times. At dismissal, he gave the prince homework.

"Now, I want you to practice these moves thoroughly at home tonight." He grinned. "Try them out on your father. Then tomorrow, you and I will have another bout and see if you can stay on your feet longer."

"Yes, sir. But you know, I could surprise you tomorrow. You might be the one lying on the floor," he ribbed.

Ephraim's left brow rose at the challenge and he laughed. "Xavier Wells, you have an ego that would rival your father's; neither one of you likes to admit defeat. But let me give you a word of advice, Your Highness. I am the best swordsman in the kingdom. Not even your father has ever managed to put me to the floor during a bout. So I seriously doubt you'll be able to, boy," he concluded confidently, patting Xavier's head.

Chapter 19

Food Fight

Xavier found Robbie waiting for him on the steps of the Academy at dismissal. A line of cars crowded the school's drive, and students were bustling in different directions. Michael Spencer was doing his best to direct the traffic as efficiently as possible.

"Hi, Xavier!" she smiled. "How was your day?"

"Not bad. Yours?" he answered, taking her bag and flinging it over his shoulder along with his own.

"Great! I started a new empowerment class: gardening. It's really fascinating," she told him.

"Gardening?" he questioned with a lazy grin.

"Yeah...I can make things grow at an accelerated rate...and I can manipulate it to grow a certain way, too."

"Geez, that sounds a lot like telekinesis," he commented.

"Well, according to Madam Applegate, it's one step away from it. Who knows, I may develop telekinesis in time," she added with a shrug. "So, are we still going to King's Cafe?"

"Yeah, a chocolate shake sounds really good right now."

"Xavier! Hey, Xavier!" Daniel called, waving wildly to get his attention. "Are you coming over later?"

"Yeah, I'll be there," Xavier answered with a wave.

"What was that all about?" Robbie snickered.

"Well, he wanted me to stop by and *play* after our date. You don't have to come with me, but I owe the little guy," he told her as he took her hand and led her down the sidewalk away from the school.

"No, it's okay. I'll go with you."

"Are you sure? I have a feeling it's going to be boring playing with a nine-year-old." he sighed.

"I'm sure," she answered, swinging their clasped hands happily.

"Thank God! I think I might need the reinforcements," he replied, snickering.

When they reached the Coliseum, Xavier pulled Robbie to stop beside him. She gave him a puzzled look.

"What?"

"There's no reason why we should walk the *entire* way to King's Café when I can just teleport us." he grinned and extended his arms invitingly.

Robbie hesitated. "Are you sure? I mean. Have you...have you ever teleported with someone else?"

"Yeah, of course! Loads of times," he lied. "Come on! It'll take us thirty minutes if we walk. This way, we'll be there in seconds."

She eyed him suspiciously but finally agreed.

"Oh, all right." She moved into his arms.

As nervous as he was to use his powers, he couldn't resist the urge to show off what he could do in front of Robbie. So with a deep breath, Xavier concentrated on teleporting them, and within moments, they stood swaying slightly in the middle of Center Square. Relief washed over his body and he felt like laughing out loud. He had done it! He not only teleported successfully, but he had done it with another person in tow! Maybe all his worries over his abilities were unwarranted. Maybe the accidents he had with his abilities were just that: accidents.

The open market was wall-to-wall with vending stands and people, but all activity froze the moment Xavier appeared among them, holding Robbie. After a moment of utter silence, murmurs began to spray from the crowd.

"It's the prince."

"Isn't that Dublin Minnows' daughter he's holding?"

Robbie stiffened in his arms.

"Oh, they must be sweethearts."

"Prince Xavier can do better than *her*. She's become a handful since her father died."

"Did you see what she wore to the Celebration? It was so bad that the king had to intervene!"

"Poor Tamarah. Dublin Minnows would roll over in his grave..."

Xavier had heard enough. "Hey! Shut it, all of you!" he spat at the gossiping women. "Who do you think you are, talking about Robbie like that? You don't know her! You don't know anything about anything! Mr. Minnows was proud of Robbie. She's the kindest, most forgiving, sweetest person I know! I could never do better than her. If you insult her, you insult me! So, if you ever talk about her again, I'll tell my father. Got it?"

The women looked at him in dismay before one responded timidly, "We apologize, Your Highness. We were insensitive and out of line." The group bowed their heads in shame.

He stared disgustedly at the women before taking Robbie's hand.

"Come on," he muttered, pulling her from the open market and across Square Avenue to Main Street. "Sorry. I didn't think about how busy Center Square would be this time of day. They're idiots."

"It's all right, Xavier. Forget it. Let's just go to the cafe and enjoy our shakes."

"Deal," he replied, flashing a quick grin.

As he led Robbie into the cafe, there was a sudden hush from the patrons and Xavier could feel every eye on him. He wasn't sure he would ever get used to the attention and awe people openly displayed in his presence. His father seemed completely at ease with it, but then, he had grown up in the kingdom. That had to make a difference. Doing his best to ignore the people gawking at him, he and Robbie made their way to a booth in the corner. Once they were seated, the cafe slowly came back to life.

"You know," Xavier began, "if you want to get more than a milkshake, you can. I can afford it."

She snickered. "Xavier, are you trying to impress me with your money?"

He shrugged, blushing. "Yeah, I guess I was. Sorry." He looked sheepishly at the girl he had known all his life. "But if you're hungry, we can share some fries or something."

"Okay, that sounds great. I'm starving," she replied.

A very timid waitress came to their table fidgeting nervously with her tablet. She gaped down at them with a slightly open mouth.

"Ah, hello?" Xavier prompted. The woman looked too stunned to speak. Realizing she wouldn't ask for their order, he took charge. "All right then, we'd like a large order of fries and two chocolate shakes, please."

The waitress shakily wrote down the order and looked back at them. Finally finding her voice, she spluttered, "Ah...ah, excuse me, sire...but...will this be cash...or..."

"Oh, just bill my father, please," he answered the unfinished question.

With a brisk nod, the waitress left to place the order.

Robbie shook with silent laughter.

"What?" Xavier questioned.

"I bet all this is hard to get used to," she snickered. "I mean, you went from an unpopular geek to a famous prince."

"Geek!" he blurted and pinched her side. "I was never a geek!"

Squealing and laughing, Robbie squirmed away from him on the bench. Her large, smiling, dark eyes made him do it. They mesmerized and hypnotized him, and he couldn't stop himself even if he had wanted to. He grabbed her arms, pulled her toward him, and kissed her fully on the mouth. Instantly, she stilled beneath his kiss and sighed. His heart thumped strongly in his chest and suddenly the café felt too hot. When he finally pulled away he couldn't take his eyes off of the beautiful girl sitting next to him.

"Wow," he whispered.

"Well, well, well. Prince Wells and Miss Minnows!"

They jerked apart and turned to see Henrick Davies grinning from a stool at the café's counter. "How did the pair of you manage to get here so quickly? If I'm not mistaken, school let out only five minutes ago." The lieutenant stood and sauntered toward them.

Xavier grinned mischievously back. "It's a little thing call teleportation, lieutenant."

"Ah, I see your cheekiness hasn't improved much since the last time I talked with you," Henrick replied.

"And I see you still get your kicks out of tormenting kids," he retorted.

"Yeah," Henrick agreed longingly as he slid onto the bench opposite them, "but I haven't had a lot of time to do it lately. So understandably, I've been going through withdrawal. It's not a pretty sight."

Xavier laughed. "Yeah. I can see that."

Henrick glanced at a blushing Robbie before returning

his knowing gaze to Xavier. He grinned broadly. "Oh, I'm sorry. Am I interrupting something, Your Highness?"

"If I told you yes, you'd only stay longer," he chided.

"Yep, but I'll show mercy this time. Besides, I have to report to work in thirty minutes, so I better finish my food and get going. The boss gets really cranky when I'm late." He snickered and shook his head. "Jeesh, the way he acts, you'd think he was a *king* or something."

Xavier laughed heartily at this. "Yeah, I know the type. See ya later, Henrick. Tell Dad I'll be home in time for dinner."

With a nod, the lieutenant stood and returned to the counter to finish his burger.

"I think Henrick is spending way too much time with Loren," he noted, watching Henrick flirt persistently with a blushing waitress.

A few minutes later, their waitress returned with their order and Xavier gulped down several large swallows of the shake and dove into the fries, shoving a handful of the salty goodness into his mouth.

Robbie giggled. "Lord, Xavier! Someone will think your father starves you if you keep eating like that!"

"Sorry," he replied ruefully before nudging the basket of fries toward her. "Help yourself."

"Thanks. Oh wait, there's no ketchup." She frowned down at the fries before searching for the waitress, who was nowhere in sight.

"Don't worry. I'll take care of it," he whispered, looking toward the counter.

The ketchup bottles sat in a line on a shelf behind the counter. Xavier smirked. He couldn't resist the chance to show off again, and he flicked his finger at one of the bottles. The bottle rose from the shelf and slowly drifted toward them. He turned and gave Robbie a triumphant grin. But, his grin quickly dropped as one bottle turned into a dozen. Alarmed, he tried to put the ketchup bottles back on the shelf, but they didn't respond to his command. Instead, dishes, glasses, orders waiting to be served, customers' belongings, and everything else not bolted to the floor flew into the air and hovered there. The crowded restaurant erupted with a collective gasp.

Xavier tried to disconnect from his telekinesis, but this turned out to be a very terrible mistake for the items floating slowly around the room were suddenly whizzing and crashing into walls, tables, and people. It was a full-fledged telekinetic food fight! Xavier and Robbie ducked under the table as a bowl of applesauce smashed into the wall beside them. Pandemonium erupted among the cafe's patrons. Many dove under their tables, a few darted for the door, and a couple, who Xavier suspected were telekinetic, stood in the center of the restaurant with their hands raised, trying to "catch" the food missiles. It took the telekinetics several minutes to get the last of the food out of the air.

As people slowly began to reemerge from under their tables, a large, burly man with a fat, sweaty face threw open the swinging door from the kitchen. He scanned the crowd suspiciously.

"Okay! I want to know whose idea of a joke that was!" he bellowed.

Of course, no one responded, and Xavier glanced anxiously at Robbie, who was staring back at him with large doe-like eyes.

"Come on! Who did this?" the man shouted again.

"Beau, I'm sure it was an accident. Several people darted out of here when the ruckus began. It could have been any one of them," Henrick stated, but as he did so, he glanced at Xavier. "I'm sure these gentlemen would be more than willing to help clean this mess up." He nodded at the two men who had helped to stop the ruckus.

"Sure, it won't take any time at all," one man told Beau.

The tension in the air seemed to melt away as the men began to clean up the mess.

Xavier turned to Robbie. "I don't know about you, but I think I've had enough fries and shakes. What do you say we head out?"

Without a word, Robbie nodded, and they exited the restaurant in silence.

Once outdoors, they hurried from the café in a shocked silence. After they were a block or two from the café, Xavier, feeling less anxious, reached for Robbie's hand, but she pulled out of his grasp, and continued to walk, staring at her feet.

"What's wrong?" Xavier asked.

"*What's wrong*? You know *what's wrong*, Xavier!" she retorted, looking at him with worried eyes. "It happened AGAIN! When are you going to admit that it's getting worse not better? You need to tell your dad."

"No," Xavier hissed. "It was...I can handle it!"

"No, you can't! Xavier...I'm afraid..."

"Xavier? Hold on a minute." Henrick called from behind them.

Xavier gave Robbie a warning look as the lieutenant jogged up beside them. Henrick looked at Robbie's downcast head before his eyes settled quizzically on the prince. "So? What happened in there?"

"I don't know what you mean," he muttered.

"Come on, Xavier. I wasn't born yesterday. I saw that ketchup bottle floating toward your table before all hell broke loose!" he told him.

"It wasn't me!" he lied.

"Are you sure about that?"

"Of course I am! You don't think I'd do something like that on purpose, do ya?" he spat defensively.

He studied the boy a moment before finally answering, "No, of course not, not intentionally."

"All right, then. Can we go now? My cousin is expecting us at his house." Not waiting for a response, he turned and walked away with Robbie reluctantly following.

Chapter 20

The Fort

As they walked to Michael Spencer's house, Xavier tried to make light of what happened at the café, but Robbie wasn't buying it.

"Stop it! Just stop, Xavier," she hissed irritably. "We both know your powers got away from you again, so stop trying to make it seem like it was all a practical joke! If it had been just a joke, we wouldn't be walking the entire way to the headmaster's house. You would have teleported us! And you know what? I'm not really in the mood to go to your uncle's with you. I'm sorry, Xavier. I care about you, but I can't pretend that everything's fine."

"Robbie! Oh, come on! Don't be like that!"

He watched her walk away until she was inside the palace gates and out of sight. With a heavy sigh, he turned and trudged along the street that skirted the palace walls. Uncle Mike lived in a modest little house in the merchant end of the kingdom. This surprised many because his status as royalty would permit him to live within the palace walls. Xavier wondered what made his uncle choose to live where he did.

It hadn't occurred to him until he knocked on the door that he had never been inside his uncle's house. He had *decorated* the outside of the house during a mummering prank, but he'd never seen inside.

The door opened on the second knock and standing in the doorway with bare feet, tattered jeans, and an old t-shirt was his uncle. He looked completely out of character for the headmaster of Well's Academy.

Mike smiled down at him. "Hey, kiddo. Come in. Daniel's very excited you could stop by. Where's Robbie? He told me that she was coming with you."

"Oh, well, she was, but she had to go home," he answered dismissively, stepping into the house. He studied the interior and found it masculine yet neat and homey. Most of the furniture looked old and well used, and the pictures on the walls were landscapes and historical renditions.

"Daniel? Your cousin's here," Mike called down the hallway that most likely led to bedrooms.

Xavier heard a thump from the back of the house followed by a shout. "Ouch, darn it! Okay, Daddy. I'm coming!"

Seconds later, Daniel skipped out of his room and down the hall with a large grin.

"Hey, Xavier! Thanks for coming. So, whatcha wanna do?"

He shrugged. "Whatever you want to do. It doesn't matter to me."

"Can we go outside, Dad?"

Michael smiled down at his son. "Yes," he answered as he cupped the small boy's chin with his hand, held his face steady while rubbing at a smudge of what looked like chocolate pudding on the boy's cheek. "You have an hour before dinner. Okay?"

"Okay," Daniel whined trying to pull out of his father's grasp. "Dad! Come on! It's fine. You're embarrassing me!"

He released the boy and smiled. "If you'd wash your

face after snacks, I wouldn't need to embarrass you." He winked down at Xavier, who stifled a smile.

"Fine," Daniel muttered, grabbing Xavier's arm and dragging him through the kitchen and out the back door.

"Remember, one hour!" Mike called after them.

"Come on, Xavier. Check it out! Dad built this fort for me! Isn't it awesome!"

Xavier had to admit the fort was pretty cool. It was three stories tall with a fireman's pole from the top level to the ground, a hanging ladder to climb to the upper levels, a rope swing, and from the top level, a swinging bridge stretching from the fort to a small platform erected in the tree next to it. He grinned. Maybe spending time with Daniel wouldn't be as boring as he had first thought.

"Come on, Xavier!" he called, already half way up the ladder.

He raced to the fort and climbed the ladder to the top level where his small cousin stood waiting for him.

"It's cool, isn't it?"

"Yeah, it is," he answered, looking around admiringly. Magazines, comics, books, and cards were stacked haphazardly on a milk crate and four beanbag chairs were scattered around the space. The guys would go nuts over the fort. Maybe Daniel wouldn't mind if he brought his friends over sometime.

Grinning, Daniel fell into one of the beanbag chairs. Xavier moved to a beanbag next to him and flopped into it.

"What did you and Robbie do on your date?" he asked, digging into a small cooler next to him, producing two ho-hos, and handing one to Xavier.

Xavier took the sweet and answered, "We had a couple of shakes and some fries."

"Oh," Daniel replied, frowning.

"What?"

"I don't know. Dates sound like the kind of stuff you'd do with your friends is all. I just figured there'd be more to it than that."

Xavier snickered. "Well, Robbie is my friend. But I like her differently than my other friends."

The smaller boy started giggling. "Yeah, cuz you want to kiss her, huh?"

He laughed. "Yeah, I guess I do."

"Have you? Have you ever kissed her?"

"Yeah, a few times."

Daniel made a face. "Sounds gross."

He smiled. "It's not, believe me."

"Hey, can you make your electro-force change its shape? I saw Court with a force on his shoulder at school today during break. It looked like a dog."

"Yeah, I can."

Daniel sat up eagerly. "Will you teach me how? Please?"

"I don't know, Daniel. We're not supposed to use our powers outside of school." This had been a long-standing rule for students of Well's Academy, but Xavier and his friends had never abided by it. However, after recent events, he wasn't too keen on conjuring anything, and suddenly, he was thankful for the rule.

"But you're the Prince of Warwood! You can do anything!" he said with a measure of awe in his voice.

Xavier smiled. "Thanks, but even kings and princes have to follow the rules."

"Oh, come on! Please? You've gotta show me!" he begged.

"I don't think it's such a good idea, Daniel."

"But that Jonas kid keeps teasing me. He says I don't belong at the Academy. He says I'm only there because my dad's the headmaster and I'm royalty. I got to show him that I *do* belong there and that I can do stuff. Please,

Xavier! Please?"

He looked down at the smaller boy and sighed. Surely there wouldn't be any harm in telling him how as long as he didn't engage in his own powers. "Okay, okay. Stop looking at me like your puppy died. I'll tell you how and help you practice."

"Yes!" Daniel cheered, punching his fist skyward in triumph.

Xavier couldn't help but laugh. "So, first you conjure your force and control it so that it stays in your hand."

"Okay," Daniel replied, furrowing his brow in concentration as he conjured a force in his hand and worked to control it.

"Good! Now, what you need to do is to think of an animal you want it to change into and concentrate on that animal."

Daniel closed his eyes, his brow furrowing into deep lines. The force changed shape, but not into anything recognizable. Panting, Daniel opened his eyes and his force evaporated.

"I can't do it. It's too hard. Can you show me?"

"No, just try again."

"But if I could see how you do it, I might be able to do it. Come on, Xavier! You've got to help me! It's probably really easy for you to do. You're powers are really strong."

Xavier smiled, feeling flattered and confident. "Well, I do have more powers than most men," he bragged.

"Yeah, I know," the smaller boy replied with awe. "Dad says that you're going to be a very powerful king when you grow up."

"Really? Uncle Mike said that?"

Daniel nodded enthusiastically. "Yeah, he did. So it would be easy for you to show me how you do it, right?"

"Well...yeah, in theory. Oh, okay. I'll show you but just

once, so pay attention," he told him. Surely if he concentrated hard enough, he could maintain control of the force.

"Okay, I will," Daniel promised eagerly.

"Okay, whenever I do something new, I meditate first," he explained softly, closing his eyes and breathing rhythmically for several long seconds. "Then I picture in my head exactly what I want. I picture every detail: how it looks, feels, sounds, and smells." He began picturing an electro-force in the shape of Robbie's face.

"Whoa! That's cool. It's Robbie!" Daniel exclaimed.

Xavier opened his eyes and saw Robbie's face a second before the force popped and fiery missiles flew in every direction, setting the fort on fire. Both boys sprang to their feet and Xavier stomped at the nearest flame, trying to put it out. It wasn't working! The flames grew larger.

"Xavier! What are you doing?" Daniel yelled. "Put it out! Put it out!"

"I'm trying!"

Picking up a magazine, he swatted at the flames, but only managed to catch the magazine on fire. He dropped the magazine, which then caused another fire. The fire was rapidly growing out of control! Xavier couldn't stop it.

"Stop it, Xavier! Stop it! I'm telling Dad!" Daniel whined.

"I'm not doing it on purpose!" he shouted at the younger boy. "Come on! We've got to get out of here!"

He pushed the smaller boy toward the fireman's pole. Daniel slid easily to the ground and Xavier followed. He didn't need to look at the fort to know it was completely engulfed in flames.

"Why did you do that?" Daniel accused, tears streaming down his face.

"I...," Xavier looked up at the tree that now resembled

an enormous torch.

"What the..."

Mike sprinted from the house, jutted his hand toward the fire, and a great wave of water crashed over the tree. The act put out the fire, but the force and weight of the water split the tree into two, and a large part of the tree toppled to the ground feet from where they stood.

Mike turned to the boys, who both cowered at his furious face.

"What happened," he growled between tightly clenched teeth.

The boys seemed suddenly interested in their shoes and neither answered.

"Both of you, inside, now!" he spat.

They didn't hesitate and scurried into the house.

"Sit!" he ordered, pointing to the kitchen table.

It was then that Xavier realized his uncle was wearing an apron with yellow daisies on it, and he had to bite his tongue to keep the laughter from bubbling up inside him and escaping. Laughing at his uncle at this point in time would be suicidal.

"Who's going to talk? You know I don't need you to in order to determine the truth. I can find out easily enough on my own."

Daniel darted a dark look at Xavier, but as angry as he was, he wouldn't squeal on him. In an ordinary life, his cousin's silence would be beneficial, but with an uncle who possessed telepathy, it was futile.

"I did it, Uncle Mike," Xavier muttered, trying not to look at his uncle in his ridiculous apron.

"Explain to me what happened, Xavier?" he asked with a cold and hard voice.

"It was an accident. I didn't mean to set it on fire."

"You did too! I saw you!" Daniel yelled.

"No I didn't, Daniel! I wouldn't do that! If you hadn't yelled out and scared me, the electro force wouldn't have gotten out of control!" he hissed at the younger boy.

"Liar!"

"I'm not lying!"

"Okay, that's enough, boys!" Mike ordered. He directed his attention to Xavier. "Why would you even consider conjuring an electro force in a wooden tree house to begin with?"

He hesitated, glancing briefly at Daniel, who visibly shrank at the question.

"I...I don't know. I guess..."

"Don't. Don't stammer around as you think up a lie. I don't need telepathy to know that what you're about to say isn't going to be the truth."

"Daniel asked me to. He wanted me to teach him how to change his force into different forms and figures."

Mike looked down at his son. "Daniel, what have I told you about using powers outside of school?"

"Not to," Daniel muttered. "But it wasn't me who started the fire!"

"No, your cousin did because you coaxed him into conjuring his powers," Mike concluded sternly. "I will deal with you later. Go to your room, son."

Daniel stood and slunk from the room.

Mike walked to the phone and dialed a number. Xavier didn't need to ask who he was calling. He knew he would call his father. He anxiously listened as Uncle Mike explained into the phone what happened. Then he went silent for several long seconds, his face impassive.

Finally, he glanced at Xavier and spoke. "Okay, Jer. We'll see you in a few minutes."

"So, how much trouble am I in?" he asked his uncle timidly.

Mike turned with his hands on his hips. "What do you think? You are the older boy here. You know better. Why did you let him talk you into doing something you knew was wrong?"

"I tried to tell him no! He wouldn't listen! He kept begging me and looking at me with those big, sad eyes!" he blurted.

"So you let a nine-year-old boy coerce you into doing something you knew was not only wrong but dangerous? Pathetic! That is absolutely pathetic, Xavier! What kind of king lets others make his decisions for him?"

Xavier's face ignited with heat and he bellowed, "You want to know what I think is pathetic? You standing there, trying to be all superior wearing *that thing*!"

Mike gave him a quizzical expression, not sure what he meant. Then he looked down at his apron before glaring back at the insolent boy.

"Watch yourself, boy," he spat as he peeled the apron off and tossed it onto the table. "Your father will be here shortly. You stay put while I talk to Daniel."

Without waiting for a response, Mike left the room, and Xavier slouched in his chair. Sighing loudly, he stared out the back window at the charred remains of the tree house. *"Could this day get any worse?"* he wondered.

Of course it could, and it did. When his father arrived, Xavier found himself staring into two pairs of hard, livid grey eyes.

"First, I want you to tell us exactly what happened in the tree house," the king demanded. "Then, I want you to explain to me why you would be so stupid that you would use an electro force in a small, enclosed, *wooden* tree house!"

"Daniel said Jonas was picking on him because he's not very powerful. I guess Daniel wanted to show him that he was powerful. So he asked me to show him how to make his electro force into a shape. I felt sorry for him. I know what it's like to be picked on and teased. So I showed him. I guess he got excited and yelled when I showed him. Well, when he yelled, he startled me, and I lost control of it. The next thing I knew, the fort was on fire. It was an accident. I wasn't showing off or anything. Really! It was just an accident. I tried to put it out, but it spread too fast. I got Daniel out of there before we got barbequed."

Mike sighed, ran his hand through his hair, and glanced at Jeremiah before speaking, "Xavier, are you supposed to use your powers outside of school?"

"No, but everyone does!"

Jeremiah bristled at his son's response. "Everyone does, eh? Should a king do something he knows is wrong just because everyone else does it?"

Xavier deflated and slouched in his chair. "No, sir."

"I understand you thought you were helping Daniel," Mike continued calmly, "but that doesn't excuse you from going against the rules. I'm sure your father has told you no one is above the law, not even the king."

Xavier nodded, still pouting. "Yeah, I tried to tell Daniel that."

"You did, did you? Well, I'm sure that message really sank in for him when in the next breath you disobeyed that rule," Jeremiah hissed sarcastically.

He slouched further into his chair. At this rate, he'd be lying flat on the floor in shame before too long.

"All right then, all that's left here is to determine an appropriate punishment," Mike announced and looked at Jeremiah.

The king gave his brother a nod of consent, and Mike squared his shoulders and faced Xavier with his hands on his hips.

"Okay, for starters, you'll have the same punishment as Daniel. You are grounded for four weeks; no TV, no computer, no hanging out with friends, no games."

"*Four* weeks!!" Xavier jerked upright with indignation.

"Yes, four weeks!"

He huffed loudly and slouched back into his chair.

Mike ignored him and continued, "You'll go to school, come home, do your assignments, and go to bed. The only entertainment you'll be allowed to have is reading a book. Secondly, this weekend, you'll come to my house and help clean up the mess you created. Got it?"

Xavier didn't answer and continued to sulk.

Mike lifted his head so that their eyes met and repeated, "Do you understand?"

"Yes!" he spat, feeling disgruntled, yanking his chin from his uncle's grasp.

"Xavier!" Jeremiah barked. "Show a little respect."

"You'll only make things worse with your attitude!" Mike remarked.

"Whatever," he muttered so softly he was sure his father and uncle couldn't hear him. He was wrong.

The words barely left his lips when Michael grabbed him, hauled him out of the chair, and held him inches from his face. The unfurling fury Xavier saw in his uncle's eyes sent chills down his spine, and he nearly whimpered.

Mike's hands dug painfully into his arms as he hissed, "I'm a breath away from busting your butt, boy. Do you really want to continue with your attitude and make things worse?"

"No," Xavier managed to choke out as his voice broke. Tears pooled in his eyes, and he quickly looked everywhere but at the man holding him. "I mean, no, sir. I'm sorry."

Mike relaxed marginally, set the boy on his feet, and nodded. "Ok. You can go home with your father. I'll see you Saturday at 8 am to work on cleaning up my backyard."

He nodded, not trusting himself to speak.

"Let's go home, son," Jeremiah told him, laying a large hand on his shoulder. Then, his father looked at Mike. "I'm sorry about the damages, Mike. I can send supplies or more manpower if you need it."

He shook his head. "That's not needed. The boys and I will take care of it. Xavier isn't the only person carrying the blame for what happened today. Daniel has repeatedly tried to use his powers outside of school. I've had countless discussions with him about it and why the rule exists. He was quite deviant to manipulate Xavier into doing it for him. When I'm through with him, he may regret wishing for a father for all those years."

"No he won't," Xavier muttered. He looked up at his uncle, blinking through the remnants of tears left unshed. "He wants you to punish him. It...it'll make him feel...I don't know. I guess it makes you feel *normal*."

Chapter 21

Invisibility

The next day, Xavier walked to school with his thoughts swimming in a sea of anxiety. What he had told his uncle and father about the fire had been true, but he neglected to tell them the entire story. After being startled by Daniel and losing control of his electro force, three more forces had erupted from him, making it impossible to extinguish the fire. His abilities couldn't be trusted any more. After lying in bed for over an hour trying to understand what was happening to him and his abilities, he was no closer to an answer. He was scared and confused. Maybe the King's Key corrupted his powers when it drained LeMasters' life force. It seemed to fit. All his problems began shortly after that confrontation. Had the key damaged his ability to control his powers or was it simply taking them bit by bit?

"Are you okay? You're awfully quiet," Court noted, elbowing Xavier out of his thoughts.

"Just thinking," he responded as they climbed the stairs to the Academy.

Daniel stood next to his father, looking sullen and grumpy.

"Hey, Danny," he called timidly to the younger boy.

Daniel glanced in his direction, but quickly looked away

without responding.

"Whoa. You just got snubbed by your seven-year old cousin," Court exclaimed.

"He's nine, and he has a right to be mad at me. I burned down his tree house yesterday," he muttered.

"You *what?*" Court exclaimed, grabbing his arm and stopping him.

"Well, I didn't do it on purpose," he snapped. "Most of what I do anymore isn't on purpose!"

"You mean *it* happened *again?*"

He nodded, not meeting his friend's serious stare.

"Tell your dad!" Court pleaded. "God, Xavier! You could have killed yourself or your cousin! You *have* to tell him!"

"No, I don't! I don't want him looking at me like I'm a disappointment. Besides, I can't run to Dad for everything! What kind of king runs to other people for help?"

"A good one," Court retorted.

"I just need a rest; that's all!" he barked, glaring at the other boy. "Dad is NOT to know, Court. Do you hear me? Don't you dare say a damn word!"

His best friend scowled at him, mumbled something about him being barking mad, and stomped away. As he watched his friend walk into the academy, Xavier tried to convince himself of his own words that all he needed was a rest from his powers. With his decision made, he marched into the building, steeling his nerves for what would surely to be a long day.

The morning went pretty well, but then there wasn't a need for him to use his empowerments in his academic classes. His afternoon classes were a different matter. However, when Spencer found him just before lunch and told him that his telepathy lesson would be postponed until after school due to an issue at the Governing Hall detaining his father, Xavier thought for a moment that making it through the day without using his powers would be easier than he first thought. Although within moments after entering anima lingua class, he was volunteered to demonstrate infiltrating and terminating an opponent's bond with an animal. His hopes crumbled.

"Prince Wells has done this technique before," Sir Blaire commented with a smirk. "Sire, would you please demonstrate it for the class?"

Blaire referred to the bat attack incident on Drew last year at the Mountain. Growing tired of Drew's taunts and teasing, Xavier had bonded with his bat and instructed it to attack him. He regretted the act now that he and Drew had worked past their differences and had become friends. Court, on the other hand, still loved to tease his older brother and remind him of the incident whenever he annoyed him.

When Xavier didn't respond immediately, the instructor stepped toward him holding out the large snake wrapped around his arm. "Sire?"

"N...no thank you, sir."

"I apologize. That shouldn't have come across as a question. You *will* demonstrate this technique for the class." Sir Blaire responded, nodding insistently toward the animal.

"No, sir. I won't."

"No? What do you mean, no?" he growled. "When I tell you to do something, boy, you do it!"

Xavier flinched, but he stood his ground. "No, sir. I won't do it. I don't feel like it today."

"You don't feel like it?" his anima-lingua teacher shouted and shoved a finger in his face. "You don't get to decide when and when not to use your empowerments, Prince Wells! I do! It is my job to teach you and help you perfect your abilities. Now you *will* use your powers while you're in my class!"

"No, sir. I won't."

"Get out!" he boomed loudly, pointing to the door. "If you're not going to do your lessons, then you can spend the rest of the afternoon with Headmaster Spencer!"

As he shuffled toward the door, he could feel Drew trying to catch his eye, but he tucked his head and left the room without looking at the older boy. He went straight to the headmaster's office. When he opened the door, Janice, the secretary, saw him and stood.

"Can I help you, sire?" she asked.

"Sir Blaire sent me."

"Yes. So I've heard," Mike called from the door to his office. "Enter my office, Prince Wells." He nodded toward the interior of the room.

He slumped through the door and sank miserably into a chair in front of a long walnut desk. His uncle lightly closed the door behind him, strolled to the desk, and sat on its edge in front of him. For several long minutes, Michael simply stared at him in a painful silence.

Finally, he demanded, "Well? What do you have to say for yourself?"

"Nothing. I...I'm just not in the mood to use my empowerments. That's all," he mumbled.

Mike stared at him a moment and then sighed. "Xavier, does this have anything to do with what happened yesterday? I think you're overreacting. What happened was an accident, but even if you lose control of your abilities here, there are trained, empowered adults who can stop the power before any real harm is done. Your teachers are trained to help you gain control and improve your command over your abilities. Okay?"

He swallowed and muttered, "It's not that, Uncle Mike.

I...I just don't...feel good. I...I just figured a rest from my powers would be the best thing to do."

"You don't feel well? What is it?" Mike asked, pressing a hand to his forehead.

"I don't know. I'm kind of tired, and...I just don't feel up to using them."

Mike dropped his hand and studied the boy in front of him. "Xavier, I'm sorry, but using or not using your empowerments in school isn't your decision. If your teachers tell you to use your powers, then you use them. Understood?"

When he didn't respond, his uncle reached down and lifted his chin, forcing him to meet his eyes. "Understood?" he repeated firmly.

"Yes, I understand, but...what if I refuse? You can't *make* me, Uncle Mike," he answered quietly.

"It's Headmaster Spencer at school, sire," he intoned stiffly. "If you refuse to do as you're told, your father will be called in to persuade you."

"And if I still refuse?"

Mike looked at him incredulously. "Then I will suspend you from school, and if that appeals to you in the slightest, Xavier, let me give you something to think about. Imagine your father's reaction if you're suspended from school for insubordination." After pausing to allow the boy to ponder the idea, he continued, "So? Will you return to class and do as you're told?"

Xavier's courage fell apart. His uncle was right. His father could and would make his life miserable if he continued with this plan. With a gulp, he briefly met his uncle's eyes, "Yes, sir."

Luckily, nothing out of the ordinary happened the next two class periods, and he entered his fencing class harboring the hope that it would be an uneventful day.

"All right, everybody! Settle down! Find your partner and let's begin," Ephraim stated, watching as the class divided into pairs before turning to Xavier. "Ready to do a bit of sparring, Your Highness?"

"Yes, sir."

When the sparring session began, Xavier was feeling pretty good about the moves Ephraim had shown him the day before. He kept his distance from his larger opponent and used his quickness to his advantage. Timing his counter attacks were the hardest thing to perfect, but after practicing the moves for over an hour last night he managed to have them at near precision.

Ephraim was impressed at his progress and he paused to beam down at him. "Nicely done, sire! You've learned those techniques quickly. Now, let's try increasing the stress and see if you can hold it together."

Suddenly, the general feinted, spun, and caught him squarely on the back. Xavier went sprawling face down onto the floor. He barely managed to roll onto his back and parry an attack inches from his face. He scrambled to his feet, and instinctively pummeled an electro force directly at the general. It hit him like an atom blast, and he flew backwards nearly fifteen feet before hitting the floor unconscious. The class went suddenly still and silent.

"DAD!" Drew bellowed, racing to his father's side.

Xavier approached the fallen general in a daze.

"Someone go get Nurse Turner! Now!" Drew yelled.

Xavier dropped to his knees beside Drew. "I...I didn't mean to...it was an accident! Why didn't he block it? He said he had blocking abilities!" He shook Ephraim's shoulder, as he closed his eyes and pled quietly, "Please, don't be hurt."

A shocking surge of warmth erupted from his hand, and

Xavier's eyes flew open to find the general engulfed in a brilliant white light. The students around him gasped and simultaneously stepped away from the prince and fallen general. Even Drew with large, stunned eyes scurried away from them. Xavier tried to pull away but found his hand was stuck to Ephraim's shoulder like crazy glue. The growing power hummed and vibrated through his body before bursting from him in an intense, blinding light. The group around him cried out as they collectively retreated to the sides of the room, a few escaping out the classroom door. Xavier paid no attention to the other students as he watched with a mixture of horror and fascination as a small scar on the general's chin slowly melted away. Again, he struggled to pull away but to no avail, and the pulsating energy continued to work on the small, fine age lines around Ephraim's eyes and mouth. Fear consumed Xavier. He had no control over this uncharted, unknown power. Who knew what the power would do to General Hardcastle if it continued. Finally, grunting with effort, he managed to tear his hand away from the unconscious man and the light instantly evaporated.

The class was dead silent, and Xavier looked around from face to face seeing shock and fear. No one spoke, but they didn't need to for suddenly their thoughts slammed into him. He clutched his head and closed his eyes to block out the accusing stares and thoughts. He wished he could vanish, run away, or disappear, anything to escape the judgment of his classmates. Suddenly, the room erupted in fevered outbursts.

"Where'd he go?"

"Wow!"

"What happened to him?"

"He's invisible!"

Xavier opened his eyes and saw why the room was in an

uproar! He was invisible! Startled, he jumped to his feet and looked frantically down at his missing arms and hands as students cautiously moved toward him.

"Whoa, that is freaking awesome!"

"Do you see that? It's like his clothes are standing on their own!"

A group of girls giggled. Drew looked up at him in awe.

"He's gotta be the first person in over a hundred years to get that ability!"

"How many powers does he have now? He's only thirteen. Isn't that really *unusual*?"

A boy approached him curiously and poked his arm as if testing to see if it was real. Xavier stumbled away from the boy and other students slowing making his way toward the door. Their thoughts and fears slammed into him again, and he flinched at the pressure in his head as he continued to back away from the group. Then, Ephraim moaned and the students' eyes darted toward their instructor. Panicking, Xavier took advantage of the distraction and scrambled from the room, down the hall, and out of the school. Without any thought of where to go, he plunged into the woods, tripping over rocks and roots. He didn't stop until he reached the lake, where he finally stooped to catch his breath. He looked down at the smooth, clear surface of the lake and saw only the blue sky above him. He had no reflection! He sank back onto the pebbly shore and sighed.

How could he undo an empowerment that he didn't even know he had, or how he conjured it? Trying not to panic, he began meditating to calm his overwrought nerves. It took several long minutes before he was calm enough to consider disengaging his newly found power. Taking a deep purifying breath, he imagined himself visible. He pictured his arms, his legs, and his face. Slowly he opened his eyes and looked down at himself. It didn't work. He was still invisible!

A horrifying thought invaded his mind. What if he couldn't undo it? What if he had to spend the rest of his life invisible?

"Prince Wells? Xavier? Where are you, boy?" Mike's voice was faint, but it would only be a matter of minutes before his uncle reached the lake.

He scurried to his feet and looked around frantically for a place to hide. Hide? He didn't need to hide! He was invisible! But his clothes weren't...

Recklessly, he stripped. He managed to hide his clothes behind a rock just as Mike and Sir Blaire emerged from the dense foliage.

"I thought for certain he would come here," Michael muttered, peering around.

"Well, Headmaster, the boy is invisible. Try telepathy," Sir Blaire suggested.

With a nod, Michael closed his eyes, and Xavier instantly felt the chill. With a lurch of anxiety, he immediately began pushing back at Michael's ability, but he couldn't.

"Xavier?" Michael began, stepping in his direction.

He sank against the rock behind him and held his breath.

"Xavier? I know you're there. Answer me!" Michael continued.

He didn't answer. He quietly shuffled towards the edge of the clearing.

His uncle found his carelessly hidden clothes and turned to stare bewilderingly at Sir Blaire.

Xavier slipped into the woods and carefully put as much distance as he could between himself and the men. Once he was sure he was out of his uncle's hearing range, he turned and ran. Soon he found his path blocked by the palace wall, and he followed the wall southward until he came to the field adjacent to the school. A cluster of Royal Guards were fanned out across the grounds calling his name. His father stood a few yards away holding Xavier's clothes and talking to Michael and Sir Blaire. Trying desperately to keep his mind blank and clear, he scurried past the men, along the palace wall, and toward the secret passage. He had to find a place to hide until he figured out how to undo his invisibility and decide what to do next. He slipped through the secret passage and nearly ran into Loren, who was guarding it. Covering his mouth to muffle his breathing, he silently slipped past the massive general and darted around the palace. He walked purposefully toward the stables. It would be the best place to hide since the stable hands would be gone for the day. When he slipped into the stable, invisible or not, he couldn't fool the horses. They sensed his presence immediately and whinnied uneasily at the peculiarity.

"Whoa! Easy, fellas. It's okay. Brewster, tell them it's okay. It's just me," he whispered and instantly the animals stilled.

Finding an empty and fairly clean stall, Xavier slipped inside, piled up fresh hay and sat to contemplate what to do about his predicament.

"I got myself into this! I made myself invisible. I should be able to undo it! I've just got to concentrate," he muttered.

He tried. He really tried, but nearly an hour later, he flopped back into the hay, sweating and frustrated.

"ARRGGHH! God! I'm sick of being invisible!" he groaned bitterly, hitting himself in the head. "Come on, come on! Undo it!"

He closed his eyes again and pushed at his brain to

work the empowerment until he was grunting loudly.

"God damn it!" he spat, as he pounded his fists on the earth and threw a fistful of hay. Finally giving in to self-pity and exhaustion, he curled into a ball, and sobbed himself to sleep.

Chapter 22

Fountain of Youth

"Lord almighty, boy!" Loren's voice boomed, startling Xavier awake. "Do you have any idea the trouble you've caused?"

Xavier sat up and looked up at the angry general. "You...you can see me?"

"Of course I can see you! I see a little too much of you actually," Loren added, peeling off his Royal Guard cloak and wrapping it around him. "Do you have any idea how much trouble you've caused? You've been missing since yesterday afternoon."

"What?" he exclaimed, hugging the cloak closer. "What time is it?"

"It's nearly 8 am."

"Oh, shit," Xavier moaned, getting to his feet.

"Exactly. Come on. Your father is in a near panic," Loren told him, clamping a hand on his shoulder and leading him out of the stables.

"Oh, man. He's going to be pissed."

"Yep," Loren answered shortly. "I'd bust your butt now if your father didn't already have first dibs on it."

"Oh, man. Loren, you have to listen to me. It was all an accident! I didn't... Wait. Is Ephraim okay?"

"He's fine."

"Thank God. It was an accident. I didn't mean to hurt him. I was just trying to do what he taught me..."

"Xavier!" Loren interrupted stopping and turning the boy to look down at him. "This isn't about Ephraim. What happened to him is par for the course when you teach at an empowered school. You are in trouble because you ran off and hid! You worried your father. You worried your uncle. You worried Ephraim. You worried me! Jer had the entire Royal Guard sweeping the kingdom looking for you, which was damn near impossible since you were invisible!"

He tucked his head, guiltily. "I'm sorry, Loren. I...I guess I just got scared."

"Man up, Prince Wells," he retorted harshly as he continued toward the palace, pulling Xavier with him. "Learn to face the consequences for your actions like a man."

Jeremiah stood at the palace's entrance looking imposing as he gave several Royal Guards their orders.

"Don't tell me you've looked everywhere, damn it. Find my son!"

"King Wells?" Loren called out to him.

The king's eyes whipped in Loren's direction and settled on Xavier.

"Oh, thank God," he moaned and started toward them. Then, growing impatient with the pace of walking, he ran the remaining distance to his son. He swept him into his arms, held him close, and released a shaky breath. "Jesus, boy. You scared the hell out of me," he murmured into his ear.

Xavier voice broke as he whispered, "I'm sorry, Dad. I...I'm so sorry."

Later that morning, Xavier sat on his bed, waiting for his father. His father hadn't even yelled at him, and to be honest, he was shocked. After what Loren said, he had expected him to whip him out in the driveway as soon as he got over the initial relief of finding him. But he hadn't. Instead, he calmly asked him if he was okay and sent him inside to shower and get some clothes on.

"Son?"

Xavier jumped and looked guiltily up at his father as he walked into the room, dragged the chair from his desk toward the bed, and sat in front him.

"Yeah...yes, sir?"

"Do you realize how much mayhem you caused in the last twelve hours?" he asked stiffly.

"No...I mean...I didn't think about that, sir."

"Oh really? What were you thinking about then?" his father asked, his temper wedging into his voice.

"Uh, just...that I hurt Ephraim. That I...that you'd be mad."

"Uh, huh. And how happy do you think I am now having spent hours looking for you, scared to death that something happened to you?" he asked sarcastically.

He met his father's glare briefly. "Uh, not very."

"Oh, not very happy is describing it mildly. Ephraim knows injury is possible, even probable when teaching the use of empowerments. You did nothing wrong in class yesterday. But you chose to act like a coward and run and hide instead of facing your problems head-on."

Anger and shame rushed across his face in a sea of red. "I'm not a coward!" he spat. "I faced William LeMasters by myself without anyone's help!"

"Then why did you run?"

"I...well," Xavier couldn't admit to his father that he was ashamed he couldn't undo his empowerment. He was supposed to be the Prince of Warwood, the Chosen! He was supposed to be strong, capable, and brave. He was supposed to be a man that everyone would depend upon to protect and save them from darkness. The fact that he wasn't these things made him fearful his father would be ashamed of him. "I...I don't know."

"That is not an acceptable answer."

"It's the only answer I have," he retorted cheekily.

Jeremiah studied the brazen boy sitting in front of him. Xavier was hiding something. He could extract it from him, but it was time he learned to make his own decisions and accept the consequences. He wouldn't be doing his son any favors by prying the information out of him and forcing him to face his demons. He would have to learn to do that on his own in order to develop into a strong, dependable, competent king. Jeremiah expelled a deep breath.

"Son? You need to learn to make good decisions on your own, but as long as I still draw a breath, I will always help you when you ask for it. Just know that sometimes there are problems a man cannot solve alone. Sometimes being a man is knowing when to ask for help. So, although I'm sure there's more to this than what you've told me, I will not infiltrate your mind to learn of it. You must learn when to ask for help. Do you understand what I'm trying to tell you?"

"Yes, sir," he whispered, relief rushing through him.

"Good. Now, let's discuss your punishment."

Xavier stiffened.

His father folded his arms across his chest and regarded him thoughtfully. "What do you think would be a fitting punishment for running away from school, staying out all night, and worrying me and countless others?"

"I don't know. Uh...grounded for a week?"

"A week? You truly believe that grounded for a week is a fitting and just punishment for the amount of trouble you've caused?"

"Um, Loren said you were going to spank me."

"Do you think that would be a suitable punishment?"

No! "Uh, I don't know. I...don't want to be spanked."

Amusement filled his father's eyes. "Then, maybe you should think of that before you do things like this."

He nodded, tears flooding his eyes.

"I can't just ground you for a week, son. But, I won't spank you. Instead you will be assigned chores. Since you have experience with horses, you will be assigned to help the handlers clean out stalls."

Xavier looked at his father in disbelief. Was he really going to get off that lightly? "Yes, sir. I can do that."

"Wait a minute, son. I'm not done. In addition, you will clean up after dinner each night. You'll clear the table, wash the dishes, clean and mop the kitchen, and take out the trash."

His jaw dropped, and he whined, "What? But, we have maids for that! Why do I have to do it?"

"It's your punishment. I'm sure the maids would enjoy getting off early for a couple of weeks. "

"A couple of weeks! But..."

His father interrupted, "There's no discussing it. The punishment stands. Now, Ephraim is downstairs. He wants to speak to you."

Xavier stiffened.

"He's not angry," he soothed. "He has some interesting news he wishes to share with you."

With a nod, he moved to the door but his father's voice stopped him.

"Oh, and son? I think it goes without saying that you're grounded for an additional two weeks."

Xavier winced and without turning to face his father, nodded dejectedly, before exiting the room.

Ephraim and Loren sat next to the fire in quiet

conversation as he descended the stairs and approached them.

"Get some rest, mate. I'll talk to you more tonight," Ephraim finished as Loren clapped him on the shoulder, stood, and walked toward Xavier. He paused next to him and tousled his hair before yanking him against his hip and striking his backside with two painful swats.

"Ow! Jeez, Loren, that hurt!" he blared.

"Yeah? Well, too bad, kid! You're lucky that's all I'm giving you!"

"God, I said I was sorry. What do you want from me?"

"Better choices! I want better choices from you! And you know something, Xavier? Sometimes "sorry" isn't enough!" He glared down at the boy until he was confident that his message sank in. Then, with a glance at Ephraim, he left the residence without another word.

Xavier shuffled to the sofa and sat heavily with a groan. After a moment, he looked at Ephraim. "Are you going to punish me too?"

The general laughed throatily. "Having a bad morning, eh, laddie?"

"Try a horrible week," he muttered grumpily before looking at Ephraim apprehensively. "Are you really okay? I'm so sorry I hurt you! It was an accident."

"Xavier, of all the poor decisions you made yesterday, what happened with me wasn't one of them. It was superb fighting. Well, done," Ephraim noted with a grin.

"Thank you, sir. But, why didn't you block it?" he asked.

"It caught me off guard. Though, I'm not sure I would have been able to completely block the effects of it anyways. It was one bloody powerful electro force!"

Xavier smiled meekly.

"The fight isn't why I wanted to see you, young sire. I wanted to talk about what you did afterwards, while I lay unconscious. What exactly happened, Xavier?"

He hesitated. It all happened so fast that it was a blur to him. "Uh, I ran to you, so did Drew. I got really scared because you wouldn't wake up. I was shaking you and wishing you weren't hurt. Then this white light appeared all around us. It scared me. I tried to pull away, but it was like my hand was glued to you. Then I saw your face change. Like it got ...younger."

Ephraim nodded. "It did, but there's more. The healers informed me today that when you healed me, you took ten years off my chronological age. Physically, I'm ten years younger," he declared.

"What? I...I didn't mean to...I just got overly excited. I was really scared that I had killed you..."

He held up his hand against the boy's onslaught of bumbling excuses. "Xavier, it's okay. It's to be expected. I'm sure your heightened emotions caused a hyper-response from your empowerment." Ephraim smiled slyly. "Besides, I'm not complaining. I feel like I took a swim in the fountain of youth. I feel like a kid again!"

Xavier smiled with relief.

"Now, why don't I show you a couple of new moves so we could try them out tomorrow? You did fantastic with the others."

His grin grew as he swelled with pride.

Ephraim winked down at him. "But something tells me that I'll be more agile and more of a challenge for you from now on."

Chapter 23

Jackass (The Donkey)

The next morning, Xavier followed Court to school lost in his desperate thoughts of how to deal with his erratic powers. There didn't seem to be anything he could do about it. He couldn't avoid using his abilities, but he couldn't use them either. He couldn't keep up this façade much longer. He had to do something! There had to be a reason why his powers were going rogue. Frowning in concentration, he pondered over the occasions he lost control of his abilities. Then his face lifted into a grin.

"I've got it! God, I'm so stupid!" he exclaimed, nearly tackling Court out of giddiness.

"What? Xavier, mate, I think you've finally gone barmy." Court eyed the boy hugging him with a bewildered expression.

"No, you ingrate!" He released Court and lowered his voice as they reached the school's steps. "I know why my abilities have been off! The only times I've had trouble with my powers were when I lost my temper or was upset or something."

Court looked at him. "Are you sure? Every time? Even with my dad?"

"Well, I wasn't angry with your dad, but I was scared. He nearly sliced open my face!"

"He wouldn't have hurt you, Xavier. Dad's the best swordsman in the kingdom. He was in complete control. He wouldn't have ever, ever cut you!" he responded a bit defensively.

"Well, yeah. I *know* that, but caught up in the moment, I forgot," he replied.

"Okay, what about with Robbie?"

He frowned in thought. "Well, yeah. She was showing me up and it made me mad."

"What about what happened at the café and with Daniel?"

"Well." Xavier frowned. Those occurrences were tougher, but he was certain the link was there.It had to be! "I...I was...I guess I was embarrassed because everyone at the café was staring at us." He grasped desperately for a reason, no matter how flimsy. "Yeah! That has to be it. The waitress could barely take our order because she was too busy bumbling over me. Then, Henrick came over and embarrassed me in front of Robbie. And Daniel...well, he startled me when he yelled out after seeing my electro force."

Court gave a nod of understanding. "Okay, it sounds like that's it then. So, what are you going to do about it?"

"Well, I'm going to try to avoid those kinds of situations," he answered.

"How are you going to do that?"

"I don't know, but I'll figure something out."

By lunchtime, Xavier hadn't figured anything out. How could he prevent something that wasn't preventable? How could he prevent people from ogling at him? How could he keep others from sparking his anger? There was no way he could possibly control what others say or do.

"Xavier," Robbie began, interrupting his thoughts, "I

know you think you can handle this, but you should really talk to your father. He can help."

"Yeah, mate! I agree with Robbie. You've got to tell your Dad," Court responded.

"I can't run to my dad for every little problem. Some king I'd make always running to *Daddy* when things get too tough. I'll figure something out."

"That's what you said this morning, mate. Empowerment classes are after lunch, and you still don't have a bloody plan. Besides, this isn't a little problem; it's huge! You've gotta talk to your dad!"

Court and Robbie were right. Xavier was no closer to a solution than he was a couple weeks ago, and they both knew it. Nothing he had tried so far worked, and he had no idea how to avoid the next mishap that was certain to occur. Why was he having problems with his abilities? None of his friends' powers seemed to be floundering so it couldn't be a phase in his development. So, why was it happening? He could only surmise that his troubles weren't ordinary or small. Maybe his confrontation with LeMasters had damaged him somehow. Maybe the Key not only took William LeMasters' powers but bits and parts of his as well.

"Look, Xavier. You're my boyfriend and I care about you. But if you don't talk to your dad, I will," Robbie concluded quietly.

He looked at his friends, who anxiously awaited his response. Hadn't his father told him that part of being a man was knowing when to ask for help? Finally, he whispered, "All right. I'll talk to him during telepathy class after the lunch break."

Both Robbie and Court exhaled loudly and exchanged relieved smiles.

After lunch, the children made their way out into the courtyard to unwind before their afternoon classes. They had just settled around a large tree when Jonas approached them smirking.

"Well, looky, looky! Isn't it the great invisible boy? Personally, I don't think you need the ability, Pipsqueak. You're so small that you're practically invisible as you are," the older boy mocked, and his burly thugs laughed.

"Shut up, Jonas," Court hissed.

"What? Come on, Hardcastle! If he'd nearly killed my father, I would have beaten the crap out of him! Why are you still sticking up for him?" he asked.

"That was an accident and no one asked you!" Robbie blurted.

He gave a soft whistle of contrived appreciation. "Well, well. Look what we have here, boys? Pipsqueak's girlfriend has a mouth on her. Good thing she's bigger than you, runt; she can serve as your bodyguard! Tell me, do you have to get a stepladder to kiss her?"

His friends stooped over, holding their stomachs and howled with laughter. Jonas looked down at them smiling appreciatively before looking back at Xavier in triumph.

"Shut it, you...you jackass," he growled as he clambered to his feet, his hands balling into fists at his sides.

The smile slipped from the older boy's face, and his features melted into an expression of fury.

"What did you call me, Pipsqueak?" he spat, swelling in size.

The confrontation had begun to draw a large crowd around them. Aside from a few moans of ominous anticipation, the group was quiet.

"You heard me. You're a jackass, and everybody here knows it!" Xavier snapped loudly. Was he insane? Jonas was a good foot taller than him and outweighed him by a hundred pounds! He would be rat bait if he didn't shut his mouth. But, it appeared his mouth had a mind of its own.

The bigger boy stepped closer, his chest swelling with anger as he hissed in Xavier's face, "Call me a jackass again, and you'll be sorry."

"You. Are. A. JACKASS!" he spat at Jonas.

"You little..." Jonas growled, grabbing him by the collar.

"Stop it, Jonas!" Robbie yelled, shoving the boy and causing him to stumble backwards. Jonas quickly righted himself, but Xavier was wrenched off balance, stumbled, and landed unceremoniously on his butt.

Why did that always seem to happen? Why did he always end up on his butt during a confrontation? Why did goons like Jonas always single him out to torment? Was he a bully magnet or something?

Jonas and his friends burst into laughter.

"Oh, God! I... knew.... it!" he managed through his fits of laughter. "She... IS... your... bodyguard! I'd keep her close, runt. There are a lot of insects in the yard who could take you out. Oh no! Watch out for that gnat!"

Anger and humiliation swelled inside Xavier, and he scrambled to his feet, glaring at the older boy. A rush of energy surged through him, and his head began to tingle. It was happening again! But this time, he had no desire to stop it, even if he could.

In the blink of an eye, Jonas was no longer *Jonas* any more. In fact, he was no longer human. The older boy's image simply molded into...well, a jackass.

The crowd around them released a low groan of surprise, and for several long seconds, there was simply shocked silence. Then, as though a dam ruptured, laughter burst from the group.

"What's going on here? Come on, come on! Move aside!" Sir Blaire ordered from the back of the crowd.

The laughter dropped away, and within seconds, Sir Blaire stood at the front of the crowd with Lana sidling up beside him. For a moment, the two adults gaped at the jackass. Then, slowly their gaze shifted to Xavier. The seconds ticked by slowly until finally, Lana spoke.

"Xavier Wells? Did you do this?" The disappointment in her voice was unmistakable.

He looked at his feet and shuffled. "Yes, ma'am."

Sir Blaire cleared his throat. "Well, I'll take the animal to my classroom and see if I can undo this...it may take a while." He looked down at Xavier. "Who's the jackass?"

Stifled laughter erupted from behind them as he whispered, "Jonas McKnight, sir."

"Right. I'll take care of him," Sir Blaire noted with a nod to Lana. "I'll leave the rest to you."

The group watched Sir Blaire push, pull, and muscle the stubborn animal into the building. Several students exploded in laughter when the animal bucked and kicked Sir Blaire in the stomach. He released a string of curses before muttering loudly, "It's no wonder he turned you into a jackass, you ungrateful little heathen!"

"Prince Wells?" Lana's sullen voice drew his eyes to her formidable face. "Come with me, young man."

He felt like a condemned man as he followed Lana into the building, down the hall, and into her classroom. He lingered near the door and fidgeted nervously with the edge of a nearby desk.

"Well? What do you have to say for yourself? What in God's name were you thinking? You know better than to use your empowerments against another citizen to humiliate or harm him! You *know* better! Your father has been very patient and understanding about this thus far, but he will blow his top over this. And I will not intervene this time; do you hear me? I am so disappointed..."

"Stop yelling at me!" he interrupted, his temper still very close to the surface. "I didn't start it! Ask anyone there!"

"You may not have started it, but you're the Prince of Warwood!" she chastised. "How do you think the other kids will think of you in the future?"

"They were all laughing!" he responded desperately. "They think it was a joke."

"Yes, but do you think they'll remember you as a patient and just ruler?" she persisted.

"I don't care! I don't care how people remember me!" he bellowed. "Jonas deserved it, and I'll do it again if he starts running his mouth!"

Lana was losing her patience. "You don't care? You don't care? Xavier Wells, as future king, you need to set an example on how..."

"Shut up, okay? I didn't ask to be future king or an example for anyone!" he shouted, his hands clenching into fists.

Her eyes flashed with anger. "Do not use that tone with me, young man!"

"NO! Don't *you* use that tone with me! You're not my mother! My mother is DEAD!" he shouted as a surge of power pulsed and throbbed inside him. It fought to escape and he desperately tried to squash it, but like an erupting volcano, it couldn't be stop. An icy sensation shuddered through his body moments before a blue, almost transparent force burst from him. In a blink of the eye, Lana stood stone-still; the remainder of her reprimands left unsaid.

"Lana?" he yelped, racing to her. She was cold to the touch. In fact, she felt like ice, frozen and stiff. "Lana? Oh, God!"

Panic-stricken, he raced out of the classroom and

stumbled down the hall, yelling at the top of his lungs.

"HELP! Someone help!"

Classroom doors burst open, and Xavier's eyes immediately fastened on Sir Underwood.

"Sir Underwood, please help! It's Lana...she's...she's frozen! She's not moving!" He barely got the words out before Sir Underwood jumped into action.

"Get the headmaster. Now!" he shouted at a student as he sprinted past Xavier and into Lana's classroom.

He followed the tall, thin man wearily and idled by the door. Sir Underwood approached the immobile woman cautiously. His long nose nearly touched hers as he studied her eyes. Then, he straightened, placed his hands on either side of her face, and closed his eyes, but nothing happened.

"Matt? What's happened?" Michael questioned, brushing past Xavier and hurrying into the room.

Xavier didn't stick around to hear Sir Underwood's explanation. He bolted out of the building and paused at the top of the steps unsure of where to go or what to do. If he went to the lake, they would find him, and hiding among the kingdom's population was impossible. Most people could accomplish getting lost in a crowd, but not Xavier. He was too well known and would stick out like a neon sign. Then, like a horrible ghost, he remembered the Ruins. He could hide in the Ruins until dark and then....then what? He would have to figure that out later.

He was scared to death to use his empowerments again, but he was desperate. He had to get away from the Academy and fast! Closing his eyes, he summoned his teleportation power and teleported flawlessly to the Ruins. Shakily, he shuffled toward the decrepit building and lingered in the doorway but didn't enter. A low hum and a distant echo of dripping water sifted out of the structure's depths.

The sounds, the smell, the energy from the Ruins still frightened Xavier, and he shivered as goose bumps spread across his body. It had been nearly a year since he been here when LeMasters kidnapped and held him captive in its dark depths. The Ruins held nothing but horrible memories. Struggling to regain his courage, he slowly walked through the entrance and into the blackness. The last time he was here, lanterns lit the passage, but now he couldn't see his own hand an inch from his face. He couldn't risk conjuring an electro force for light. With his recent track record, he would more than likely blow himself into smithereens! Instead, he shuffled a few feet down the corridor, keeping his hand on the wall to guide him before sinking to the floor. Alone and safe from being found, he simply broke down. He had hurt Lana. He had used his empowerments against her! Would she be all right? He shuddered to think of his father's reaction when he discovered his son had used his powers against the woman he loved. If Lana died, his father would hate him. Xavier buried his head in his arms and simply cried. He had no idea what he should do next.

Chapter 24

Out of Control

"Loren! Get in here, now!" Jeremiah spat as he stomped into the palace, shed his jacket, and tossed his brief case onto the small table next to the door.

Loren strode into the residence behind the king, shutting the door behind him.

"How many guards do we have out there looking for my son?"

"All but the gatehouse core, sir," Loren answered.

"Good. Tell them to comb the woods. I felt his presence there before I lost the connection."

"Yes, sir," Loren responded and turned to leave.

"I wouldn't do that if I were you, sire," a low voice whispered from the receiving room.

The men spun, their bodies tense and at the ready. The prophet stood next to the fireplace, leaning casually against the mantle and stoking the fire. The men relaxed marginally and the prophet smiled dryly.

"Abe, we don't have time for this." The king sighed impatiently. "Xavier is missing. He attacked a child at the school, not to mention..."

"Lana Applegate, yes, I know," the prophet answered. The men waited for the old man to continue.

When he didn't, the king growled edgily, "I don't have

time for a damn guessing game, Abe. My son is missing! Now, spit it out!"

The prophet smirked, but turned to face the king, meeting his eyes unflinchingly. "That is why I am here, sire. It's time. Xavier's powers are at an influx. He's gaining new powers at an exponential rate and as a result, his ability to control and focus his powers is faltering." The men exchanged uneasy glances as the prophet continued, "He must be isolated from the public. He must begin his training. And you must acquire the powers needed to keep the boy from hurting himself or others in the process."

"Abe, I appreciate what you're saying, but there's just not enough time, and it doesn't change anything. I need to find him! If what you say is true, he's probably scared witless," Jeremiah responded, grabbing his jacket. He stomped out of the residence with Loren and the prophet on his heels.

"Sire! Sire! It's dire that you listen to me!" Abe insisted.

"If you haven't noticed, we're in a bit of a crisis here! If the boy has begun his convergence, I do not have time to be endowed with powers! He must be found before he does something that cannot be fixed!"

"You must make time, Jeremiah! Why do you have to be so damn stubborn?"

"You're crossing the line, Abe. Remember who you're addressing," Loren hissed as they exited the palace.

The prophet glared briefly at the general before grabbing the king by the shoulder and spinning him to face him. "If you go after him without the powers necessary, you will only make matters worse! He's unpredictable, he's afraid, he's guilt-ridden, he's ashamed, and he's full of strong, powerful emotions that will only exacerbate his control issues!"

"Abe, I'm not disagreeing with you, but there just isn't

enough time to acquire them! First, I'd have to call the High Council to arrange a meeting. Then I'd need to make the proposal and wait while they deliberate..."

The king stopped abruptly, and both he and the prophet turned toward the woods and listened to something only they could hear. Loren watched the pair in awe and was struck by how similar the men were although they were decades apart in age.

Jeremiah was the first to break the trance-like state. "He's in the woods. He's calling Robbie to come to him. I didn't get all of it; his telepathy pulsated in and out of focus. I think he was trying to block me." Jeremiah looked at the older man. "I have to go now, Abe. Robbie is in danger. I must get to him before she does!"

Abraham nodded. "Yes, you must. He will kill her tonight if you don't get there in time. Take care, Your Highness! He's extremely volatile."

Jeremiah gave the older man a nod, looked at his general, and the pair walked toward the palace gate.

"So? What's the plan?" Loren asked quietly.

"I've contacted the entire Royal Guard platoon to report to the edge of the woods near the school. We'll meet them there and begin the search. No one will search alone, and there must be at least one strong blocker in each group."

Loren nodded as he followed the king to the Academy. He only hoped the plan would be enough.

Xavier stepped out of the Ruins some time later and found that the sky had darkened considerably. He couldn't hide all day; he had to face this thing, but he needed Robbie. Only Robbie could help him figure out what he should do now. He had no choice. He would have to use his telepathy and risk being overheard by his father. After breathing evenly for a minute or two to calm his nerves, he connected easily to his powers.

"Robbie? Robbie, can you hear me? I need you, please," he pleaded.

"Xavier? God, everyone is looking for you! Your dad is going nuts!" she replied.

"I know, but I need your help! Can you please meet me at the lake?" he begged.

There was a long silence. Had he lost his connection? He couldn't hear her thoughts, which was odd.

"Robbie, are you still there?"

Finally she answered, *"Yeah, I'm still here. I'll meet you in fifteen minutes."*

"Okay. See you then. Thanks, Robbie!" he disconnected and began the trek back to the lake.

By the time he reached the lake, Robbie was sitting on a rock waiting for him. She stood the moment he emerged from the wood.

"Hi," she greeted carefully.

"Hi," he muttered back. "How's Lana?"

"She's in the hospital, but the healers say she's going to be fine."

He collapsed to his knees and moaned, "Oh, thank God!"

"Xavier, you need to tell your dad," Robbie told him firmly.

"I...I want to...I just..." He peered up at Robbie desperately. "I don't know how to tell him."

Robbie knelt next to him. "Xavier, it's going to be all right. We'll figure it out together. Okay?"

The moment Robbie wrapped her arms around him, Xavier felt relief and comfort wash over him, and he desperately clung back. They were so close he thought he would fall into her. Then his innocent need for comfort changed, and he felt heat and an intense need to kiss her.

Slowly, he pulled away and looked at her. When she looked at him with those large chocolate eyes, he simply reacted. He leaned toward her and brushed his lips to hers. His inhibitions cracked as the building heat exploded inside him. He was so consumed with the kiss that he didn't feel Robbie pushing him away until she finally gave him a hard shove. He fell backwards onto the ground and landed on his butt. Annoyed and confused he looked up at her and saw fear in her eyes. One quick glance around him and he realized why. The forest was on fire! He jumped to his feet!

"How did that happen?" he shouted.

"How else? You!" she shouted as she stood and looked around desperately for an escape from the ring of flames.

A loud whoosh made both children jump as a ball of fire flashed overhead and crashed into a nearby cluster of shrubs. Robbie screamed. The concussion from the impact sent them to the ground. The earth rumbled and shook like a giant waking beneath them.

"Robbie, come on! We've got to get out of here!" he shouted, scrambling to stand.

He helped her to her feet and pulled her toward the only part of the lake's perimeter that was not aflame. They darted into the woods and clambered through the thick foliage, but the inferno continued to stalk them, bombarding them with fiery missiles. Robbie was beyond afraid; she was petrified. Xavier could feel it in her thoughts, her words, and in the way she squeezed his hand. She was terrified of *him*! He swallowed back tears as he continued fighting his way through the woods. Then the earth shuddered and growled beneath their feet, they staggered into one another.

"Xavier! Make it stop! Please, make it stop!"

He shouted fearfully. "Don't you think I would if I could? I can't, Robbie. I can't!"

Suddenly, a ball of fire thundered out of the sky above them and slammed into the earth just feet in front of them. They were thrown several feet backwards and collapsed into a tangled heap.

"Robbie?" he called anxiously, squirming out from under her limp body. She was out cold and a cut on her forehead was bleeding profusely. Oh, no! "Robbie!"

Xavier tried to lift her and carry her from the woods, but he wasn't strong enough.

"Robbie? Please wake up! We've gotta get out of here! Please! I can't carry you!"

But, she wasn't waking and the fire was intensifying around them. Desperate, he began to pull her through the forest, but it was slow going with the fallen foliage and debris on the ground.

Then, like a savior, his father emerged from the smoke and fire with Loren, Ephraim, and Henrick behind him.

"Dad! Please help me! I can't lift her!"

"I've got her, son," Jeremiah told him as he scooped the girl into his arms and turned to retrace his steps through the woods.

The three guardsmen surrounded Xavier, but he paid no attention to them as he followed his father through the burning forest, his tearful eyes fixed on Robbie's bleeding, unconscious face.

"Is...is she..." He couldn't finish the question. Robbie was hurt and he had been the one who harmed her! Nothing he said or did would make that okay. What if she died? He whimpered miserably at the thought and the fire pounding the earth around them intensified.

Abruptly, his father spun and pinned him with a steady, firm look. "Calm yourself, boy!"

He tried to do as his father demanded, but it was next to impossible. In just a few short hours, he had managed to injure two people dearest to him. Anxiety tightened its grip in his chest.

"Xavier, calm down and breathe!" his father ordered.

He nodded and inhaled a deep, shaky breath.

"Again."

He inhaled another deep breath.

"And, again."

After one last cleansing breath, the fire storm around them lessened marginally, and his father nodded satisfactorily before turning and leading the rest of the way out of the woods.

When they finally emerged from the woods, it was completely engulfed in flames like a giant orange monster, but Xavier's eyes were fixed on Robbie as his father settled her to the ground to look her over. He looked at his general.

"She's breathing. It could be a mild concussion, but I don't have scanning abilities to be certain. Loren, can you check her over?"

Loren stepped out from behind Xavier and moved toward the girl. He knelt and placed one hand on Robbie's abdomen and the other on her head. Xavier watched restlessly as Robbie was engulfed in a fantastic white light. A moment later, the light evaporated. Robbie groaned and her eyes briefly fluttered open. Xavier expelled a tense breath and closed his eyes with relief.

"She'll be fine. As you said, she has a mild concussion," Loren responded, standing.

"Thank God," Xavier muttered.

For the first time, he noticed the large crowd gathered in the field adjacent to the school. Although he was taken aback to see the group there, he was completely shocked to see the entire Royal Guard dressed in combat gear standing rigidly in front of the crowd. A chill of fear crept down his spine as he studied the rigid, stone-faced soldiers.

"Dowler! Get the girl to the infirmary," his father barked at a guard standing nearby.

Dowler hurried forward, lifted Robbie into his arms, and carried her toward the palace gates.

Then the king turned toward his son with unreadable eyes. With a sigh, he and Loren cautiously stepped toward him.

"You need to come with me, son."

Xavier stepped backwards before becoming acutely aware of Ephraim and Henrick's presence behind him. Instinctively he tried to side-step his father and his men, but they countered the move. Fear like he had never experienced before gripped him, clawing at his soul. There was only one explanation for the presence of the Royal Guard: his father planned to have him arrested and punished.

"D...Dad. I...I didn't meant to! I swear! My...my powers, I can't control them any more...I...I swear...I'd never intentionally hurt Lana or Robbie!" he pleaded, his fear and anxiety growing by the second.

"Xavier..." his father began but was interrupted.

"PLEASE, Dad! It's the truth! I don't know what to do anymore! I can't control it...any of it!" he continued to move away from the men who were slowly and calmly matching his every step.

"Stop! Please! Stay away! I don't want to hurt anyone else!" he cried, tears streaming down his face. "I SAID STOP! I don't want to hurt you! PLEASE!"

The earth beneath their feet began to tremble. There was a collective gasp of fear and confusion from the crowd. The closer the men got to Xavier, the more intense the trembling became until it was bone-rattling.

"Xavier!" his father barked. "Calm down! It'll only get worse if you continue to get worked up!"

With a sideways glance from the king, Loren, Ephraim, and Henrick rushed at the boy, but the men never reached him. An invisible, ear-popping compression exploded from the prince, and the three men were hurled twenty feet away.

Jeremiah stared at his fallen men, stunned. The boy had just tossed his best guards across the field like dolls. His gaze swept from the men to his son's stunned, panicked face. Large crocodile tears pooled in Xavier's eyes as he hugged his shaking body. He was terrified. The king could feel the fear rolling off him in overwhelming waves. Cautiously, he crept toward him and spoke in a low, soothing tone, "Son, please, just calm down. It's going to be okay."

His wide eyes darted away from the fallen men to his father. "No, it's not!" he cried miserably. "It's not! It's never going to be ok! NEVER!" He released a shuddering sob before continuing. "How can I calm down when I'm about to be arrested and caned for using my powers against people? But, I didn't do it on purpose. I can't control my powers anymore! They just go haywire without warning. It's not my fault, Dad. Please! I'm telling you the truth! You've got to believe me."

As the boy shouted, tremors rocking the earth intensified with a sudden jolt and sent every person within a mile radius stumbling and staggering.

The king staggered but managed to right himself as he continued, "Xavier, you're not going to be arrested or caned!"

"Liar! You told me I would! You said if I ever used my powers, intentionally or not, you would cane me!" he bellowed, fresh tears pouring down his cheeks.

The pressure building against the unstable terrain

finally reached a climax, and the Earth expelled a loud report as an enormous crack snaked across the field. The crowd screamed and scrambled away from the widening crevice.

"Xavier! You won't be caned...please, son! Calm down. I don't want to have to hurt you!" his father yelled over the rumbling earth and cries from the crowd.

"I don't want to hurt *you*, Dad. Stay away! Please! Get back!" he screamed.

The boy was out of control and beyond reason, and Jeremiah was terrified the prophet had been right. Xavier was about to do something he would regret for the rest of his life. He was a danger to every man, woman, and child in the kingdom. *"I have to protect my people! I have no choice! I'm so sorry, son. I hope you'll forgive me for what I am about to do."*

His father's thoughts slammed into him like an alarm. Xavier only had a fraction of a second to decipher the meaning behind the thoughts before his father launched himself at him. Fear prickled through his body and into his extremities. Then, a blazing force blasted from him, striking the king with the intensity of an atom bomb. His father was thrown into a group of guardsmen thirty meters away, knocking them down like bowling pins. Then, all hell broke loose!

The guards on his left rushed at him with their weapons at the ready. He screamed something incomprehensible, dropped to a knee, and slammed his fist against the earth. The ground broke apart around him and a guard tumbled into the ravine. Xavier cried out in agony, and the sky erupted in lightning and thunder. Hail bombarded the earth and sent the crowd scrambling for cover. The last thing he saw of Warwood before he teleported was a group of guardsmen rushing his father's limp body to safety.

Chapter 25

The Fall-out

Xavier wandered through the wooded area adjacent to his grandparents' house. He wasn't sure why he had teleported here. He had nothing but bad memories of his grandparents, their house, the woods, this town... Nonetheless, he made his way through the woods to the rear of his grandparents' home. The lights in the kitchen were on and his grandmother was standing at the window washing dinner dishes. She didn't look so formidable and cruel from a distance. She looked like a frail, old woman. The grimace she always wore in his presence was replaced with contentment, her brow line was smooth, and her mouth soft and relaxed.

Her shrill, angry voice was still clear in his memory, though. His grandmother had never thought much of him. She had always believed he was a wicked, dangerous boy who should be locked up! Xavier sighed heavily. Maybe she had been right all along. He was dangerous. In one day, he had attacked a boy from school, his father's girlfriend and quite possibly the future queen of Warwood, his girlfriend, three high-ranking guardsmen, and his own father. What kind of son does that? What kind of prince attacks his own people? How could he be the Chosen? How could he be the King of the Light destined to free humanity from the tyranny of the Dark King when he created chaos and misery wherever he went? Maybe the prophet got it backwards. Was it possible that he wasn't the Chosen at all but the Dark King? His recent actions only seemed to confirm this.

Blinded by tears flooding his eyes, he sank to the muddy ground and sobbed, but feeling sorry for himself didn't change anything. His powers were still uncontrollable, and he was still a fugitive from his home for attacking his people. Wiping the tears from his face, he looked back at his grandparents' house. His grandmother had finished the dishes and turned out the light to the kitchen. Standing, he dusted himself off and darted across his grandparents' backyard to the barn. The barn was empty and bare. His mother's stallion, Brewster, was now stabled at the palace, but he found a spare barrel of hay and spread out a thick layer to sleep on. Even with a turbulent-filled mind from the events of the day, he slipped quickly into a welcomed peaceful sleep.

When Jeremiah opened his eyes again, it was to anarchy. A group of guards carried him through the palace gates, what was left of the palace gates. The tremor Xavier had created in his terror had rocked the earth and split the palace wall's foundation. Giant fractures in the earth split the drive into two, and many of the Grand Hall's windows had shattered. People filled the streets, some crying, some simply dazed and shocked.

"Release me," Jeremiah muttered hoarsely.

"Sire! Thank God! We had feared the worse!" A young guard sighed as he and the rest of the guard set the king to his feet.

"I'm fine, Sergeant. Where's my son?"

"He teleported after he attacked you, sir. We tried to

apprehend him, but he...he...well," the young man gestured at the destruction around them, "he did this. Private O'Neal and Private Duncan are in the infirmary in serious condition as a result."

The king nodded grievously. "And what's the status of General Hardcastle, General Jefferson, and Lieutenant Davies?"

"I don't know, Sire."

"I need trackers, the best in the kingdom. Find them and send them to the castle within the hour."

"Yes, sire," the young sergeant responded, bowing slightly before rushing off toward the Governing Hall.

Jeremiah looked at the remaining guards. "The rest of you, clear the streets and get these people back in their homes. Assure them that the danger has passed."

"Yes, sir," the men responded in unison and dispersed into the crowd.

Jeremiah watched the men begin to usher people away from the fissure and coax them back into their homes. Satisfied the task was in good hands, the king turned and headed to the infirmary to check on his most trusted friends.

The infirmary was a fury of action. There were several people sitting in the waiting area with cuts, abrasions, sprains, and broken bones. The king walked past the receptionist in the triage, through the double doors, and into the treatment area. Ephraim's gruff voice flooded him with relief.

"Oh, bloody hell, I'm fine, Rebecca! Stop fussing over me and let's get out of here!"

Jeremiah rounded a corner and entered a small treatment room. Ephraim was sitting on the edge of the bed, wincing as he tried to pull on his boots.

"Ephraim, you were thrown more than twenty meters!

You have a concussion and a cracked rib. You are not fine!" Rebecca spat, standing in front of him with her hands placed firmly on her hips. She was a force to be reckoned with, and Jeremiah knew in a knock-out, drag-out fight, who he would bet on.

"I'd listen to her. I think she has the gumption and audacity to take you," Jeremiah called, leaning against the door.

Ephraim and Rebecca both looked up at the king, and Ephraim snickered. "You're not telling me anything I don't already know, mate. The woman bore and raises four Hardcastle boys. You don't have to tell me that I don't stand a chance," he retorted with a wink.

"I sometimes think I'm raising five boys, Ephraim Andrew Hardcastle! Now lay back down in that bed this instant before I break another rib!"

Ephraim muttered to himself, disgruntled, but did as his wife asked. Jeremiah smirked.

"How's the boy?" Ephraim asked.

"Gone. He teleported out of the kingdom. I'm meeting trackers at the palace within the hour. I'll find him. With the state his powers are in, there's no way he'll be able to keep them under wraps. As soon as he engages his powers, the trackers will determine his location."

Ephraim nodded. "I should be healed by the time you're ready to go after him."

"No," Jeremiah stated firmly. "I'm going alone."

"What?" Ephraim shifted on the bed. "Jer, you mustn't do this on your own! He's very powerful, out of control, and dangerous! You need backup!"

"Bloody hell, Ephraim. If you get any louder and you'd wake the mortuary!" Loren ribbed, edging into the room with Henrick behind him. Both men had a few cuts and bruises but otherwise looked fine.

"He's going after Xavier, *alone*!" Ephraim spat.

The two men turned to their king.

"Alone?" Loren asked in disbelief.

"Yes, alone," Jeremiah repeated. "I should have the powers necessary to immobilize and subdue the boy by morning."

"Jer, you should still have backup. You saw what he can do! He's dangerous!" Loren exclaimed.

"He's right, sire," Henrick agreed. "You need us. We'll stay out of sight; the boy will never know we're there. Don't try to capture him on your own."

"Henrick, the boy is telepathic! It won't matter if you're out of sight. I can't risk it! I'm the only one who can stop him." Jeremiah sighed and met each man's eyes with unwavering resolution. "There's no other way."

The men exchanged weary glances, but not one disputed the matter further.

"However, I still need your help with something. The upper level of King's Mountain is the only place built to withstand his powers. It needs to be prepared for his long term care."

Loren nodded. "Consider it done."

"Good. Rest up, men. Once I have the boy, the real work begins."

The king left the men and wandered up to the second level where Lana was being kept under observation. She was asleep when he entered her room, and he sat next to her on the bed and stroked her hair from her face. She stirred and opened her eyes.

"Hi," she murmured weakly.

"Hey, baby. How are you feeling?"

"Tired, but better. How's Xavier?"

Jeremiah hesitated and his eyes dropped from hers. "Not well. His powers are at a massive convergence. He has very little control over his abilities."

"Oh, God. It all makes sense now! He must be so afraid." Lana studied his downcast head. "What is it, Jeremy? What aren't you telling me?"

He looked at her again, anxiety creasing his brow. "He attacked Ephraim, Loren, and Henrick tonight. Then he attacked me and the entire Royal Guard. Now he's missing. He teleported out of the kingdom after the attacks."

"Oh, Jeremy," she gasped, taking his hand and squeezing it.

"I know," he whispered. "I have to go after him. I'm meeting with trackers who will help me locate him, and when I do, I will be taking him to King's Mountain. He's not safe to have here. I'm afraid all my spare time will be spent helping him get through this."

"Of course. I wouldn't expect any different. Xavier comes first. He needs his dad right now. Don't worry about me. I'm fine."

Jeremiah looked down at the woman he loved and felt so very lucky to have her in his life. Julia had been his first love, and their love had been a whirlwind. It had nearly killed him to lose her. He would have wallowed into an abyss of self-pity and depression, never to recover, save for the fact that he had a young son who desperately needed him. Lana felt like a second chance at happiness and fulfillment. She made him feel like a complete man, a complete father, a complete king.

"I love you," he murmured, kissing her. "I'll keep in touch and let you know what's going on."

"Good. I'd have to kick your butt if you didn't," she joked with a sly smile.

When Jeremiah entered the royal residence, the prophet was waiting for him.

"Okay. I'm expecting trackers in thirty minutes, and I've arranged for the High Council to report to the palace in an hour and a half. What powers do I need to get my son back?" he asked, striding to where the older man sat in the receiving room next to the fire.

The older man looked at the king's determined face before answering. "You'll need abilities that will help you contain and control the boy as well as protect yourself and others."

"Which ones, Abe?" he asked impatiently.

"You'll need an upgrade to your blocking abilities, tracking, negation, and apothecary."

"Telekinesis? Why would I need that?"

"Since both negation and apothecary require physical contact, you'll need a power that can restrain the boy when necessary until he either calms down or you're able to touch him to apply a subduing power. Ephraim will be of use in this since he already possesses the ability of apothecary."

"Okay, anything else?"

"No. Those abilities added to those you already possess should be sufficient."

"Will you stay long enough to assist in my proposal to the Council? There will be less reluctance if you back me up."

"Yes, I will stay and see to it that the High Council agrees."

It was nearly 2' o'clock in the morning when the last of the High Council finally arrived at the palace. Jeremiah wasted no time with filling the Council in on the circumstances behind Xavier's attack on the kingdom.

"So, his powers are at a tremendous influx and he's unable to control them?" Governor Wilks clarified.

"Yes. He's been displaying symptoms of this for months, but the boy was too ashamed and afraid to tell me what was going on. I wish I had paid better attention to the signs that it was happening. I bear the bulk of the responsibility of what has happened as a result of his influx. But now that I'm fully aware of what I'm dealing with, I need the proper abilities to capture and control him. Once I succeed, I will take the prince to King's Mountain until his influx has passed." The king paused and glanced at the prophet.

On cue, Abe stepped forward and continued, "King Wells will need an upgrade in his blocking power, negation, apothecary, gravitational manipulation or telekinesis, and tracking abilities. Is it necessary for me to explain how each power will be used?"

"No, no. That's not necessary, Abraham," Governor Bracus answered.

"Wait a minute, I'd like to hear it," Marcus stated. "This is a big decision, and we need to be thoroughly informed."

"I completely understand," Abe replied nodding, "and since time is a luxury we cannot afford to waste, I will make this short and to the point. Although King Wells has kingdom trackers working on locating the prince, they will only be able to tell him a general location of the boy from this distance. The king will need tracking abilities to narrow the search when he's on the move. He will need gravitational manipulation and telekinesis so that he has a means in which to immobilize the boy so he can get close enough to touch him and employ either negation or apothecary. And, obviously, negation will be used to temporarily remove the boy's powers and apothecary will be used to sedate the boy when necessary."

The group stood in silence as they mulled over the information. Then, the prophet turned to Jeremiah and upped the ante.

"Sire? I think we need to tell the council of the boy's destiny. If they knew how important he is to the future of mankind, we may be able to forgo the customary deliberation."

Jeremiah hesitated and looked from the group to the prophet and back again. He cleared his throat nervously. "All right. What I am about to tell you must never leave this room. It's far too soon for Xavier to confront the responsibilities and attention this news will undoubtedly bring." Jeremiah took a deep breath. He had always known this day would come, but the instinct to protect his son at all costs was hard to overcome. "Xavier is the Chosen, the King of the Light, and responsible for defeating the Dark King, Fox LeMasters."

There was a collective gasp from the group.

"But he's just a boy," Governor Wilks whispered. "Does he know who he is, King Wells?"

"Yes, he does. It's been hard for him to come to grips with it."

"Dear God! It's just been one thing after another for him; hasn't it, King Wells?" Governor Bracus hissed.

Jeremiah could only nod as the lump in his throat painfully restricted his ability to speak in that moment.

"In light of this news, I think we can vote on the king's request now. All in favor of authorizing the use of the King's Key to endow King Wells IV with the said powers say aye," Judge Stull announced.

"Aye," all four Council members announced in unison.

"Motion passed," Governor Bracus announced. "The Keeper of the Key must be called upon. Let's get this done tonight so that King Wells can get our prince back safe and sound."

Chapter 26

Capturing the Prince

"What in God's name are you doing here, boy?" Grandfather's gruff voice woke Xavier with a start, and he jumped to his feet.

"Ah...I ...ah...," he stammered, not knowing what to say.

"Does your father know you're here?" he asked shortly.

He stared silently at his grandfather.

The old man sighed and shook his head. "All right, let's go. We're calling your father!"

"No!" he yelled as sparks erupted from his fingertips, igniting the hay at his feet. He jumped away from the fire as it quickly began to spread.

"Lord Almighty, boy!" Grandfather yelled, racing to get an old wool blanket and began beating at the flames.

Xavier ran from the barn and darted into the woods, putting as much distance as he could from his grandparents' house. He didn't stop until he found himself downtown in a small shopping square where vendors had set up to sell their delicious treats and snacks. His stomach gave a tremendous growl at the smells there. It had to be close to noon. Ruled by his hunger, he set to work to find some food. He didn't have any money, but if push came to shove, he would use his invisibility to steal a hotdog or something.

One vendor attracted his attention. A small crowd had gathered around the small trailer. A few people stood in line to the right of a large open window where a young woman took orders and passed it along to a pot-bellied, gruff man. He busily assembled the orders and set them out on a small metal shelf running the length of the window as he shouted out an order number into the group. Slowly, Xavier crept into the crowd and worked his way toward the window. Once in position, he looked around him for a quick escape route. There were half a dozen intersecting streets and small alleys that broke up the buildings surrounding the small square. The closest was a small alley more than 200 yards from the vendor. He would have to run his butt off to get away.

He looked back at the vendor as the man dropped another order onto the metal tray.

"Order 23!" he bellowed.

A woman sitting at a picnic table stood and ambled toward the window, but she was preoccupied with her cell phone.

Xavier turned back to the window to find the vendor busy preparing the next order. It was now or go hungry. With a quick glance around, he hurried to the window, snatched the food from the shelf, and ran. He raced around the building and sprinted down the alley. Trying to put more distance between him and the scene of the crime, he turned at the end of the alley and ran down the intersecting street before turning again and racing down yet another street. Panting, he slowed and ventured a look behind him. No one was chasing him. He stopped and doubled over, gasping to catch his breath. Then, he straightened and looked around the familiar town. His old school was just down the block across from the park. It was a good place to rest, eat, and figure out what he was going to do next. He quickly walked the distance to the park, his mouth watering at the thought of devouring the food taunting him with its delicious smells. He collapsed on the nearest bench and took a large bite out of the spicy chicken sandwich in the Styrofoam box. He inhaled the sandwich before attacking the accompanying fries. He moaned and closed his eyes with satisfaction.

Across the street, a shrill bell blared. He looked up at the school. It must be lunch time. He didn't miss the school at all. It was just another place in this stupid town that held nothing but bad memories. Sighing, Xavier slouched comfortably on the bench, feeling full and sleepy. His lids drooped heavily, but he forced them open as movement from the school jerked him to attention.

Four boys scurried from a side door and darted to a crop of large pine trees separating the school from a skate park on an adjacent lot. A large, burly boy led the group. Xavier would have recognized the boy anywhere. Matt Windom! The very same Matt Windom who had tormented him, bullied him, and made his already-unhappy life at school downright miserable. If only his powers had manifested before then. Matt would have been toast! A small sly smile slid across Xavier's face.

"Let's see if you can take me now!" he muttered as he stood. He jogged across the street and toward the row of trees where the boys had disappeared.

"Hey, man. Give me a drag! It's my cigarette. I swiped it from my old man!"

"Wait your turn, numb nuts!" Matt spat as he inhaled from the lit cigarette.

"Numb nuts? Are you speaking from experience, Matt? I thought yours had been castrated at birth," Xavier taunted with a smirk.

All four heads whipped in his direction. Matt studied

him with narrow, angry eyes.

"What's the matter, *Matty*? Don't you recognize me?"

Matt's eyes suddenly lit up with recognition and he sneered haughtily. "Why, look at what we have here, boys. Is that you, Q-tip head?" He stood and took a step toward Xavier. "What are you doing here? Last I heard, your *daddy* showed up and took you away to some *special* school for losers and freaks."

Xavier smiled and strolled nonchalantly toward the older boy. "Yeah...I've learned lots of stuff at that special school for freaks. Wanna see?"

He didn't wait for an answer as he launched himself at the bigger boy and knocked him to the muddy ground. Matt scrambled to his feet with murder in his eyes. Xavier jutted out his hand at him, trying to conjure his telekinesis, but nothing happened. Matt paused, staring dumbfounded at his outstretched, impotent hand before he and his friends burst out in uncontrollable laughter.

"Oo! Scary hand," one boy guffawed, mocking Xavier's gesture.

"Dude! What was that supposed to do?" another boy blurted, still laughing.

"What a freak!" the third boy spat.

"Oh my God, cotton balls. No wonder your daddy sent you away. You're completely nuts!" Matt jeered, spraying Xavier with spittle as he did.

Xavier dropped his hand, his face red with humiliation. He stared heatedly into the other boys' taunting faces. Of all the times for his powers to disappear, it would have to be now! Powers or no powers, he was fed up with being humiliated and teased. He was a king by God! No one would ever put him down again. Ever! Tightening his hands into fists, he punched Matt squarely on the nose, sending him stumbling backwards before falling on his butt. Blood gushed from the bigger boy's nose, and tears streamed from the corners of his eyes. The other three boys stared down at their fallen friend in shocked silence.

Matt gurgled a string of obscenities before shouting at his buddies, "Get him!"

The group jumped Xavier and wrestled him to the ground. He struggled against them, but it was no use. He was sorely outnumbered, and without his powers, he didn't stand a chance against four older, bigger boys. Matt climbed to his feet and loomed over him, wiping blood from his face.

"Stand him up," he spat nasally.

The three goons holding him jerked him to his feet and held his arms. Matt shuffled forward and stood nose-to-nose with him. Fury and hatred filled his eyes and without a word, he sucker-punched him in the stomach. Xavier grunted loudly, doubled over, and gasped to regain his breath.

"You crazy freak! Did you really think you could take *me*? Did you?" Matt bellowed, this time punching him in the face.

An explosion of white blinded him followed by throbbing, hot pain.

"Hold him still, guys," Matt barked, glee sticking to his voice.

Xavier looked up just as Matt swung and punched him again, this time in the nose. He would have fallen to his knees if Matt's cronies weren't holding him upright. He could feel the bitter-sweet taste of blood as he tried to swallow.

"I think he's gonna pass out, Matt," one boy sneered.

"Look! He's crying like a little girl!" Another laughed.

"He'll be doing more than that when I'm done with him," Matt spat out, punching him again.

Xavier could taste bile after the last blow and struggled not to throw up. Fear and anger surged through his body. He knew Matt wouldn't stop until he couldn't stand, lost consciousness, or was dead. He prayed desperately for his powers to return. He would repay their brutality in kind. He would cause them unmentionable pain and suffering. He would make them wallow in pain and cry for their mamas! They would rue the day they laid a finger on him.

Suddenly, the three thugs holding Xavier dropped to the ground screaming in agony. Large, painful-looking blisters surfaced over every inch of their bodies. Matt stood transfixed and horrified at the sight before turning to the small, pale-haired boy.

"My turn," Xavier whispered with a smirk, slowly wiping the blood from his face.

He thrust his hand out at Matt, striking him instantly with an electro force that propelled him several feet backwards. The larger boy landed with an unmistakable snap as his left leg shattered on impact. He screamed. But, Xavier took no pity as he strolled arrogantly toward him and stood over him, another force spinning wildly in his hand.

"Please! Please don't kill me! Please," Matt cried.

He lowered his hand, stunned by the boy's fear and pleas, but the force continued to spin in his palm. He closed his eyes and tried to concentrate on pulling the force back, but it had no effect. It continued to swirl, growing more and more out of control. He stumbled backwards, trying to put as much distance between his out of control force and Matt. He couldn't squelch it. It would erupt in a matter of seconds.

He looked wildly at the other boy. "I can't...I can't stop it! Run! You've gotta run!"

Matt struggled to his feet, but his deformed leg

wouldn't support his weight and crumpled underneath him. He screamed, tears running freely down his cheeks now. "Please! Please don't!"

With a blinding white light and a loud crack, the king appeared a few feet away looking angry and dangerous.

"Daddy's here," he intoned softly just as Xavier's force exploded from his hand.

His father jumped into action, and in less than a blink of an eye, the king surrounded Matt with a shielding force. The rogue force struck and bounced harmlessly away. Xavier expelled a sigh of relief and before he could turn to his father to explain, a force slammed him painfully to the muddy earth. He tried to push himself to his feet, but he couldn't move a single muscle, not even his pinky finger. He was helpless and defenseless. His father strode toward him, squatted, and smiled sadly down at him. Xavier's heart hammered in his chest and plump tears filled his eyes and dropped heavily to the ground.

"It's time to stop running, son. Everything's going to be okay," his father whispered as he stroked his cheek softly. It was the last memory Xavier had before he drifted off into oblivion.

Chapter 27

Quarantine

When Xavier opened his eyes, he found himself in an unfamiliar chamber. Ignoring the throbbing pain behind his eyes, he sat up and looked around the small, bare enclosure. Aside from the small twin bed he was sitting on, the room was sparsely furnished with nothing more than a small plastic table and chair, a small bookcase with a few magazines and books, a small sink, and a toilet. It was a prison cell. His father had thrown him in prison! Panic gripped him and he struggled to breathe properly. He would face charges for using his empowerments against the people of Warwood. He would be caned! Tears flooded his eyes and plopped onto his cheeks. He deserved it! He could have killed people. Heck, he might have! The lump wedged in his throat grew bigger, making it painful to swallow. Robbie! He had nearly killed Robbie! Her unconscious image still haunted him. Then there was Lana. She was the closest thing he had to a mother and he had attacked her! She probably hated him now. She might even decide she didn't want to be a mother to a boy like him and break up with his dad. His dad would be angry and hurt, and it would be entirely his fault! Yes, his father would cane him. He deserved at least that much.

Slowly he rose from the bed and approached the metal

door. He wasn't surprised to find it locked. Isn't that what they did to prisoners, after all? Lock them away in a tiny cell and forget about them until it was time to punish them? A restless, sullen energy grew in the pit of Xavier's stomach and fought to explode. Fighting against the energy, he paced around the small chamber. Where was he? The Governing Hall? A cell in the palace itself? Where was Robbie? Was she all right? What about Lana? He sank onto the bed and released a bitter sigh. He fought back the fear and tears threatening to overtake him as his mind reeled from the strange events that had occurred over the past few months. Why had his empowerments suddenly gone haywire? Was something inside him broken? Maybe deep down the darkness inside him was taking over. Maybe, just maybe, his worst fear was coming true— the prophet had gotten it backwards. Could it be that he was not the Chosen at all but the Dark King destined to destroy the kingdom and bring misery? The latest events seem to confirm this thought. He'd already brought about fear and pain to much of the kingdom. Tears plopped heavily onto his cheeks. What would happen to him now? Only his father could answer that. He needed his father! Panicked and desolate, he lunged toward the metal door.

"Hello? Hello? I want to see my father! Please!"

Silence.

"Hey! Can anyone hear me?"

More silence.

"Open the damn door!" he blared, pounding on the door as his temper heated. "I have rights!" He wasn't sure what rights a prince had after attacking his own kingdom, but he was certain he should be allowed a phone call, a visitor, a lawyer, *something*!

Anxiety mounted inside him and he felt the urge to cuss, scream, hit, and kick at the door until someone listened. But before he could implement the idea, there was an echoing click and the door swung open. He staggered backwards and stared into his father's grave face.

"You're awake," the king muttered, entering the room and closing the door behind him.

Filled with apprehension, he whispered weakly, "Where am I? Jail?"

"No, son. We're at King's Mountain," he responded, sinking onto the bed and patting the mattress next to him.

Xavier sat on the bed next to his father as the questions racing inside him rushed out. "Why are we here, Dad? Did the High Council banish me or something? How are Robbie and Lana? Are they okay? What about Loren and Ephraim?"

The king held up his hand against the onslaught of inquiries. "They're all just fine, son. Robbie has a small bump on her head, but she'll be okay. Lana has a mild case of hypothermia, nothing serious. And, no, you haven't been banished. I've brought you here for your protection as well as for the protection of our citizens."

Xavier's eyes filled with tears. "I didn't mean to hurt anyone, Dad. I swear it! I just...I can't control them anymore. I could have killed Robbie and Lana! I nearly did! I nearly killed them, Dad!" His tears dropped heavily from his eyes and rolled down his cheeks.

"I know you didn't intentionally mean to harm anyone. It's all right," Jeremiah replied, pulling the boy into his arms and rubbing his back soothingly. "It's not your fault. I blame myself for not recognizing you were in trouble. The prophet warned me this day would come."

He straightened and looked at his father with disbelief. "What? The prophet *told* you I would lose control of my powers? Why didn't you tell me? God! I thought I was going insane...that maybe I wasn't worthy! I thought...maybe...maybe the prophecy got it wrong. *You should have told me, Dad!*"

"You're right. I should have told you, but so much has happened over the past year that I didn't want to burden you further. I'm sorry, son," his father told him softly, stroking his cheek with the back of his hand. "However," he continued, lifting the boy's chin and forcing him to meet his unwavering eyes, "if you had just told me when all this began, you could have avoided much of this."

His head dropped. His father was right. He should have gone to him when he first started having problems. He should have listened to Court and Robbie.

"I know. Robbie and Court told me to talk to you, but..." Xavier mumbled.

"But what?"

He glanced briefly up at his father. "I guess...I was afraid."

"Afraid? Lord! Son, I don't want you to ever be afraid of telling me anything!" Jeremiah replied quietly.

"I know, but I don't want to disappoint you. I'd rather you cane me within an inch of my life than for you to be embarrassed of me again," he answered, bashfully meeting his father's eyes.

The king shifted uncomfortably beside him. "Xavier, don't you know that no matter what happens, I'll always love you? Nothing you do will ever change that."

Xavier nodded, and Jeremiah pulled him into his arms. He felt the knot of anxiety and guilt he had fought with over the last few weeks melt away. Relief washed over him and soon, he was sobbing like an infant in his father's arms. When he could cry no more, he dropped into a deep, peaceful sleep in the security and comfort of his father's arms.

When Xavier woke again, he felt his father's warmth around him and smiled. He opened his eyes and looked up at the man who still held him.

"Hey," he whispered awkwardly.

"How are you feeling?" his father asked quietly.

He shrugged. "Tired. My body is kind of achy."

Jeremiah nodded. "I'd be surprised if you weren't exhausted, son. You're experiencing a surge, an increase of new powers at an extremely high rate, which makes it difficult if not nearly impossible for you to control them. The volume of empowerments you've been exhibiting would drain anyone. It takes a lot of energy to conjure and control those powers. Therefore, your bedtime until further notice is 9 o'clock."

Xavier smiled at his feeble attempt at lightening the mood. "Dad?"

He hugged him closer. "Yes?"

"Well, I was just wondering...when did you get the ability to control gravity?" He looked up at his father's stunned face. "Wasn't that the power you used to hold me to the ground like a magnet? I never knew you could do that, or that knocking out thing either!"

He laughed. "Your old man impressed you, eh?"

Xavier blushed and smiled. "Maybe a little."

Snickering, his father explained, "The prophet and I made a presentation to the High Council to obtain the abilities I would need to save you. They didn't even choose to deliberate on the matter. They voted on the spot that I should be endowed with everything necessary to help you."

"Why? Why would they give a crap about me after what I did? I mean... maybe the prophet got it wrong. What if I'm not the Chosen? What if I'm really the Dark King," he blurted out his fears as fresh tears dropped onto his cheeks.

252

"Xavier," his father began firmly, sitting up and turning the boy to face him. "Listen to me, son. I have no doubt in my mind that you *are* the Chosen. There is no way you could possibly be the Dark King. You are far from being dark in any way. You are a good, kind boy. You will be a superb leader for our people, a far greater king than me."

He quickly wiped the tears from his cheeks and looked up at his father. "No, I won't. You're the best king Warwood has ever seen. I can't possibly be better than you. I just want to be as good as can to make you proud."

Jeremiah smiled. "Oh, son, I am proud. And, I appreciate your words, but as your father, I want better for you. You wait and see. You will surpass me in every way!"

"Not if I can't control my powers, I won't," he muttered grumpily.

"With some training and some time, you'll regain control of them, but before we can start working on your powers, you must learn to discipline your emotions. An uncontrolled emotion makes it difficult to control anything else."

"Yeah, I figured that out already. It seemed that most the time I lost control of my powers whenever I got mad or upset...or...uh...well, whenever I had *any* strong feelings," Xavier answered with a blush.

His father nodded and asked, "Did you only lose control of your powers when you lost control of your emotions?"

"Yeah, pretty much. Well...except... I nearly dropped a boulder on Mr. Sims. I wasn't upset or anything when that happened. It just...happened."

"Yes, Loren briefed me about that incident after it occurred," Jeremiah noted. "At the time, we believed it was a result of your injuries from your encounter with William."

Xavier paused, thinking through all the times when his

powers had failed him. "Well, there was the fire incident at the theater. I wasn't upset at all then; I just lost control. Oh, and the first day of school when I was really sick? I wasn't sick. My telepathy was working in hyper-drive. It was like everyone's thoughts in the kingdom attacked me at once. Man, did that hurt."

Jeremiah smirked. "I bet it did. So aside from the boulder, fire, and first day of school, there wasn't any other time when your powers faltered or surged without cause?"

He shook his head.

"What about the food fight at the dinner?"

He could only stare up at his father. "H...how did you know about that?"

"Henrick," Jeremiah answered simply. "He told me about it after you ran away. He felt the incident was relevant. So, was the food fight unprovoked?"

"Ah, no...not exactly." Xavier blushed. "I just...I wasn't mad or scared or anything, but...I was with Robbie, and....she's just...she's really beautiful."

His father smiled and nodded. "I see. You were feeling attracted towards her. Right?"

He nodded, avoiding eye contact. He was grateful he didn't have to go into detail explaining what he had felt.

"Well, we'll begin training this evening. You will train twice a day for the next few months..."

"Whoa, wait a minute! Few months? Just how long am I going to be here?"

"As long as it takes to accomplish control."

"And how long will that be, Dad?"

His father hesitated before responding, "At least until the spring equinox."

"The what?"

"Spring equinox, March 20th."

Xavier looked up at his father incredulously. "But...but,

that's nearly six months away! You mean I'm going to be locked up here for six months?" he blared.

Jeremiah tensed and his hands flexed out at his sides. The boy was working himself up into another eruption. "Xavier," he intoned firmly, "settle down before you lose control and I'm forced to restrain you."

He lowered his voice a decibel. "But...but six months? Six months of solitude stuck here? Six months trapped underground? Six months without my friends, without Robbie?" Xavier jumped to his feet and began pacing, his voice rising with each word. "It's not fair!" He could feel the powers surging inside him and he tried to push them back.

His father sensed the building powers and approached him cautiously. "Son, you need to stop it now. Close your eyes and think calming thoughts."

"No, damn it! I want to know why I have to stay here for six months!" he shouted and the room lurched, sending the king to the floor.

"Damn it, boy!" he shouted, army-crawling over to him and grabbing him.

Xavier felt, saw, and thought nothing as everything went black and he sunk into the sweet abyss of sleep.

Chapter 28

First Training Lesson

When Xavier woke again, he was alone in his bed chamber. A covered tray of food sat invitingly on the table. He could smell the roast beef from his bed and his stomach rumbled.

He sat up and nearly passed out from the pounding in his head. Slowly, he sank back into the bed and released a long sigh. It was several long minutes before he ventured to sit up again, and when he did, he did so very slowly and made his way over to the food. When he lifted the tray and saw the food, his stomach growled again in response. He eagerly grabbed the plate, hurried back to his bed, and wolfed down the first sandwich without tasting a crumb of it. He savored the second, closing his eyes to the juices and flavors exploding in his mouth. God, it tasted heavenly. When he was finished, he brushed the crumbs from his shirt and stared at the metal door. He knew it would be locked, but he got up and tried it anyway. Confirming his suspicions, he walked to the small shelf with books and magazines, picked up *Rugby Today*, sat on his bed, and began to leaf through it.

An hour ticked by and Xavier tossed the magazine to the floor. Energy swelled in him, and he itched to move, to explore, to do something, anything! He jumped to his feet and did a hundred jumping jacks, but the energy continued to eat at him. He dropped to the floor and did as many push-ups as he could before collapsing. He lay against the stone floor, worshipping the cool surface before rolling to lie on his back to do sit-ups. Another hour ticked by as Xavier tried to work off the excessive energy pulsating inside him. Finally, a loud click from the metal door announced he had a visitor. He scrambled back to his bed as the door creaked open and his father and Ephraim entered the room. Ephraim closed the door and leaned casually against it as the king approached him.

"How are you feeling, son?"

He shrugged, staring at his father's shoes, embarrassed to make eye contact.

Jeremiah grabbed the plastic chair from the table and twirled it around to face Xavier. As he lowered himself into the chair, he studied the boy sitting meekly before him and chuckled softly.

"There's no need for the long face. I expect you to struggle with control, son. If this was going to be an easy fix, I'd never have brought you here. All that I ask is that you make every attempt to follow all directions and instructions given to you," he requested, softly.

Xavier nodded, still staring at his feet. For a brief moment nothing was said. Finally, he looked at his father and muttered, "Why do I have to stay here until March, Dad? Why can't I return to the kingdom when I've learned how to control my powers?"

He sighed deeply and stared at his hands clasped in his lap for several seconds before answering. "Son, the prophet has provided us with a lot of insight into this period of your life. You must stay here until the Spring Equinox because, quite simply, you're still a danger until then. Even if you think you have complete control over your abilities, there is still a chance you will hurt someone. Do you really want to risk that, son?"

He squirmed under his father's questioning stare before sighing with resignation. "No, sir. I don't."

"I thought not," his father replied firmly and patted his knee. "I know it's tough to be isolated from your friends and the kingdom. But it's for the best."

"Yes, sir," he muttered.

Jeremiah tousled his son's hair and stood. "Why don't we get out of this chamber and get some training in before dinner?" He returned the chair to the table and waited expectantly for the boy to get to his feet.

With a nod, Xavier followed his father out of the room and into the hall. Ephraim followed close behind as Loren and Henrick filled in on either side of Xavier with tense, taut bodies as though expecting him to attack them at any moment.

Loren and Ephraim entered the fencing room with father and son, fanning out in strategic positions across the chamber. Only Henrick remained outside the doorway. Once the men were in place, Henrick closed and locked the door behind them. Xavier's brows rose with surprise and he looked at his father.

"Henrick's orders are to secure the room until Loren, Ephraim, or I tell him otherwise," he responded to his son's alarmed, questioning stare.

Xavier's eyes widened. It had to be some kind of joke. "You're kidding. Right?"

But the men weren't smiling and they exchanged knowing, anxious glances.

"You're serious. Why? Why would you lock the door?" he questioned, his smile disappearing.

"Son, your powers are out of control. And during these exercises, I'm afraid we must simulate highly stressful circumstances," his father answered.

His stomach dropped with dread and he whispered, "What? What does that mean?"

Again, the generals looked at their king apprehensively.

"Xavier, we must provide situations that produce strong emotional responses from you. How else will you learn to control your emotions?"

He shrugged. He understood what his father would need to do, but he didn't like it. He was still afraid.

"Now, are you ready to begin?" Jeremiah asked.

His entire body tensed. "Y...yes, sir."

"Okay, then. Your fencing lessons are suspended until you've learned some control over your emotions and powers. In the meantime, we'll start hand-to-hand combat training," he announced, stripping off his sweatshirt and tossing it aside.

Ephraim tossed boxing gloves into the center of the room. Xavier approached the equipment, butterflies going mad in his gut.

"Hand-to-hand combat? So you're going to teach me to box? How is that supposed to help me control my feelings?"

His father smiled dryly at him before answering. "Are you saying that the thought of fighting your father doesn't worry you in the least?"

He frowned. "But it's training. You wouldn't really hurt me. It's just boxing."

"First of all, hand-to-hand combat isn't a sport. It isn't boxing. It's survival; it's war. As for me hurting you, I don't *want* to hurt you, son, but there's a war coming, and I'm more interested in you surviving that war. I'm sorry, but I will not hold back my skills or abilities. I will fight you with all my strength," his father answered solemnly.

Xavier gulped, suddenly very nervous about the

training he was about to begin.

"So," Jeremiah began, picking up a pair of gloves and fitting them to Xavier's hands, "the first rule in hand-to-hand combat is that there are no rules."

"No rules?" he responded weakly as his father pulled on his own boxing gloves.

He nodded. "That's right. Before I teach you techniques and strategies in fighting, let's see what skills you already possess. It will help me determine what we need to work on. I want you to give me all you've got, son. Don't hold back because you know I won't."

Xavier gulped and nodded. When his father began to dance around him like a professional boxer, his anxiety pulsated throughout his body. Trying his best to mimic his father's actions, he moved with him, his hands instinctively rising to protect his face.

"Come on. Hit me, Xavier! We're not here to dance!" Jeremiah taunted.

He hesitated, still unsure.

As if sensing weakness, his father jabbed hard at his face, striking his gloves and knocking them into his face. Tears swelled to the surface almost immediately. As he tried to readjust his hands, another punch barreled at his head and he barely ducked and avoided it.

"Jeez, Dad!" he snapped.

"If you don't want my punches to connect, you better start blocking or dodging my blows," Jeremiah answered nonchalantly as he threw a hook, grazing the boy's left temple.

Xavier backpedaled quickly and stumbled to the floor. His father was over him in an instant, his left foot sweeping toward his ribcage. Xavier rolled quickly to avoid the blow, jumped to his feet, and scurried away from the king. But Jeremiah was relentless and was on the attack again. Xavier dodged another jab, ducked under a left hook, before straightening and striking his father's exposed underbelly with a quick, hard jab. With a soft grunt, the king spun around and swung his gloved fist at the rapidly moving boy, missing again.

Loren's snicker echoed from the corner and Xavier's confidence soared.

"Seems the boy isn't the only one who could use some work on his technique," Loren commented dryly.

Xavier advanced, dancing within range, throwing a jab at his father, and dancing out of reach again. "What's the matter, Dad? Am I too fast for you?" he bantered, giggling.

The king answered his son's insolence by lunging forward and using his forearm to shove the boy backwards. He continued to advance in long, powerful strides as his son staggered and wobbled backwards, struggling to keep his footing. Xavier toppled and landed hard on his butt, jarring his confidence and pride in the process. Embarrassment and humiliation clung heatedly to his face and rushed into his extremities.

"Get to your feet, boy," his father ordered, standing imposingly over him.

He scurried to his feet and was met with a quick jab to his chest that knocked the breath from his lungs. Again, he stumbled backwards, barely managing to remain upright.

"Not feeling so cocky now, are you, son?" he taunted.

Heat exploded over Xavier's face and began to gather in his hands. A left hook swept into his view a split-second before pain exploded across the right side of his face and a burst of white flooded his vision. He staggered into something hard and unyielding. Disoriented, he started to push away but strong arms encircled him, holding him in place.

"Xavier, listen to my voice. Listen, breath, and relax

your body and mind," Ephraim whispered.

Xavier took a shaky breath. "I...I can't. I...I'm afraid. I can't do it. I can feel it coming."

"Son." Jeremiah stripped his gloves and tossed them aside. "Son, take deep breaths. You can do this!"

He looked up at his father, shakily. "I...I don't...I don't think..."

The room lurched throwing its occupants to the floor.

"Holy Hell!" Loren yelled.

"Xavier!" Jeremiah barked. "Stop it, son. Concentrate!"

"I can't. I...I..." Another tremor rattled the chamber and a loud crack echoed around the room as a long, thin fissure snacked across the floor.

"Ephraim!" Jeremiah yelled. "Stop him!"

The general's arms tightened around him. Then Xavier felt, saw, and thought nothing.

When he opened his eyes again, he was back in his "cell". He had no idea what time it was or for that matter, what day it was. Moaning, he rubbed at the dull ache behind his eyes.

"Lie still for a few minutes," Ephraim instructed softly from the plastic chair across the room. He stood and moved toward the bed with a glass in one hand and Tylenol clutched in the other. "Here. This will help the headache."

Xavier tried to sit up, but the room spun.

"Take it easy," Ephraim whispered, moving to sit next to him. He helped him up enough so he could take the pills and drink a bit of water. "How do you feel?"

"How the hell do you think I feel?" he blurted, pulling himself out of the general's grasp and propping himself up against the wall in a sitting position. "What time is it?"

Ephraim's brow rose at the boy's cheek, but he answered, "It's 8 o'clock in the morning."

"What? You mean that I've been asleep since yesterday afternoon?"

"Aye."

"Where's Dad?"

"Working."

"Oh," he muttered, absentmindedly rubbing his right cheek.

"It was a rough lesson, eh, laddie?" Ephraim commented, not missing the boy's action.

He nodded. "Yeah, no kidding," he muttered before finally meeting the general's eyes.

"What techniques did you use to try to control the surge?"

"What's that supposed to mean?" he snapped. "I'm trying! Okay? I tried the mediation techniques Mike taught me in telepathy lessons. They don't work. I don't know what to do! I just don't know how to stop it, okay?"

"Calm down, lad. Letting yourself get worked up to begin with doesn't help. Controlling an influx of power is a lot tougher than wielding telepathy. It will take more than mediation to command it."

"Like what?"

"You'll need to develop a strong focal point."

"A focal point? How is staring at a stone in the wall going to help anything?" he spat.

Growing tired of the boy's disrespectful tone, Ephraim shook his head. "That's not what I meant and I'd appreciate it if you'd keep your temper in check and a respectful tongue in your mouth, young sire." After pinning the boy with a hard stare to let the message sink in, he continued more conversationally, "As for the focal point, I was referring to an emotional focal point since it's your emotions that hinder your ability to control your powers. You need to choose a memory, a person, a feeling, something that gives you the greatest sense of peace and emotional strength."

Xavier sank against the wall with a furrowed brow. After giving the boy a moment to work through his thoughts and memories, the general pressed him. "Can you think of something that could serve as a strong focal point?"

"Uh, maybe."

"No maybes. If you're not sure the thought will work, then it won't. Keep thinking."

"Well, the memory I'm thinking of calms me, but it's complicated. It calms me, but makes me a little sad at the same time."

"What's the memory?" Ephraim asked.

"Horse riding with Mom. It makes me smile thinking about riding with her and hearing her squeal whenever Brewster would take off in a full gallop." Xavier smiled as the memory flooded into his thoughts. "But then I remember she's dead...and... how she died."

"I see. Under those circumstances, I don't think it would be the best memory to choose, young sire. Keep thinking." Ephraim stood and crossed to the door. "We'll be back around lunch time for training."

"Mr. Hardcastle? C...could I go look around? I'm tired of being stuck in here. I feel like a prisoner. Please!"

The general began shaking his head long before the boy finished his plea. "I'm leaving the mountain and won't be able to supervise you."

"What about Loren or...or Henrick?"

"Sorry, Loren's not here and Henrick doesn't have clearance to open this door unless your father, Loren, or I permit it."

"Great, thanks for nothing. Why don't you just lock me up in a real jail then?" he spat, scowling.

"I'm sorry, laddie. It's for your own good."

"Yeah, I'm getting tired of hearing that," he muttered, pouting.

"Well, work on finding a good focal point. When you've got that out of the way, you could write letters to your friends. I know Courtney would like to hear from you."

Xavier nodded but continued sulking.

Chapter 29

A Focal Point

It was after lunch before Xavier's door opened again, and his father walked in, smiling.

"Hey there, kiddo! Sleep well?"

"Is that a trick question?" he responded sullenly. "Ephraim used that mojo on me. Of course I slept well. I slept like the dead!"

"Well, look at it this way; you'll have plenty of stamina for this afternoon's training."

Xavier moaned. "More boxing?"

His father stifled a grin. "No. More *hand-to-hand* combat. Ephraim told me he talked to you about a focal point. Did you find one?"

"Yeah."

He had put a lot of thought into his memories and had determined that the relief and security he had felt when his father rescued him from the Institute was extremely strong. This was the memory he chose as his focal point, but it felt awkward to tell his father this, and he hesitated to say more. Fortunately, the king didn't ask him to reveal his decision.

"Good, let's get started then."

He got to his feet and followed his father out of the room. As before, Ephraim, Loren, and Henrick flanked him. Xavier, the king, and his two generals entered the fencing room as Henrick once again closed and secured the door behind them.

Ephraim dumped the boxing equipment onto the floor between father and son before stepping back and standing against the wall.

Xavier stared down at the gloves, his mind suddenly blank as to what to do with them. Jeremiah turned, pulled off his shirt, threw it aside, and approached the unmoving boy. Xavier's eyes widened as he studied the well-defined muscles across his father's torso and arms. Next to the king he was nothing more than a puny, little boy. There was no way he'd ever beat his father at hand-to-hand combat.

"Hand-to-hand combat techniques are a lot like fencing. You seem to do innately well with avoidance maneuvers, but your balance is atrocious. A man can't fight if he's flat on his back," his father stated, raising one eyebrow disapprovingly.

"It's not my fault! You're bigger and stronger! It's not a fair fight!"

"No excuses! Find an advantage! Find a weakness! Every opponent has a weakness. Find mine and use it against me!" his father barked. "Now, just like in fencing, you can feint. You can feint a punch to the body in order to go in for a more devastating hook, uppercut, or jab to the face. And it goes without saying that the use of empowerments during a fight is very beneficial."

"What? You want me to use my empowerments? The same empowerments I can't control? Are you nuts?" he blared, suddenly very nervous about this training session.

"Eventually, yes. Xavier, calm down," Jeremiah ordered softly. "Pay attention to what your body is telling you. Right now, you should be aware of the sensations in your fingertips and toes."

Xavier took a deep breath and closed his eyes. Yes, he felt the surge of powers beginning again. How had his father known? His thoughts whirled and he started to panic. Wait, the focal point, his dad. Concentrating, he focused on seeing his father for the first time at the Institute and his commanding, reassuring voice saying, "Fear not, son. I'm here to free you. I am your father." The tingling in his extremities stopped immediately. He opened his eyes, looked up at his father, and smiled triumphantly. "I did it. I got it to back off!"

"Well done, son," Jeremiah commended, smiling and patting his shoulder.

"How did you know it was about to happen again?"

"Xavier, my telepathy has been connected with you since I entered your chamber. Didn't you feel it?"

He shook his head, blushing at the implications. His father knew that he was his focal point.

"No matter. I'm sure the silence of your telepathy is just another symptom of the influx. Right now, we're more concerned with the more violent effects," his father stated simply. He picked up a pair of boxing gloves and began securing them to Xavier's hands.

"So, the important thing to remember during this exercise is that no matter what is going on around you, be mindful of what your body is trying to tell you."

He nodded. "Yes, sir."

After securing his own gloves, Jeremiah bounced lightly from foot to foot. "Ready?"

Xavier mimicked his father's actions and nodded. "Yeah."

The king attacked suddenly and feinted a hard jab straight to Xavier's face. He pulled the punch just before contact, but it had the desired effect. Xavier's hands jerked up protectively and exposed his waist and ribs. The king hit him with a sharp uppercut to the ribs.

Xavier coughed and gasped, trying to catch his breath, but his father gave him no time to recover and barreled down on him again. Still wheezing, he struggled to counter his father's aggressive moves.

"W...wait," Xavier gasped. "Wait a second."

But the king wasn't waiting. He feigned an uppercut to Xavier's sore abdomen before jabbing at his face. The punch grazed his right cheek. If he hadn't stepped back and turned his head, the jab would have knocked him out cold. Fear and anger sprang him into action, and he tried to answer his father's attack with a right hook. Jeremiah lazily batted his fist away, and then, using the boy's momentum against him, he sent Xavier stumbling past him and gave him a swift, hard kick on the butt as he went.

"Ouch! HEY! That hurt!" he bellowed, rubbing his backside.

The king straightened, looking mildly amused. "Son, it's not supposed to tickle. This is combat training. Now, stop opening yourself up and be prepared for your enemy to feint," he commanded firmly and without pity.

He glared at his father. "But..."

"No buts! Now fight!" he shouted and lunged at the boy.

Xavier scrambled to avoid the attack but was caught off balance, and he fell hard to the floor. Why did he always end up falling on his butt?

"Dad!" he griped, standing and rubbing his sore backside. "Will you stop? God! You're not my enemy! Give me a chance to prepare, would you?"

"Xavier, do you think Fox LeMasters will give you the courtesy of preparing?" he growled impatiently.

"No! But you're not Fox! You're my father!"

"Yes, I am, but I wouldn't be doing my duty as your father if I didn't prepare you for what you'll face. Now, damn it, boy, stop whining and fight!" his father bellowed as he charged toward him again.

Xavier had barely raised his gloves when Jeremiah struck him with a force that rattled his teeth. Sloppily, he swung at his father, but the king simply pushed him away.

"Come on, boy!" his father shouted. "Move your feet, remember your avoidance techniques, and keep your balance!"

Xavier's face ignited with anger. "I'm TRYING! Damn it!" he bellowed and suddenly, electro forces began to shower the room.

Jeremiah froze, looking both anxious and triumphant. "Xavier! Stop. Control it, son. Think of your focal point. Control the anger," he ordered firmly.

Xavier tried. He really did, but the anger he felt toward his father had invaded his entire body, even his head hummed with it. The calming memory of his father didn't seem so calming now. He vaguely heard his father's voice before he felt the familiar warm, relaxing sensation and then, nothing.

Xavier awoke just moments later to find his head cradled in his father's lap where he had caught him as he fell unconscious. Ephraim knelt next to them, his hands lingering above Xavier's head, and Loren stood behind Ephraim, staring down with apprehension.

"Welcome back, son. How do you feel?" Jeremiah asked.

"Fine," he muttered and tried to sit up, but his father stopped him.

"No, Xavier, not yet. I want Loren to check you first," he commanded, holding him in his lap as Loren stepped forward and bent over them.

"God, this is stupid. I'm fine!" Xavier muttered.

"Quiet down, boy," Jeremiah ordered with quiet

authority.

Huffing indignantly, he lay quietly as Loren closed his eyes and slowly waved his hand over his head. As his hand moved over the span of Xavier's upper body, a faint white light flooded over him, soothing his aches and relaxing him.

After a moment, Loren straightened. "He's fine, Jer. His blood pressure is slightly above normal, but he's fine."

With a nod of satisfaction, Jeremiah released him and helped him to his feet.

"It doesn't appear that I'm a good focal point since I'll be the source of much of your anger over the next few months. I think you should find another."

"No, really? You think?" he spat condescendingly. "Why would *that* cause me to need another focal point?" Agitatedly, he jerked out of his father's grasp, but Jeremiah caught him by the arm and spun him to face him.

"Xavier, I understand that you're under a lot of stress, but you are not permitted to talk to me or any other adult like that. You know better than that. Don't be under the delusion that I won't punish you if you're disrespectful. Understand?"

"What are you going to do, Dad? Ground me? Lock me in my room? Oh, wait, you already do that!" he spat sarcastically.

"Xavier, do I need to take you over my knee while Loren and Ephraim look on?"

Xavier's anger and irritability evaporated, and he muttered meekly, "No sir. Sorry, Dad. I'm...I'm just frustrated."

"I know. It'll get better," Jeremiah acknowledged his expression relaxing. "But, you need another focal point for that to happen. Take a few minutes and determine one."

With a nod, Xavier began the task of finding a new focal

point. He knew he couldn't use the calming memories of his mother for they always led to the memories and the premonition of her death. So he considered Robbie. He thought of her large doe-like eyes, her laugh, and her soothing voice. He remembered visiting her bedroom a month ago. He had felt so at ease, so calm, so at home with her leaning against his shoulder listening to him. She was a piece of his soul. He thought about how he would someday marry her, and the thought made him smile as he looked back to his father, who had been waiting and watching silently.

"I've got one. I can do it," he announced.

Jeremiah eyed him for a moment and then, smiled knowingly. "Excellent choice."

Xavier blushed and grinned at his father sheepishly. Loren chuckled behind Jeremiah.

"Are you two ready, yet?" the general asked, mocking impatience.

The king gave a nod and began dancing from foot to foot. Xavier matched his movements and shortly his father swung at him, but this time, he was ready. He ducked under the punch, and unleashed a hard uppercut to the king's ribs. Jeremiah coughed as his breath was forced from his lungs. Feeling triumphant, he stood relaxed as his father righted himself, but the king was a skilled, merciless fighter. He attacked Xavier with quick repetitive blows that sent him stumbling backwards until he slammed against the wall. Pain shot through his entire body, but he had no time to languish in it. He scrambled across the room and tried to prepare himself just as the king turned, yanked off his right glove, and propelled an electro force at him. He dove to the floor as the searing heat of the force passed over him. Livid, he jumped to his feet.

"Geez, Dad! What if you had hit me?"

"Both Loren and I can heal injuries," Jeremiah responded and lunged another force at him.

Again, he dove to the floor as fear and anger overwhelmed his senses. Electro forces began ricocheting around the room and balls of fire fell from the ceiling.

His father lowered his hands. "Calm yourself, boy. Think of Robbie."

He tried to picture Robbie and think of all the things that made him so content just moments ago, but he couldn't. He closed his eyes and desperately tried to push away the anger, but it was still consuming his body.

"I... I can't. I can't!" Xavier moaned. "It's too hard...too powerful."

"Damn it, boy! Stop whining and concentrate!" Jeremiah barked loudly.

His father's sudden, harsh order jolted him out of his pessimistic thoughts. He closed his eyes and concentrated on Robbie, starting with her eyes. They reminded him of chocolate. Her thick dark eyelashes curled on the ends and somehow made her eyes seem larger. Her skin was beautiful, creamy, and smooth. He itched to touch her soft, silky skin. Then there was her hot body. She was so beautiful, and he loved the new curves she had developed.

"Okay, son. I think you'd better stop there," his father snickered interrupting the course of his thoughts. "We don't need another influx that those thoughts would undoubtedly bring."

He opened his eyes to his father's smiling face. Slowly, he peered around the calm, tranquil room.

"I...I did it?" he questioned, looking back at his father.

"You sure did! Well done, son. Well done!" he exclaimed, pulling off his other glove and clapping the boy's shoulder.

"Let's see if he can repeat it," Ephraim stated with a

grim expression.

The king's smile dropped marginally and he looked from Ephraim back to Xavier. "He's right. Controlling your powers once is not what we're aiming for here. You need to be able to command them easily, every time. Let's have another go at it, but this time I want to spar only with powers."

"What? You want me to *intentionally* conjure my powers and attack you?"

Jeremiah nodded, pulling off Xavier's boxing gloves and tossing them aside. "Yes, that's exactly what I want you to do."

"But...what if I hurt you like last time?" he questioned, his brow furrowing with worry.

"You won't. Not this time. I'm a very powerful blocker, thanks to the Kings' Key," Jeremiah noted, winking playfully down at him.

Xavier wasn't convinced, but it appeared he had no choice in the matter. He would have to trust that his father was right. With a heavy sigh, he nodded.

"Don't look so worried; it will be fine. Trust me." His father laughed as he walked to the other end of the room and faced him.

"Well, if you're wrong, at least I have witnesses that will testify on my behalf," he retorted, attempting to make light of the anxiety he felt.

"That you do, young sire," Loren remarked, nodding to him.

With a chuckle, Jeremiah warned, "Make ready, son."

He got into a boxing stance, not knowing how else to stand during an empowerment spar.

"Okay, now conjure an electro force and attack me," he ordered.

Xavier tried, he really did, but nothing more than a

faint glow would materialize in his palm. After five minutes of trying to simply conjure the force, Jeremiah was growing impatient.

"Xavier, what in the Hell are you doing?" he spat out. "Stop worrying about me and conjure the bloody force already!"

He couldn't help but worry about hurting his father and the other men in the room! He still had nightmares about the night he had nearly single-handedly destroyed his own kingdom. He still woke up in terror dreaming that his father had died and the council had banished him.

Jeremiah grazed his hip with a stinging force.

"Ouch! Bloody Hell, Dad. That hurt!"

"Good! Maybe it'll snap you out of it!"

He peered down at his hand again, and sure enough, he found a spiraling, glowing electro force in his palm. Grimacing, he propelled it at his father.

The king ducked, easily avoiding the force, and sent another force barreling toward Xavier, who barely managed to sidestep the attack.

"Well, done! Now, again!" Jeremiah barked.

Concentrating greatly on conjuring another controlled electro force in his hand, Xavier didn't see his father's force until it was too late. The force hit him squarely in the chest and knocked him on his butt. Pain shot up his spine and a string of profanities slipped from his mouth before he glared at his father.

"Why did you do that?"

"You're taking too long!"

He slowly got to his feet, gingerly dusting off his backside. "Well, *excuse* me if I can't conjure forces easily anymore! I'm going through an *influx* after all!"

"No excuses! Just do it!"

"I am! Would you just give me a freaking minute!" he

blared at his father before conjuring another force and launching it angrily at him. Jeremiah couldn't duck to avoid this one and barely managed to lift his hand to block it.

"Wow!" Jeremiah exclaimed, grinning. "That was terrific, son!"

Still annoyed at his father, he barely managed a weak smile, but it quickly dropped from his face. Something was wrong! The tingling sensation still raged in his fingertips. He looked at his hands and recoiled at the force he saw swirling wildly there. It was gaining momentum and strength. He stumbled backwards.

"Control it, son. Pull it back."

Xavier didn't get the chance before the force shot sparks and eruptions across the room, narrowly missing Loren and Ephraim. Panic and terror filled every fiber of his being. The sensation felt eerie like the force that set fire to the woods and nearly killed Robbie.

"Xavier! Control your emotions!" his father shouted.

He couldn't do it! The force was too strong!

"I...I..."

Another stream of pure energy erupted from his hand, and then another.

Suddenly, his body went cold, ice cold, and the force vanished. Shivering, he looked up at his father and then to the large hand on his shoulder.

"W...w...what was th...that?" he managed through chattering teeth.

"Negation. I wasn't sure I would be able to wield it so easily the first time," the king answered, staring at his hand in awe.

"I...I th...think I like the oth...other power bet...ter."

The men laughed heartily at the boy's declaration. Jeremiah pulled his cloak around the boy, still snickering.

"I bet you do."

"Sire? He won't be able to acquire his abilities for at least an hour or two, until the negation wears off," Loren told him. "Maybe this would be a good time for a hot meal?"

Jeremiah nodded. "I think you're right, Loren. Come on, Xavier. Let's get something warm and tasty in you. It'll make you feel better."

Chapter 30

Love Triangle

One morning during his third week at the mountain, Xavier awoke stiff and sore from the previous day's training. Stretching, he sat up and yawned loudly. The clock on the shelf next to his bed read just after eight; his father would be coming soon for his morning lesson. He stood slowly and started to shuffle toward the toilet but stopped. A small yellow envelope was on the floor next to the door where someone had slid it under the crack. Xavier immediately recognized Robbie's handwriting and lunged for the letter. He tore open the envelope, and the pendant Robbie had given him for his 13th birthday fell out onto the floor along with a piece of flowery yellow and blue paper. He picked up the pendant and looped it quickly over his head before reading the letter.

Dear Xavier,

I miss you so much! Of course I'm not mad at you for what happened in the woods. I know you'd never try to hurt me. It was an accident. So don't worry about it. Ok? I was really honored that you decided to use me as your focal point in your training. I know it's hard training, but maybe the pendant will help. It'll be like a piece of me is with you. I wish your dad would let me come and visit. He won't even consider it! He just says that it isn't safe and there's no discussion. You know how he gets.

Things here are going ok. Court got a new ability the other day when he was arguing with Erica. She got really angry with him and tried to slap him, but the next thing either of them knew, Erica was hanging upside down five feet in the air. It surprised Erica so much that she forgot she was mad at him and roped him into playing a practical joke on Sara. Every time Sara tried to put on lipstick, Court would make the lipstick jerk and horribly messed it up. He did it six times before Sara realized something dodgy was going on. It was funny. Erica seems to always be in trouble with Loren. I overheard Erica's mom telling my mom that Loren's cracking down on her inconsiderate, wild ways.

I'm doing fine other than I miss you so much! Beckley has finally stopped calling me the royal concubine. Actually he's been really nice to me since you left. Like, the other day when I was really upset and missing you, he sat and listened to me blubber. He's actually a sweet and sensitive guy when he's not around the other boys. Anyway, I think of you all the time. I wish I could be there to help you in person. And, I love you too, Xavier.

Love always,
Robbie

Xavier read and re-read the letter half a dozen times. Finally, unable to sit still any longer, he jumped to his feet and began pacing the width of the small chamber. He could feel energy crackling around him, but for the first time since he arrived at the mountain, he didn't care. A cold, black emotion was swelling inside him, clawing its way to the surface. Overwhelmed and aching for a release from his misery, he turned and punched the stone wall. Pain exploded up his hand, and his bed burst into flames.

Anger, not fear, pulsated through his body, and he threw the bed across the room, crashing into the small bookshelf on the opposite wall. Books and magazines ignited and the flames raged into a wild inferno. The stone floor, walls, and ceiling acted as a conductor for the heat, and it wasn't long until the chamber felt like an oven. The fire continued to grow like a living, breathing beast and spewed out thick, poisonous smoke that filled the small chamber. That was when the fear came. Xavier panicked and launched himself at the locked metal door.

"H...help!" he choked out, banging frantically on the door. "Help! Oh, God, please! Please, open the door. My room is on fire! Help!" he screamed, beating on the door and choking on the suffocating smoke.

Within seconds, the door swung open with a loud screech, and Loren grabbed him and pulled him out into the safety of the hallway. He pinned Xavier against the wall, his arms on either side of his head. Henrick and another guard Xavier didn't recognize raced into the room while he leaned against the large general coughing and fighting to clear his lungs of the poisonous fumes he'd inhaled. A loud whirling sound and a splash came from his room followed by a crash and scuffling. Finally he regained the ability to breathe without coughing up a lung, and the two men exited his chamber with a nod at Loren.

"Good job, Henrick, Turner. Clear out of the corridor and contact King Wells. I'll secure the Prince in the alternative chamber." The general didn't move until both men were out of sight. In that moment, Xavier realized that Loren had shielded him with his massive body the entire time in order to protect Henrick and Turner from *him*. "Come on, Xavier. Let's get you settled in your new room."

Loren stepped back, but Xavier didn't budge. His legs were shaky and weak. If he tried to walk now, he would collapse. The terror he had felt moments ago morphed into a dark depression, and he felt dangerously close to tears.

"Come on, kiddo," Loren encouraged gently wrapping an arm around him and guiding him into a small chamber across the hall. It was identical to his old room. There was a small twin bed, a table with two chairs, a toilet, a sink, and a small bookcase. "Are you okay?" he prodded. "Do you have any burns?"

Xavier shook his head and managed a hoarse croak. "I'm fine."

"Are you sure? Does it hurt to breathe? You inhaled a lot of smoke."

Again he shook his head.

Loren rubbed his crown affectionately. "All right. I need to help Henrick and Turner with the report and make sure your old room is dealt with." He paused and shifted his weight anxiously. "Your dad will be here soon." Then without another awkward word, he left the room, closed the door, and jammed the exterior lock into place.

Slowly Xavier shuffled to the bed and sat down. Pain finally registered in his hand, and he gazed down to find the letter still clutched in his hand. Slowly, he loosened his grip on the paper; his hand was already swelling. With his uninjured hand he tried to smooth out the wrinkles in the letter.

It wasn't fair! Why did he have to be here? Why couldn't he see his friends? Why couldn't he see Robbie? Beck was making moves on her and there wasn't a damn thing he could do about it trapped in this freaking mountain. His father was being overly protective and a complete ass about it!

Frustrated and overwhelmed, he hugged his knees against his chest and rocked anxiously. He sighed miserably. He would never see Robbie or any of his friends now. Destroying his room would only confirm his father's fears that he was still a danger to others. He would be stuck here by himself for months! Xavier let the tears come then. He simply cried, feeling lonely and sorry for himself. He wished he could see Robbie, just once! He would feel better if he could see her, hear her laugh, touch her, but he knew his father would never allow it. So, he cried.

It was nearly a half hour later when the door finally opened and the king marched into the room. Without a word, he grabbed a chair from the table, spun it around to face Xavier, and sat.

Xavier's eyes dropped to the floor as his father studied him intently.

"What happened, Xavier?" he asked quietly.

He glanced up at his father's penetrating eyes before looking back down at his bare feet. He shrugged.

"A shrug isn't an answer. Explain to me how the fire started."

Xavier sniffed, but he didn't answer and continued to stare at his toes. He wiggled them nervously.

The king sighed heavily, his patience waning. "Xavier, I want verbal answers, son! No more shrugs. What in the hell hap..." his words dropped away when he saw the pendant dangling around the boy's neck. He lifted the pendant into his palm and rubbed his thumb over the gleaming tree etched into the surface before letting it drop back into place. He looked at his son's down-cast head. He shoved his hand through his hair as he began to put the pieces together. "Did you get a letter from Robbie today?"

He nodded meekly and sighed shakily.

"Did something in the letter upset you?"

Again, he nodded.

Jeremiah sighed sympathetically before pulling the boy

into a warm hug, stroking his head and back. "Love can be a double-edged sword sometimes, but I know how much Robbie loves you, Xavier. The girl has pestered me on a daily basis with questions about how you're doing, how your training is going, and when she will be allowed to visit. Anyone can see how much she cares about you." He withdrew enough to peer into his son's eyes. "But all of that pales in comparison to her thoughts about you. I can hear her thoughts so clearly, she might as well shout them from the turrets of the castle!"

Xavier's eyes lit up. "You heard her thoughts? What did you hear? She said in the letter that she's not mad at me about what happened. Did she mean that? Does she still want to be my girlfriend? What does she think about Beck?"

Jeremiah held up his hands to the boy's onslaught of questions and chuckled. Upon hearing his last question, he dropped his hands and looked at his son, bewildered. "Why would she be thinking about Beck?"

He shrugged but answered, "I guess he's been really *chummy* with her since I left the kingdom. He listens to her and hangs out with her when she's missing me."

Jeremiah nodded. "I see. Now this all makes perfect sense. You're jealous."

"Well...he's moving in on her! I know he is! I...I just feel so helpless stuck here and not able to protect what's mine!" he whined. His steely glare met his father's. "She's my girl! He'd better back off!"

"Xavier, Robbie chose you, right?" After the boy nodded his response, his father continued quickly, "Then why are you so insecure about losing her to anyone?"

"I don't know. I guess because I miss her and because I can't see her every day."

"Do you trust Robbie?"

"What?"

"Do you trust her?"

"Yeah...of course, I trust her. I'd trust her with my life."

"Then why don't you trust her about this?"

"I...I trust her. I just don't trust *him*!"

Jeremiah nodded his understanding. "Son, it takes two to tango. You can't lose her to Beck unless she chooses him. So, instead of threatening Beck to stay away from Robbie, you should have faith in Robbie."

His father's words made sense, but it was hard not to feel animosity toward Beck for making moves on Robbie. After all, Beck was supposed to be his friend. It was disrespectful to their friendship. Not to mention, he was future king. Surely it would be like...treason or something!

The king was obviously reading his thoughts. "Xavier, even if Beck is trying to win Robbie's favor, how is that any different from what you did here at the mountain last year?"

Ouch! That was a low blow, but his father was right.

"How do I not feel jealous, then? I don't want to feel like this, but I don't know how not to," he mumbled.

"Just let it go. Keep yourself busy with other things, like your training. Write letters to Robbie often so that she misses you less..."

"If you'd let her come for a short visit, we'd miss each other a lot less!" he interrupted.

"No, son. It's just not the right time. It's not safe for either of you."

He sighed weightily before muttering, "I knew you'd say that."

"Sorry about that, but you know it's true."

Xavier groaned as he buried his face in his hands before hissing at the throbbing pain in his right hand.

"Here. Let me have a look at that hand."

Chapter 31

First Success

Xavier's training on controlling his emotions during hand-to-hand combat and empowerment spars continued. After several weeks of this, the time had finally come to combine the two. All his previous successes seemed inconsequential as he struggled to conjure and utilize his powers while fighting hand-to-hand. As the day wore on, his ability to control his abilities was quickly diminishing, along with his father's patience.

"Focus, boy!" Jeremiah growled, perspiration beading on his forehead as he sent a stinging electro force at Xavier.

The force hit Xavier's left side, tossing him off balance and sending him hard to the floor. They had been at it for hours. His empowerments were hit or miss at best. Some simply refused to present themselves at any level, whereas the others came out with an uncontrollable vengeance.

"I AM FOCUSING!" Xavier blared angrily at his father, unintentionally bombarding the king with baseball-sized hail.

Jeremiah held up a shield to deflect the majority of the frozen missiles his son had unwittingly directed at him. "I can see that," he responded dryly when a chunk of ice came uncomfortably close to his groin.

Xavier closed his eyes and concentrated on Robbie and soon the smashing of icy debris vanished. He opened his eyes and found his father nodding approvingly.

"Good! Now that you're focused, try again."

"Awe, come on, Dad! I'm so tired that I can hardly feel my feet! Can't I stop now? It's hard to concentrate."

"Xavier, the more tired you become, the more important it is for you to be able to effortlessly control yourself and your powers," he stated matter-of-factly. "Now, fight!"

The king threw the first punch, but he saw the punch coming, ducked, and struck him in the ribs before dancing out of reach. Jeremiah sent a blazing force at him, knocking him backwards. Barely managing to stay on his feet, he answered with his own force, but the king lazily blocked it.

"Good! Again!" his father commanded.

His next attempt at conjuring an electro force proved less successful. The force simply swirled weakly in his palm, impotent. When he attempted again, the force refused to materialize at all and Xavier lost his patience.

"GRRR! This is hopeless!" he blared, throwing his hands into the air.

"Xavier, if you quit, you'll never learn to break through these dry spells," his father stated bluntly. "The Prince of Warwood is not a quitter."

"Then I guess I'm not the Prince of Warwood because I'm not doing this anymore! I'm tired and I'm going to bed!" he spat out, turning and stomping to the door. When the door didn't unlock and open, he glared up at Loren. "Open the door, Loren. I want to go back to my room."

The general looked at the king before responding. "Sorry, young sire. Your father's right."

"This is stupid!" Xavier blared, angrily. His eyes darted

to Ephraim, who stood tensely a few feet away. "Let me out!" he yelled at the second general.

Ephraim slowly shook his head, his eyes never leaving Xavier's.

"GOD!" he shouted and kicked the door, before pacing angrily. Energy crackled around him and all three men watched the boy warily.

"Stop whining, Xavier. Do you think Fox will care if you're too tired for battle?" his father challenged.

"This isn't a war!" he screamed, glaring at his father. "This is training! And I don't give a damn about Fox!" Sparks erupted from his fingertips as he pointed at the reinforced lead-lined door. "Open the damn door, Dad!"

"No," his father answered as he stepped toward him. "Do you really think we're not at war, son? Are you truly that foolish? Of course this is war! We are in a desperate war to win control over your powers!"

"Shut up! Just shut the hell up! I'm tired, and I'm not going to do it!" he shouted, stepping toward the king with his hands clenched at his sides.

"Watch it, Xavier! Don't talk to me..."

"I SAID SHUT UP!" Xavier shouted.

Suddenly, the king clutched his throat, gasping and wheezing. Unable to catch his breath, he sank to his knees, his eyes wide with fear.

Loren raced to the king's side and glared angrily at the boy. "Xavier! Stop it! Stop it now!"

He stared down at his father unbelievingly, not quite grasping what was going on.

"Xavier!" Ephraim shouted. "You're killing your father!"

He snapped his head up toward the second general as if not quite hearing him. He looked back at his father, who was close to passing out.

"Oh, shit!" he mumbled, looking back at Ephraim.

"Knock me out! Knock me out!"

"No, *you* must stop it! Just stop it, Xavier!"

"I don't know how!"

"Try! He doesn't have much time!"

"Then knock me out! Please!"

"Not until you make the attempt on your own!"

He looked back at his father helplessly. He frantically looked around as if the solution to stopping what was happening could be found in the room.

"Damn it, Xavier. Search inside yourself for the answer! You can't stop it by looking around the bloody room! Concentrate on yourself!" Ephraim demanded.

Xavier snapped his eyes closed, fighting the panic mounting inside him. *"Oh God, oh God, oh God! How am I going to do this? Okay."* He took a deep, shaky breath. *"I've gotta calm down. I've gotta calm down and imagine Dad breathing."*

He concentrated on his own breathing and calming his thoughts. Soon his father's gasping breaths were forced to the background until he could no longer hear him. Keeping his eyes clamped tightly shut, he began to visualize his father breathing normally, until he thought he could hear his father breathing steadily right in front of him. His heart leaped with hope and he concentrated more intently on the image in his mind. He was so deeply implanted in his vision that he jumped when a firm hand grasped his shoulder. His eyes snapped open, and he saw his father's face, a bit flushed but alert and aware.

"Dad!" he croaked, relief flooding his voice as he propelled himself into his father's arms. "Oh, jeez! I'm so sorry, Dad. I didn't mean to do it. It was an accident."

"It's okay, Xavier. I know. I know," his father soothed hoarsely as he stroked his head. Then, pulling the boy at arm's length, he whispered eagerly, "But, son, you did it!

You overcame your strongest insurgency yet! You controlled it all by yourself without any help from us! You did it, Xavier!"

The relief he felt was so overwhelming that he started to cry. He had controlled a strong rogue power; it hadn't controlled him. For the first time in months, he started to believe he would beat this thing. Everything would be okay.

Well into the second month at King's Mountain, Xavier's abilities had increased rapidly in number. It seemed that each day brought a new empowerment. He acquired so many powers so quickly that the men were in utter awe over the powers he now exhibited. It wasn't a surprise that Xavier had trouble controlling these pubescent powers, but after extensive training, he quickly developed a fairly firm command over them. The work was hard and exhausting but the success he was experiencing made it worth it.

By the fourth month, training began to wind down in intensity as the volume of new powers had lessened considerably. Control over his abilities had improved so much that it was no longer necessary to lock him in his room during the day, although he wasn't allowed to go anywhere alone. Xavier was confident that the worst of his control issues were behind him. So, when he asked his father if his friends could come for a visit, he was sure his father would allow it. He was wrong. Without hesitating, the king denied the request. Certain his father was over-reacting, he kept pressing him to reconsider.

"Absolutely not," the king stated simply, taking an enormous bite from his burger.

"Why not? I don't have hardly any trouble with my powers anymore! You said yourself that I was doing great.

Besides, you or Ephraim could be there just in case," he pleaded for the third time that week.

"Xavier, I'm not going through this again. It's still not safe for you to have visitors. I will not put their lives at risk," his father insisted firmly.

"But, Dad..."

"Xavier, I said no. That's the end to this discussion! Maybe in another month or so you'll be ready for visitors."

"This is bullshit!" he retorted, standing and throwing his napkin to the floor.

"Xavier Wells!" his father's voice boomed. "Curb the foul language. It's unbecoming for the heir to the throne."

He scowled at his father before turning and stomping out of the hall muttering, "That doesn't seem to keep *you* from cussing."

The king and his generals watched as the boy stormed away. Henrick nodded to the king and followed.

"He needs a real test. He needs to realize that even though he's come a long way, he is still dangerous and has a lot of work to do. I know he's going to try something stupid," Jeremiah noted quietly.

"Do something stupid? Naw. Not your son!" Loren guffawed.

Jeremiah looked at his general soberly. "He's thinking about sneaking out of the mountain and returning to Warwood."

"What do you have in mind, sire?" Ephraim asked.

"We need to up the ante," he answered.

Chapter 32

Test

The next morning, Xavier reported to the fencing chamber as usual for his training and found his father and the generals already there, dressed in full combat gear with swords in hand. He froze at the sight of them.

"Come in, Xavier. Thank you, Henrick. You may secure the chamber," his father instructed.

Henrick nodded dutifully, exited the chamber, and locked it behind him.

"Secure the chamber? He hasn't done that for weeks. What's going on, Dad?"

"A test. You say that you're in control of your abilities and that you're ready for visitors. I'm afraid you must prove it to me."

Jeremiah despised that it had come to this. He didn't enjoy the idea of putting his thirteen-year-old son up against fully grown men trained, skilled, and experienced in combat, but he had to get through to the stubborn boy that he wasn't ready to have visitors. If he didn't accomplish that, Xavier would find a way to get back to the kingdom on his own, and he simply wasn't ready to return.

The destruction Xavier had caused in escaping Warwood had been severe. The school's foundation had been damaged, large fissures snaked throughout the kingdom, one section of the Coliseum had collapsed, and the palace wall had been compromised. Damage, some minute and some devastating, could be found throughout the kingdom. Since the kingdom was still on high alert and much of the citizens' time was spent preparing for the inevitable war, repairs had to be prioritized, and therefore they were slow moving. The most severe, dangerous, or needy problems were dealt with first. The palace's wall had been repaired and the school's foundation had been re-enforced so that school and training could continue. However, the large cracks in the earth still remained. Temporary bridges had been built where the fissures had cut through roads and high traffic areas.

In addition to all of this, the power Xavier had exhibited during the attack on the kingdom had many citizens speculating on the prince's true identity. Rumors had spread like wild fire, and Jeremiah couldn't walk across the drive or through the Governing Hall without hearing his citizens' fevered whispers and thoughts. The boy's friends were suddenly in the spotlight and were being questioned by nosey, meddling citizens. Luckily, the children had agreed not to mention any of this in the numerous letters that weighed his pockets after each visit to the kingdom. They agreed he didn't need this additional burden. As hard as it was for Xavier to be away from the kingdom, he wasn't ready to face the consequences of what he had done, what he was, or what he was prophesized of becoming. Yes, this test was essential.

"W...what do you mean? What kind of test?"

"Fencing, laddie. Put on your protective gear and pick up your sword," Ephraim instructed, nodding to the vest, helmet, and sword on the table next to the doorway.

Xavier looked at the gear and then back to the men. With a shaky breath, he turned, pulled on the gear, and picked up the sword. He swung it experimentally. It had been over four months since he had held a sword, let alone wielded one. He turned uncertainly to the men behind him.

"You will fence each one of us. Loren and Ephraim have been instructed to hold nothing back. If an injury occurs, we'll pause long enough to mend the wound before continuing. Understand?"

"Why are you doing this?" he whined anxiously.

"Because battles are fought with swords, son. This exercise is just the next level in your training. If you can complete the exercise and maintain complete control and command over yourself and your abilities, then I'll reconsider your request for visitors."

"Really? You'll let them come for a visit? Could it be an overnight visit?"

"Don't push your luck, Xavier. I can only guarantee a day visit."

He nodded. As scared as he felt, he had to keep himself in check. He had to beat his father at his own game if he wanted to see Robbie and his friends. With a deep breath, he stepped forward and prepared himself.

Jeremiah nodded to Loren and the big man stepped forward. Immediately, Xavier's mind whirled, trying to determine the best fencing strategy for such a large, powerful man. Loren could pulverize him with sheer blunt force.

As Loren readied himself across from him, his eyes were unwavering and hard. This was not a game! This was serious business.

"En guarde," Loren barked and swept his sword in a wide arc, striking Xavier's blade with a tremendous blow that rattled his teeth. His sword clattered loudly to the stone floor.

If he had any preconceived notions that Loren would pause to allow him to reclaim his sword, he would have been sorely mistaken. The large man was advancing again. Xavier ducked, rolled underneath the attack, grabbed his sword, and stood. When he turned to face the general again, he barely managed to lift the sword in time to block yet another strike. This time, he succeeded in keeping the sword in his hands, but the contact of blade against blade jolted him and his knees buckled. Fear mounted in him with each strike of Loren's sword, and he began to feel energy crackling in his fingertips. He wouldn't last much longer with Loren's powerful blows. He had to use his empowerments if he were to have any hope of escaping pain and injury.

When Loren came at him again, Xavier dodged the attack, scurried to the other side of the room, raised his right hand, and launched a powerful electro force straight at the general. But Loren was quicker on his feet than he looked. He spun to the side, the force only grazing his shoulder. Then, Loren returned the favor. The crushing force hit Xavier and knocked him to the unforgiving stone floor. There was an unmistakable snap and excruciating pain exploded up from his elbow. Gritting his teeth against the agony, he staggered to his feet and tried to conjure an electro force to defend himself.

"Stop the fight," his father commanded firmly.

Xavier relaxed, relieved to have a break. Jeremiah approached him and gingerly lifted his right arm to examine it. He cried out in pain.

"Loren," he called, waving the general to them. "This needs mending. You're better with bones than I am."

Xavier looked down at his arm and nearly threw up when he saw it twisted at an abnormal angle.

Jeremiah noticed the boy's reaction. "Xavier, sit down

and breathe slowly through your nose and out through your mouth. Don't look at your arm."

Loren stepped up beside them and nodded. "It's a compound fracture, but I can have it mended in minutes. No problem," he responded.

"Good. Ephraim, administer a small dose of apothecary for the pain."

"Yes, sire."

With the apothecary, the healing of his arm was painless and within minutes, he was as good as new. Loren helped him to his feet and clapped him on the back before moving to the side of the room.

Jeremiah turned to Ephraim. "You're up." Then he turned and handed Xavier his sword. "Keep your balance and stay calm, son," he instructed, patting his shoulder before moving to stand next to Loren.

"Okay, lad. Let's see if you remember anything I've taught you. I sure didn't see any of it while you sparred with Loren," Ephraim taunted, flipping his fencing mask down and shuffling into position.

Grimacing, Xavier faced the second general and readied himself. He wasn't nearly as big or as strong as Loren, but he was a very skilled swordsman. Rumor had it that Ephraim was the best swordsman in the kingdom, and this made Xavier more nervous than he had been when sparring with Loren. The only advantage he had over Ephraim was that he was slightly faster and lighter on his feet. He would have to use his agility to his benefit. This thought gave him a small glimmer of hope and he raised his sword. But, the hope he felt didn't last.

He no sooner raised his sword when Ephraim feinted and jammed his sword hard into Xavier's chest. Stunned, Xavier gasped for air and staggered away from the man. He lowered his sword to his side as he examined his chest.

Ephraim's blade had struck his chest with such force that the sword had managed to gash open his protective vest. If he hadn't been wearing the vest, the strike would have surely been mortal. This realization sent his adrenaline into overdrive. The general was advancing on him again, and he tried desperately to remember his techniques, *any* technique that would help him. All thought of technique evaporated from his mind as he watched in near awe at Ephraim's swordsmanship. He launched a smooth, superbly skilled compound attack. He cut Xavier's sword to the side, feinted high to his head, and then lunged an attack at his vulnerable torso.

Xavier managed to twist his body away to avoid a direct hit, but the blow still battered his body. Recoiling in pain, his sword wasn't in position to stop the next attack. This time, Ephraim came straight at him and attacked. There were no feints and no compound moves. It was a simple, yet potent attack. The blade came crashing down on Xavier's back and he crumpled to the stone floor. It would have been a perfect kill stroke, but in the last instant, Ephraim twisted his sword and struck Xavier with its blunt side.

"Do you remember *anything* I've taught you, boy?" Ephraim hissed, disgusted. "You're sloppy, off balance, and show very little knowledge of swordplay. I've seen first year students do better than that!"

Panting and grimacing, Xavier got to his feet and squared off with the general. "I'm trying, okay? Maybe you've forgotten, I haven't picked up a bloody sword in over four months!"

"You're fighting like a drooling tot, and all you can think to do is come up with excuses?" Ephraim spat out, grabbing the boy by the collar.

Xavier was hurting. His abdomen felt like it was on fire,

his freshly healed broken arm ached, his chest throbbed, and his back hurt to stand up straight. Now, he had to stand here and listen to insults? Anger pulsated through his body and he glared up at the general.

"Get your hands off me!" he growled, knocking the general's hand away.

He felt the tingling in his extremities too late to squelch it and a crackling electro force flared up in his hand.

Ephraim glanced down at it just as it erupted from Xavier's hand, narrowly missing him. Almost instantaneously, a second force thundered from him and crashed against the wall.

"Control it, lad," Ephraim whispered.

Xavier's brow furrowed as he stared intently at the force in his hand, trying desperately to will it back, but it only seemed to be growing in magnitude.

"Xavier, focus on your focal point. Calm down and pull it back," his father intoned.

He tried to concentrate, but the force continued to grow more and more powerful. Moaning in frustration, he lost the battle for control, and forces erupted around the room.

"Xavier!" his father yelled, diving at him and knocking him to the stone floor as a force whizzed above, just missing him.

Xavier's body went bone-chilling cold, and the rogue forces around them vanished. His father rolled off of him and sat back on his haunches, eyeing him soberly. Shivering, Xavier closed his eyes in shame. He nearly killed himself with his own empowerments. If his father hadn't tackled him and extinguished his powers... Without looking at his father, he climbed to his feet and frowned at the sword still clutched tightly in his hand. Without a word, he dropped the weapon with a clatter and stomped toward the door. After a sequence of knocks from Loren, the door opened, and Xavier left the room with Henrick following quietly.

The king exhaled loudly before whispering regretfully, "Test failed."

Chapter 33

Rise of the Chosen

Although Xavier had failed miserably at his first test, it didn't deter him during his training sessions in the weeks that followed. If anything, his failure had only strengthened his hunger to conquer his abilities. It was the only way he would be able to see his friends again. The two months that followed were comprised of the hardest, most grueling work of his life. His father would give him what he liked to call "pop quizzes", which he believed would contribute greatly to Xavier's development and control of his powers. During these quizzes, the king would call out an ability, and Xavier was expected to summon it, perform with it, and then distinguish it with ease and solid command. At first, he struggled, but with concentration, hard work, and lots of practice, he improved rapidly. Soon his abilities became automatic, and he could easily wield any power he possessed. And, boy, did he possess a lot! He had more powers than Henrick, Ephraim, and Loren combined! He was uncertain about how he compared to the king since his father kept the extent of his abilities to himself. When he asked him how many powers he possessed, his father just smiled slyly and stated, "A king should never divulge the level of his power, son. It could have unwanted consequences." Xavier didn't ask him about his powers again.

The atmosphere at the mountain had altered from a tense, dangerous mood to a calm, relaxed one. Now that Xavier was in complete control of himself and his powers, the guards were more relaxed and joked with him and each other. As a result, he no longer needed constant supervision and had free reign within the mountain. He could explore and go wherever he pleased without Henrick or one of his father's generals in tow. Xavier spent most of his free time divided between the rugby pitch and the entombed river. Sometimes his father and the men would take time out of their busy schedules to play some rugby with him, but most of the time he was left to entertain himself. The times he was on his own, he would run laps around the field and practice rugby maneuvers barefooted. The feel of grass under his bare feet made him feel a little less trapped, a little more normal.

His visits to the river were a secret he kept to himself. Though he never asked, he assumed that the lower levels were still restricted as they had been when they lived in the mountain almost a year ago. Swimming the river was exhilarating, and he often went there whenever he felt lonely or depressed. Even though Xavier was an aqualung and could breathe under water, swimming the river would still send his heart hammering and adrenaline surging into his bloodstream. There was nothing like life-threatening whitewater to put those feelings into perspective.

The days began to run together. He spent every morning and evening training and the afternoons at the rugby pitch or the river. Before he knew it, his fourteenth birthday was rapidly approaching. One morning, his father strolled into his bedchamber with a large smile and a surprise.

"How do you feel about having some visitors?"

He stared dumbfounded up at his father. "What? Are you serious?"

The king nodded, still grinning.

"Really? Robbie and the guys can come and visit?"

"Yes, I think you've earned it. I'm so proud of the progress you've made, Xavier."

"Oh, man! Thanks, Dad. Thank you, thank you, *thank you*!" he exclaimed, launching himself into his father's arms.

Jeremiah chuckled appreciatively, hugging him.

"When will they be here? Tomorrow? Day after?" he asked excitedly.

"How about a visitor now?" his father asked, amused.

"Now? They're coming now?"

"Well, one visitor is on her way right now."

"Her?" His eyes widened. "Robbie's coming?"

His father nodded. "Yep, she should be here within the hour. I thought you might want some alone time with her without your friends lingering about."

"How long can she stay?"

"I promised her mother she'd be back after dinner. So, you've got the entire day to spend with her."

"Thanks, Dad. Really, thanks a lot!"

Xavier paced next to the entrance for nearly a half-an-hour before Robbie's arrival. When the door finally screeched open, he froze with his heart fluttering wildly in his chest. Then, for the first time in months, he saw her. For a moment, he could only stare, stunned by how beautiful she looked. Her hair was longer. It fell in soft curls onto her shoulders with one lock clipped to the side. Her eyes were the same doe-like brown. And her smile, his heart stopped at her smile.

"Robbie," he whispered, his voice breaking.

"Xavier!" she squealed, running and throwing her arms around him. "Oh, my God!" she cried. "I missed you! I missed you so much!" She pulled away enough to plant a long, breath-taking kiss on his mouth.

Xavier's heart soared and he moaned against the sudden shock of sensations pulsating through him. He hugged her closer and kissed her back, feeling as though a great weight had lifted from his soul. When she ended the kiss, the teenagers were startled to find themselves levitated more than thirty feet into the air.

"Whoa. Oh, my God! How...what...Xavier, what's going on?" Robbie blurted, anxiety filling her eyes.

He held the girl tighter and smiled. "What can I say? You swept me off my feet."

She laughed nervously. "Well, can you get us down now? It's making me nervous."

"You trust me, right?"

"Well, yeah, of course."

"Then, stop worrying. I'm in complete control," he whispered, winking at her.

Slowly he lowered them back to the ground, smiling at the girl in his arms. He couldn't believe she was finally there.

"Wow, you've grown," she commented once their feet were on solid ground again.

Xavier noted with pleasure that he was now taller than Robbie, by nearly three inches. "What did you expect? I've been here for nearly six months! Besides, I was bound to have a growth spurt eventually!"

She giggled. "You don't have to pretend, Xavier. I know you're happy that you're finally taller than me."

Xavier grinned down at her. "God, yes!" He sighed.

"All right you two," his father's amused voice called as he shut the door behind him. "You have some time to yourselves until lunch in an hour."

"Okay. Thanks, Dad."

"We'll need to train after lunch since we weren't able to this morning."

"But, Dad, Robbie's here. I thought I had the day off so I could spend it with her."

"Xavier, you still need to practice your skills. It's not up for a debate. Robbie is more than welcome to come and watch you train. I'd bet she'd enjoy that."

"Yeah, I would, Xavier. I want to see how good you're getting," she added sweetly.

He looked at Robbie's big smile and felt his insides go to jelly. "Uh, okay."

"All right then, we'll see you two at lunch," Jeremiah snickered and walked past the couple and into a chamber on the right.

Xavier took Robbie's hand. "Come on. Let's get away from all these prying eyes and eavesdroppers."

Jeremiah's booming laugh echoed out of the chamber. "Son, I don't need to eavesdrop! The moment Robbie entered the mountain, you've been broadcasting every thought and feeling you've had."

"What?" he blurted, hurrying to peer into the small chamber his father used as a study while at the mountain. "I'm broadcasting my thoughts?"

Jeremiah leaned back in his chair, his grin slipping. "Survey yourself and you tell me?"

Xavier stopped a moment and tuned into his body, pushing past the sensations Robbie's presence had on him. Blushing, he asked, "So, you heard my thoughts? *All* my thoughts?"

The king nodded and winked at him.

His blush deepened.

"We'll work on quieting strong feelings this coming

week. In battle, Fox could use them against you."

He nodded, knowing his father was right. "Yes, sir."

"Go on and have some fun. I'll see you both at lunch."

Xavier longed to spend some uninterrupted time with Robbie, but he needed a place where his father couldn't hear his every thought. Without a pause in his step, he grabbed Robbie's hand and pulled her to the stairway at the end of the long corridor that led to the lower levels of the facility. Moments later, they sat next to the river watching the churning, turbulent surface, amazed by its unbridled power.

"I swam that last week," he bragged.

Robbie eyed him skeptically. "Why would you even want to?"

He shrugged and smirked. "Because I can. I have aqualungs, remember? It was easy for me. I swam out to the rock and back," he answered proudly, pointing to the large outcrop fifty yards out into the water.

She glanced at the rock before looking back at him, her eyes still skeptical.

"What? You don't believe me? I'll show you," he remarked, standing and stripping his shirt off.

"N...no, Xavier," she stammered at the sight of his bare chest. The boy had grown more than just up. He was trim and had an impressive six-pack starting. Dragging her eyes back to Xavier's, she continued, "I...ah, I believe you. Please, don't do it. It scares me."

"It scares you? Why should it scare you? I won't drown; I can't drown with aqualungs."

"I know, but what if the current is too strong and you get swept away to...well, who knows where? Just don't, please. It makes me nervous," she pleaded, grabbing his arm and trying to pull him down to sit next to her again. She realized then that his muscles weren't just for show.

He was stronger, much stronger. She couldn't physically make him do anything anymore. Her gaze dropped to his chest and arms again. She couldn't help but admire the defined muscles there. Her ogling didn't escape Xavier's notice.

Smiling, he sank down next to her again. "I've been working out," he boasted. He lifted his arm in front of her and flexed his bicep. "Want to touch it?"

Blushing, she giggled but gave his arm a squeeze. "Yeah. I guess you have. You're a lot stronger and bigger."

He smiled, pleased with the compliment. He leaned toward her and kissed her. He loved the feeling of her mouth on his. His hand snaked across the stone floor to grasp hers.

"Watch," he whispered. Then, without more of a warning, he sprang gracefully to his feet, darted toward the river, and dove into the violent surface. When he emerged from the water, he was already half the distance to the stone.

Robbie jumped to her feet and ran to the water's edge. "Xavier! Oh, my God! Swim! Don't stop!"

Xavier cut easily through the water and within seconds, he was climbing onto the rock and grinning wildly back to her.

"See? It's easy!"

Robbie laughed, smitten by this cocky attitude he now possessed. He looked so cute standing soaking wet on that rock with his hands on his hips and his hair tousled. She loved his muscular body as well; she caught herself staring again and she blushed. When he smirked back at her, her blush deepened, and she wondered if he had read her thoughts. In the blink of an eye, Xavier disappeared from the rock. Eagerly, Robbie scanned the water thinking he had plunged back into its riotous depths, but she saw no sign of him. Then she felt a light tap on her shoulder and turned into Xavier, who immediately kissed her. She sighed happily. He was so different from what she remembered. He seemed a lot older somehow. He was confident, calm, and more mature. She was seeing a glimpse of the man, the king, he would someday become, and she liked what she was seeing. She liked it a lot.

Following lunch, Xavier stood dressed in combat gear across from his father, Loren, and Ephraim. Each stood primed with his sword in hand. He glanced over at Robbie, who sat against the wall, and winked at her. She grinned back at him.

"Okay, Romeo. Focus!" the king ordered and nodded to Ephraim, who moved to stand next to Robbie. Once Ephraim was in place, Jeremiah and Loren both lunged at the boy. Xavier sent an electro force at his father, sending him a good six feet across the room before lifting his sword just in time to parry Loren's attack. Then, he transported to Loren's rear and attacked. The general responded a fraction of a second too late, and Xavier's blow threw him off balance, making him stumble across the room. Xavier turned as if some sixth sense warned him of the imminent advance from his father. He parried the king's assault and attacked with a compound move he had been practicing for weeks. He pulled it off flawlessly, and his father's eyes widened with surprise, but he managed to parry the attack in the nick of time. The slight change in air pressure warned Xavier that Loren was conjuring a force behind him. He blocked another blow from his father and waited for the general's force to be released. The instant the force was launched, he teleported so that his father was between him and the force barreling down on them. The force hit the king and knocked him to the floor. In that instant,

Xavier sent a potent telekinetic force at Loren, lifting and slamming him against the wall. He stood at the ready and surveyed the men, who were slow to get to their feet.

"Well done, son," Jeremiah managed, wincing as he stood.

Robbie clapped enthusiastically from the side of the room. "Woohoo! Way to go, Xavier!"

He grinned at her before turning toward his father, who shook his head, chuckling.

The following morning, Xavier lay spread-eagled in the center of the rugby pitch staring absentmindedly at the rugby ball spinning less than a foot above his head. With a grin and a slight jerk of his head, he sent the ball rocketing toward the stone ceiling more than a hundred feet above him. Then he released the ball from his telekinesis and watched, slightly amused, as it plummeted toward the ground. Less than an inch from his nose, he caught the ball once again in his telekinesis energy. He chuckled as he grabbed the ball and tucked it under his head. He loved it here. It almost felt like he was outside with grass under him and sunlight bursting down on him in nearly every direction from the collection of crystals embedded in the rocky ceiling like bright stars. With a content grin, he closed his eyes and inhaled deeply.

"Is this how you spend your time in the mountain while the rest of us are busting our butts in classes? Seriously, I wish I had a prince's life. Don't you, Court?" Beck chided, elbowing a grinning Courtney as the boys strolled easily toward him with Garrett, Harry, Mac, and Frankie following close behind.

Xavier's grin widened, but he kept his eyes closed listening to the group's approach. His keen sense of hearing pinpointed their exact location, and he conjured a great cascade of water that crashed down over his friends' heads.

The group let out a chorus of shouts.

"Hey!" Court shouted. "What the heck!"

Xavier sat up and watched, smirking, as his drenched friends approach with crooked grins.

"Showoff." Beck laughed, stopping in front of him, shaking his hair like a dog, and showering him with droplets of water.

Laughing, Xavier stood and clapped Beck on the shoulder. Beck gave a sideways glance at the other boys and suddenly all six lunged at him, gang tackling him to the earth under a pile of giggling bodies.

"Oof! Ouch! Court, that's my spleen!" he called out, laughing.

Slowly the boys climbed off the prince, and Court pulled him to his feet.

"Boys, they just never grow up, do they, Robbie?" Erica commented, her voice rising above the ruckus and light-hearted insults. Xavier looked at Erica and smiled before fastening his gaze on Robbie's smiling face.

"Xavier, how did you do that?" Garrett asked breathlessly.

"I've gotten a few more powers since I've been here," Xavier answered, his eyes still on Robbie as she and Erica joined the group.

"You gotten a *few* more powers," Garrett repeated slowly.

"Blimey, Xavier, like what?" Court asked.

"Um, well," Xavier began, his eyes darting from eager face to eager face. "Well, obviously, I got hydromancy. I also have the aeronautic ability, transfiguration powers, tracking abilities, x-ray vision..." His voice trailed off at the weighted looks the boys were giving each other while

Courtney carefully inspected his shoes.

"What?" His eyes fixed on Beck. "What?"

Beck glanced at the other boys before answering. "Well, X, it's just that no kid in empowered history has ever had that many powers. It's...um... look, there's a lot of talk that you're not just our prince but ...that...you're the *Chosen*!"

Xavier's face grew hot and his eyes darted from Court to Erica and then to Robbie. All three kept their eyes fastened to the ground. The declaration caught him off guard, and it took a moment for him to regain his composure, a moment too late.

"Bloody Hell!" Beck exclaimed, looking at him in nothing short of shock. "It's true, isn't it?"

"What? Are you kidding, Beck?" Xavier exclaimed. "You're mental! Me, the Chosen?"

Beck eyed the other boys before replying. "Xavier, look, we're your mates. We've got your back. Just tell us the truth. We won't tell a soul."

He glanced at Courtney's unhelpful head before turning back to Beck. "Beck, really, it's crazy! Jeez, don't you think I have enough to deal with without being the savior of all mankind?" He gave a small, weak laugh.

"Then why aren't you saying that you're not the Chosen. You just keep saying it's crazy, but I haven't heard you deny it," Beck chided.

"That's because it *is* crazy and I can't believe you're falling for it."

Beck eyed him suspiciously, but he let the matter drop.

Xavier pretended not to notice Beck's doubtful look as he turned his attention to the group at large.

"Wanna play a game of rugby? I haven't been able to play a decent match in months."

Within moments, the months of loneliness and isolation slipped away as he and his friends wrestled a rugby ball up and down the indoor pitch. His friends' laughter and cheers of enthusiasm were comforting, and for the first time in a long time, he felt at home. Contentment and pride ballooned in his chest as he watched his best mates arguing over possession of the ball.

"What are you grinning at?" Court whispered beside him as Beck threw himself at Garrett and wrestled him to the ground to get the ball.

"I was just thinking," he whispered back, his eyes still on the scuffling boys. "This is what I've been preparing for these last few months." Xavier looked his best friend in the eye and straightened to his full height, now an inch above Court. "This is worth fighting for."

www.ingramcontent.com/pod-product-compliance
Lightning Source LLC
Chambersburg PA
CBHW071243170626
46809CB00001B/70